Praise for *Miranda's Vines*

"In this lustrous tale of loyalty and devotion, Kafka limns
the depths of intimacy and explores the nature of
relationships, from mother to son, father to daughter,
neighbor to neighbor, and friend to friend. In Kafka's
sensitive hands, Miranda's compassion is heralded with
insightful grace and understanding in a sublime account
of personal and emotional challenge and growth."
—*Booklist*

"A creatively penned novel, set against the beauty
of Oregon's wine country."
—*Romantic Times Bookclub*

"A spirited novel . . . Readers who like to cheer on the
underdog will relish this tale of grit and determination
in the face of daunting circumstances."
—*Publishers Weekly*

Kimberly Kafka is the author of the novel *True North*. She has
taught writing and literature at the University of Michigan and
now lives in Wisconsin.

Also by Kimberly Kafka

TRUE NORTH

MIRANDA'S VINES

Kimberly Kafka

A PLUME BOOK

PLUME
Published by Penguin Group
Penguin Group (USA) Inc., 375 Hudson Street, New York, New York 10014, U.S.A.
Penguin Group (Canada), 10 Alcorn Avenue, Toronto, Ontario, Canada M4V 3B2
(a division of Pearson Penguin Canada Inc.)
Penguin Books Ltd., 80 Strand, London WC2R 0RL, England
Penguin Ireland, 25 St. Stephen's Green, Dublin 2, Ireland (a division of Penguin Books Ltd.)
Penguin Group (Australia), 250 Camberwell Road, Camberwell, Victoria 3124, Australia
(a division of Pearson Australia Group Pty. Ltd.)
Penguin Books India Pvt. Ltd., 11 Community Centre, Panchsheel Park,
New Delhi – 110 017, India
Penguin Books (NZ), cnr Airborne and Rosedale Roads, Albany, Auckland 1310,
New Zealand (a division of Pearson New Zealand Ltd.)
Penguin Books (South Africa) (Pty.) Ltd., 24 Sturdee Avenue, Rosebank,
Johannesburg 2196, South Africa

Penguin Books Ltd., Registered Offices: 80 Strand, London WC2R 0RL, England

Published by Plume, a member of Penguin Group (USA) Inc. Previously published in a
Dutton edition.

First Plume Printing, February 2005

10 9 8 7 6 5 4 3 2 1

CIP data is available.
ISBN 0-525-94763-9 (hc.)
ISBN 0-452-28617-4 (pbk.)

Printed in the United States of America

PUBLISHER'S NOTE
This is a work of fiction. Names, characters, places, and incidents are either the product of
the author's imagination or are used fictitiously, and any resemblance to actual persons, living or dead, business establishments, events, or locales is entirely coincidental.

For Liz Grenamyer,
who has fed me body and soul
for as long as I can remember

ACKNOWLEDGMENTS

I was honored to meet and speak with Dick Erath, one of the first to recognize the potential of Oregon for growing pinot noir. Through Dick, I met one of the finest vineyardmen in the business, Mayo Alba, who spent patient and precious hours answering my questions.

Rob Stuart, Erath's former winemaker, was the epitome of stoicism and graciousness, giving up time that winemakers rarely have, imparting wisdom and facts at breathtaking speed as we traversed the hills of Oregon visiting vineyards.

Rob introduced me to two of the finest grape growers in Oregon, Elizabeth and Grant Brunker, who, even had they not fed and watered me in sublime fashion, would have charmed me to no end. I keep the vision of Brunker Hall Vineyards close to my aesthetic heart.

None of these meetings would have been possible were it not for the considerable efforts of a certain bundle of pure Irish wit, heart, and talent, Trish Rogers. God love ye, girl, there is no other like. Trish and Rob Stuart have now created R. Stuart and Co. winery, making Big Fire wines. Long may you quaff.

Special thanks is due to the beautiful and accomplished Deborah Alfaro, who put me on to Oregon and Trish within seconds of my mentioning an interest.

This loop opens and closes with Liz Grenamyer, extraordinary chef and closest friend who started it all in the first place by cooking for me and standing fast through bleak times and good.

My fine cousins, Elizabeth and Craig Fanshier of Portland, Oregon, put me up and put up with my comings and goings with magnanimous cheer, and provided limitless knowledge of area geology and history to boot. Great couch, kick-ass truck, and good food . . . life doesn't get much better among friends.

For wine talk that bordered on great sex, I owe much pleasure to friends Marty Williams and Dennis Sherman. Because of them, poetry and laughter bless my days.

Malou Cronin shepherded me through the perils of the disabled with grace, heart, and humor. I continue to be astonished by her accomplishments and grateful for her friendship. Through Malou, I was able to glean more information from Prasad Bhojaraju and Tim Turner, both formerly of Centegra Health System Rehabilitation and Sports Clinic, along with other staff at the clinic. Thanks to Todd Boyer who put me in touch with Laura Crouse. Laura's insight into paraplegia and her candidness about it were invaluable. My friend Mary Jane Miller has parked her wheelchair at my house on many occasions, and I am grateful for her contribution to my knowledge of living life with a disability.

My canine buddies, past and present, inform the characters of Fluke and Zeus; without them, my life would be poor, indeed. And without the patient and brilliant instruction of Dr. Janet Gildner, DVM at Whitewater Veterinary Hospital, my knowledge of their physiology would be poorer still.

A special blessing goes to Dr. Barbara Heinrich who advises me in all things medical. Had we known our friendship would span our lives, we might not have kicked each others' shins when we were six, or argued over who got to ride the horse first.

My sweetheart, Donald Dane, wins Saint of the Year (not to mention my heart) for his day-in, day-out contribution to my sanity and happiness.

And as always, I thank Alyson Hagy, novelist and greatest of friends, for her keen and tireless eyes.

How easily our bodies become us, our souls bound to the Material, to the joy or grief or pain we feel through our skin.

—Lee Martin, *From Our House*

MIRANDA'S VINES

1

Miranda Perry came into the Willamette Valley from the coast road. She'd gotten off the I-5 as soon as she crossed into Oregon because Ruben had lobbied hard to see the ocean. The fact that the Pacific was the same here as it was in California meant nothing to her six-year-old, so she'd taken the longer route without argument—to tell the truth, it did seem different here. The swells heaved in more lucid shades of gray and green and blue.

But Ruben fell asleep before they were out of Grants Pass, and he hadn't been awakened even by six calls to her cell phone from the restaurant. The first five had been from her sous chef, who hadn't gained much confidence in the three months he'd worked for her. Her boss, the executive chef, was the sixth call. Eric wanted to let her know he'd booked a party of twenty banking executives for the following week, and that he'd arrange the menu. The purpose of the call was, of course, to cement the fact that she had only one week off, and he'd groused royally about giving her that, as if late February were their busy season.

Fuming at Eric kept her mind occupied while Ruben was asleep, so she wouldn't have to think about why she was going home. When she'd tried to explain it to Ruben, she had not been able to say it outright. She meant to spare him his first introduction to death, but really it was herself she meant to spare; if she tried to take in the scope of the world without her father in it, her hands shook and her mouth filled with tart secretions as if she were going to vomit.

Carter Perry hadn't seen his grandson in three years. She'd meant to take time off for another trip home since then, but the timing was never right. Eric wanted a renovation of the house space to accommodate more tables, which meant additional diners, which meant hiring more kitchen staff, who needed to be trained.

In the middle of all that, investors had approached her about starting a restaurant of her own. She had achieved some cachet as the chef de cuisine at a top-notch restaurant in San Francisco. Winning the James Beard Award two years ago didn't hurt, either. When the investors asked her what she would do to make her restaurant different—and she knew they meant "marketable"—she'd tried to explain the ancient art of Shojin cooking, elegant in its simplicity and simple in its intentions: to perfectly aid the mind and body in their struggle to survive and flourish.

Miranda insisted on and knew how to choose quality, cleanly grown ingredients. She knew it mattered, because when she plated the homeliest dish imaginable—smothered pork chops with Indian-spiced mashed sweet potatoes—she had chosen the hog from a farmer she knew and trusted, had helped weed the sweet potatoes, mixed the garam masala herself. She knew again how much it mattered when she served the dish to one of her regulars, a gourmet of some repute, and watched his face pink with pleasure while his eyes closed. It was the face of an infant at its mother's breast, it was what the Japanese called *umame*, the "taste of life." The investors stared at her blankly, but her enthusiasm did not go unnoticed. They came back for a second look.

And she deserved that look. In twelve years, she'd worked her way up from prep cook, her hands aching and cut and burned because, contrary to the going notions, there were no secrets, no shortcuts. You needed good knives, strong technique, and the ability to concentrate on as well as orchestrate a situation that gravitated toward chaos.

Beyond the work, she'd suffered her share of agony along the way. She looked over at Ruben and resisted the urge to smooth the dark sprigs of hair that lay matted on his forehead. In sleep he looked so much like his father, it keened a grief she thought had dulled after six years.

She'd meant to go on up the coast to Wheeler and cut through the state forest so Ruben could see the Coastals, but she remembered how heavily logged they were now, and she did not want Ruben to see the mountains shaved and raw in the winter-gray afternoon. So she'd turned inland toward the Willamette Valley at the Salmon River and headed for McMinnville. From there, she'd cut over to Dundee, and then it was only minutes to the vineyard, to home.

As if an inner compass informed him of the change, Ruben's head rolled upright, and he stubbed his fists in his eyes. "Where's the ocean, Mom?"

"You missed it, sleepyhead. We're following the Salmon River now."

He pushed against his seat belt, fully alert, as if three hours had not just passed in sleep. "I wanna see the sammin."

"There aren't many salmon left, Ru. Besides, they're out in the ocean now, growing up."

"Let's see the ocean."

"It's the other way, honey. But we'll come back this way when we go back to San Francisco. We'll see it then."

As if some pheromone spray alerted her seconds before it happened, she was ready when he pressed his back to the seat and wailed.

"Sweetie, I'm sorry, but we've got to get home." And thought it odd as she said it. She'd lived in San Francisco for twelve years but still called Oregon home.

"But you said we're goin' to Papa's."

She didn't think she had it in her to explain right then the difference between home where she'd grown up and the home that he knew in the city, so she just said, "That's right. We're going to Papa's."

She drove on for ten minutes, Ruben sobbing so hard he choked himself, until she stopped the car at a pullout by the river and grabbed her tote bag from the backseat. She smeared some cream cheese on a slice of cherry bread, her eyes appreciating the texture of bread risen with real starter instead of with commercial yeast. She cut it into quarters on the dashboard and coaxed Ruben through the first three bites. He chewed and sobbed at first, then ceased vocalizing and chewed with only his eyes leaking, until he was well into the last bit of sandwich.

She watched the river through the window, tried to get Ruben to focus on the water. When he finished the sandwich, she watered down some pear juice and gave it to him. He drank, his throat convulsing in great throbs.

She smoothed his hair. "Better?"

He nodded, staring at the river as it foamed past them.

"Do you miss your school?" she asked.

He shook his head. He'd just started kindergarten that fall, and so far he had not been happy about it. It was hard for him to make friends, and she knew this was her fault. It was difficult for her to schedule playtime for him with other kids, because her work hours were out of sync with the nine-to-fivers. If she managed to make a playdate, she couldn't follow up on a regular basis. So most of the people Ruben knew were grown-ups, coworkers at the restaurant where he ended up spending a lot of time if she couldn't get a sitter.

She passed the miles to McMinnville pointing out hawks in the trees. She explained to him how they liked to perch there and wait for things to eat.

"Like what?" he wanted to know.

"Delicious mice."

"Yuck."

"They taste wonderful to a hawk," she said.

"Why?"

"Probably because they're juicy and crunchy."

"Gross, Mom."

"Not to a hawk."

When they got to McMinnville, she had to tell him they were just changing roads to get to Dundee.

"That's our town," she said. "The closest to home, anyway. Do you remember the name of Papa's vineyard?"

"What's a vineyard?" he asked.

"It's a farm where they grow grapes to make wine. Papa's vineyard is called Perry Hill."

"Is it our farm?"

"It's Papa's," she said.

As they drove past various places she'd taken him on their last visit, she asked if he remembered it, but he always shook his head. She thought if something joggled his memory, he might remember being with Papa, who'd held the boy close to his long, flat chest, his pale blue eyes creased by a smile. It had made her feel accomplished, the smile his response to a gift of incomparable perfection.

When she finally pulled into the driveway, she watched the boy's face, certain the old white farmhouse with hickories hovering over the roof would have etched a groove on the smooth contours of his mind.

He waited for her as she loaded her arms with luggage from the back of their old blue Toyota. She stumbled up the steps and prompted Ruben to open the door for her. He held out his hand for her keys, and she had to laugh. Most of his cognizant life had consisted of locked doors and directions for when it was okay or not to open them.

"There aren't any keys, sweetie."

"How we gonna get in?"

"Things are a little different here, Ru. It's not like in the city."

She showed him his room, which was really her old room. She'd slept there with him the last time they'd visited. She thought there'd be housework, but the beds were already made, age-thinned chenille spreads arranged just so. Of course, Petra and Madrita would have come in and cleaned the house. She put Ruben's backpack on his bed, and he sat down next to it.

"While I put the rest of the things away, would you please unpack your clothes and put them in the dresser?"

He swung his feet against the bed frame.

"It'll give you something to do until the surprise gets here."

5

"What?"

"If I tell you, it won't be a surpise."

She went back to the kitchen and stood on the cracked linoleum, stared at the bare half-moon of space in front of the sink worn away by her feet and Papa's. One hundred and fifty years of life in this spot, on this land, was a lot to get organized in one week. She'd asked Eric for two weeks off, knowing it was a stretch, but his face told her she'd be lucky to get one. There was no job protection in the food industry, no matter how many awards she'd won. You cooked or were cooked; there was always someone to take your place, always more ideas.

She turned quickly to the packages she'd set on the table and started to unpack the perishables, then stowed other things in the cupboards, before hauling her suitcase upstairs to Papa's room.

It was as she remembered it—only for once the bed was made. On the nightstand was the familiar picture. He'd kept it there in the stubborn belief that what it portrayed still existed, ever existed. Papa held Miranda in her white christening gown, her baby hair as bleached as Papa's had been. He looked happy, doting even, as he had when he'd held Ruben. And next to them stood Miranda's mother, whose small, dark eyes and hair repelled the light that emanated from the two next to her, who looked so young in the photo, she could have been Papa's daughter.

Papa had told her at first that her mother was dead. Later, when Miranda was in junior high school, Petra told her that if she wanted to know about her mother, she should ask her father. Papa had been angry at Petra for bringing it up. *There's nothing to be gained. Leave it be, goddamnit.* It was the only time she'd ever heard her father swear, and the subject was not raised again. Miranda could have insisted. Instead she told her father that she didn't care, because she was certain then that she didn't.

Miranda stared at the woman's face, but recognized nothing of herself in it. She pulled open the nightstand drawer and lay the picture inside it, then felt as if she were faulting Papa and set it on the table again as it had been.

She opened his closet to find a row of faded flannel shirts hanging there, swooped them into a soft bunch, and held them to her face. The familiar smell of him curled from the cloth until she could see him stooped in the vineyard, the red Jory soil of three generations ground indelibly into creased skin. She breathed in the apparition until her belly rounded tightly with it. Soon, even that bit of him would be gone.

Ruben called her, and when she heard him tapping up the steep staircase, she let the shirts fall away from her and pushed the bifold doors shut. She took her son's hand and led him onto the balcony off Papa's room. Papa had spent his evenings there, sucking on the one pipeful he allowed himself a day. From there, he could see the full sweep of the vineyard. The elevation gave him a good overview of the vines, told him which ones lacked vigor and needed a little care, which block would likely want harvesting first. He liked to see their orderly progression, canes and shoots trained to the three-wire trellis for maximum exposure to light and air. To the south, her eyes traveled in soothing arcs across fields of wheat and meadow foam; huge tracts of seed grass moved in smoky undulations across the valley floor.

"Which ones are ours?" Ruben asked.

She pointed out the line of trees farther up the hill that separated Perry Hill from its neighboring vineyard, Ruby Throat. "All the vines between those trees and here—all those are Papa's. All the land beyond those trees used to be Papa's, too, but he sold it to Petra and Ernest. See that house way up there? I spent a lot of time up there when I was a kid. That's where Petra lives. She calls their vineyard Ruby Throat. We'll have Papa's party there tomorrow."

"You said it was a farm, Mom. Farms are flat."

"Grape farms are different," she said. "They need to be on a hill so they all get sun. And when it rains, the extra water drains off so the vines don't stand around in puddles. Grapes don't like wet feet."

She heard the gravel crunching in the driveway out front, and looked at Ruben, her eyes wide. "I wonder who that is, Ru."

She let herself be dragged downstairs, where they could hear a car door thumping shut outside.

He stopped in the middle of the kitchen. "Whosit, Mom?" he whispered.

"I think it's the surprise," she said.

He clutched at her hand with both of his, and looked ready to cry.

"It's okay, Ru. This is a good surprise."

He caught his breath, and when Miranda looked up, Bridie was there, pushing the door in with the nose of her duffel bag, her long auburn hair catching on the doorframe and causing her to laugh and drop her bag in order to disentangle herself. She almost swore but choked it back and laughed again. Ruben looked like he'd just seen Santa Claus, though he never threw himself at Santa as he did at Bridie, who'd freed herself in time to catch the boy and swing him onto her shoulders as if he weighed no more than a handbag.

And Miranda herself felt curiously weightless now, because here was the person who mattered most to her after Papa, Bridget Marie McLewan, Miranda's best friend and Ruben's godmother, the person she'd trust to raise her own son were she incapable of it.

Bridie swung Ruben down to her chest and held him to her, and Miranda saw on Bridie's face the look she'd remembered on Papa's, and again the pleasure of having given the perfect gift washed over her.

Ruben lifted Bridie's hair in sprays of dark red that drifted over him like a shawl. "Where's the dogs?" Ruben asked.

"They're back in Alaska," Bridie said. "And boy, are they rarin' to go."

"When's the race?"

Bridie set him down.

"Four days."

"Can I come?"

"I wish you could," Bridie said. "But you've got to learn about the dogs first. Start out slow."

Miranda cringed and gave Bridie the "cut" sign, but it was too late.

"When can I get a dog?" Ruben asked.

"Well, honey, you never know. It may be soon. We'll have to see."

She ruffled Ruben's hair and changed the subject. "Right now, I need to give your mom a hug.

"Puppy sandwich!" he shrieked, and Bridie picked him up again so he could be squeezed between them.

"Sorry," she whispered at Miranda.

"I'm just glad you're here," Miranda said.

"No way you'd go through this without me," Bridie said, and Miranda knew nothing could be more true.

Their friendship had been as unlikely as it seemed natural. While they'd both gone to Reed College in Portland, Miranda was a "townie"—despite an hour commute each way—and Bridie lived in the dorms. Bridie had come all the way from Michigan to go to Reed, because, she'd said, *I've spent eighteen years in Apple Pie Land, and that's enough.* She'd have gone to the university in Alaska, but the financial aid was better at private institutions, and even Oregon sounded pretty exotic to her after Flint, Michigan.

Miranda was in the tutor program, she needed the extra money, and she'd been assigned to Bridie in their sophomore year to help her with literature.

They spent three hours a week hunched over desks in Vollum Center, but something about Bridie's physical presence always made Miranda feel as if they had trekked great distances, made her feel everything was in motion. Bridie was funny and irreverent and completely unlike anyone Miranda knew, but what impressed Miranda most was that Bridie didn't expect Miranda to do the work for her; she meant to master something, whether it was her forte or not.

Miranda knew Bridie by then, at least in the way one knows the parameters of another's social behavior, so when Bridie failed to show up at a scheduled session midsemester, Miranda went looking for her.

The door to her dorm suite was open, but Miranda smelled the illness before she found Bridie curled tightly on the rumpled bed, her face protruding over the edge just enough to reach the small garbage can she'd placed there.

Wow, Bridie said when she saw her. *Now that's dedication. But I don't feel much like literature just now. This flu's kicking my ass.*

Something about Bridie's posture, the pain on her face, told Miranda it was more than flu. She'd seen it before, when Papa brought one of the workers in from the vineyard years ago.

Bridie was in the hospital for two days until the toxins from the burst appendix flushed from her system, and Miranda stayed with her. Friends from school showed up, along with a couple of the boyfriends, loud in their greetings, but eventually silent when they shuffled out. The Bridie they knew—the six-foot-tall six-pack of energy and élan—had disappeared as far as they could tell; they neglected to see that her vitality was merely damped down for the moment.

But that power was on full blast now, and Miranda let Ruben bask in it while she rummaged through the food she brought to make them a snack. Finally, she grated a couple of potatoes, arranged them into three mounds, fried the potatoes in peanut oil, then shredded smoked salmon over the cakes, spooned on sour cream. She sprinkled that with chives, and finished with a squeeze of lemon.

Bridie smeared her lips together. "Remember the appendix thing? How you brought me back here and did nothing but cook for three days? I swear you shortened my recovery by a week."

"You would have recovered faster than anyone with or without me. I think the change of pace, being out here, did more good than anything."

"But I'd never eaten like that. I grew up on dry meat loaf and tuna noodle casserole. And here you were with lemon bread and halibut and all this shit I'd never even heard of."

"Yeah, like fresh vegetables."

"Like I said, meat loaf and tuna noodle casserole. Not that my parents could afford anything else."

"Did you get the last of the food boxes I sent up?" Miranda asked.

"They're all distributed and waiting," Bridie said.

Miranda had taken on Bridie's food preparation for the race after Bridie explained in detail what her body underwent as a result of intense physical activity in extreme winter weather.

She'd sent Bridie little dark fruitcakes full of apricots, walnuts, and bacon bits, all soaked in Tokay wine. This year she'd also made a French rillettes, which was something like the deviled ham Bridie ate as a child but made with shredded pork roast and duck fat Miranda had rendered herself. She rolled the rillettes into little balls that Bridie could pop into her mouth, where they'd slowly soften from their frozen consistency enough to be chewed. The effect of the protein and high-quality fat in the scouring cold was like spinach to Popeye. She could go on and on. Other racers called Bridie the Tundra Gourmet, which was fine with Miranda. They could gum all the Doritos and M&M's they wanted; the results were clear.

"Did Gordon give you a lot of grief for leaving right before the race?" Miranda asked.

Bridie smiled and marched her fork across the empty plate. "Grief and spleen and a few other things I won't mention in front of the child."

Bridie would be the first to admit it seemed crazy. She'd said as much to Gordon when she'd gotten the call from Miranda that Papa was dead.

Gordon had looked at her in that flat-eyed, black-and-white way of his and said, "And you think you're going down there for the funeral?"

"I know I'm going," she'd said.

"And you'll risk everything for a dead guy who won't know the difference?"

"It's not for him, I'm going. It's for her. She'll know the difference."

"You don't think she'd understand?"

"That's not the point."

"What is the fucking point?"

"It matters," she said.

Bridie thought of the time she'd asked Miranda about her mother's picture, asked if Miranda had any issues.

Issues?

Over being abandoned.

I wasn't abandoned, Miranda had said. *I've had more parents than any one has a right to.* So Bridie had let it go.

But Gordon was still ranting. "See, this is why women should never be in positions of power and responsibility."

"This is a race, Gordon. Not the presidency."

"You're right. And it's a hell of a lot more important."

When she'd started training with Gordon years ago, she knew in advance that he was a misanthrope, but she wasn't interested in his people skills. She was there to train under a four-time Iditarod champion who bred, raised, and trained racing dogs that were unparalleled in the sport, a man whose reputation for dog care was also unparalleled.

So whenever he cocked off on a rant, she tried to remember one of the many situations in which his actions told the better truth of his heart. Early in his racing career, he was running a "puppy team" of two-year-olds with his best lead dog, Zinc. The young dogs had lost heart in lousy weather and refused to run in spite of the lead dog's cue. As Gordon waited it out, Zinc fell ill with frightening rapidity. The dog's gums went pasty gray, and he would not eat or drink, a sign of internal bleeding. Unable to get the other dogs motivated, Gordon put them on their gang line and tied it off to a tree, strapped on his snowshoes, and carried Zinc five miles to the next checkpoint, where he could be flown to Anchorage. Surgery revealed a bleeding ulcer that would have killed the dog had it not been for Gordon's efforts.

Bridie thought of the story again as she ran the dogs that morning before heading for the airstrip and the twelve-seater jet that would take her to Anchorage. Her lead dog, Zeus, was from Zinc's line. Gordon had not seen any potential in the pup and intended to give him away as a pet until Bridie had convinced him to give Zeus to her. She had discovered the dog's bliss by accident, while training a yearling group. Often when running the young dogs in harness, she would stop and shuffle the order. Some ran better in certain positions than others; the idea was to figure out where each dog was most confident and comfortable. Zeus seemed lazy and uninterested, both in the kennel and in harness. *He's so laid back, he's comatose,* Gordon pointed out.

She'd shuffled the dogs on that training run until there was nothing left to try but putting Zeus in solo lead, and she'd thought, what the hell, the run was going badly anyway. She'd tried pairing him up front with a more motivated dog once before, but he'd lollygagged and sulked so much she'd put him farther back in the pack. This day, she put him in single lead and went back down the line, reshuffling. She'd thought the barking and lunging was from one of the other dogs up front, but when she turned, it was Zeus making the racket, his face wreathed in smile. It was what racers referred to as "harness-banging," a primary indication of a dog's desire to run. He'd turn to her every two or three crowhops with that smile, his blue eyes blanched white by pure joy.

Over the next two years, he'd brought her in first on a five-hundred-mile qualifying race, second in a four-hundred-miler, and finally third in her first Iditarod, the brass ring of long-distance dog racing. Over eleven hundred miles of grueling trail from Anchorage to Nome—in one of the worst weather years of the race's history—Zeus never faltered in the lead. It was a tremendous strain on a dog's psyche to be in charge for that length of time, and typically racers put their leaders back in the team on easier stretches of trail to give them a break. But Zeus would not have it, and she'd had no choice but to leave him out front. Gordon had reamed her out for pushing the dog like that, but she could only argue that had Zeus not been in the lead, she would have had to carry him in the sled.

She whoaed the dogs at the top of a cut bank that dropped onto the frozen river, and she stepped on the toothed brake that stretched between the sled runners to emphasize her voice command. It was a stretch of the actual Iditarod trail, and she anticipated seeing it again in two weeks, seeing it as she saw it now, with no teams in front of her and only the vista of the small, thousand-soul village coming into view where it perched on a flat spit thrust into the Bering Sea. At ten below zero, the weather was perfect, even windless for once.

There was speculation that dogs raised in this environment were useless for the first stretch of the Iditarod, when temperatures in Anchorage, where the race started, could reach freezing or warmer. The dogs were miserable in that heat, but when it came to the latter half, dogs that felt like they were on vacation in the face of howling, below-zero gusts were an asset. And they knew they were going home.

She scanned the low hills rolling to the coast, her eyes searching for dark specks moving against white. Caribou. If Miranda could see this, she might understand better why Bridie did what she did. Miranda supported her in any endeavor, but with little comprehension of the details. When Bridie tried to describe it—the space, the air, the sound of below-zero snow sizzling under the sled runners—Miranda's eyes glazed, and Bridie knew her heart could not stretch past the lush valley in Oregon where she was raised. Bridie didn't fault her for that. Perry Hill was beautiful in an orderly, sculpted way, and it had shaped Miranda as inevitably as weather shapes land. But here on Alaska's western tundra, motion and momentum were unimpeded by roads, trellises, or buildings, and Bridie was all about motion, as Miranda herself liked to point out.

Bridie had been raised in eastern Michigan, but this landscape must have been in her heart all along. When Bridie was twelve, her father had taken a drive north to the Upper Peninsula. It was all the vacation they could ever afford, a day's drive as far as they could go. There was a crowd gathered in a snow-thick field, with banners stretched between two posts. Her father made the mistake of stopping to see what the to-do was, and that's when Bridie had seen her first sled-dog race. They watched the teams take off, one by one, and disappear into a stand of spruce. Bridie had pulled at her father's hand each time a racer faded into the trees, certain it should have been she who was moving on, the dogs' backs straining before her.

Life took her from Michigan to Oregon to graduate school in Oklahoma to an internship with a vet in Alaska and its inevitable tangle with the place where dogsled racing was the height of sport. Her mother fought her every step of the way. *You got no business sashaying all over the place. We could use your help right here.*

Her mother had relented slightly when Bridie chose veterinary; the "doctor" thing sounded good to her.

Bridie intended to stick with veterinary, but as if she'd planned a secret life for herself and executed it, she found both of her lives merging one spring day when Gordon came to the vet Bridie interned with to stock up on supplies. She trained and raced with him for three years before he retired and passed the torch, and three more years with the benefit of his full attention and access to his entire kennel. Once Bridie threw herself into dog racing, her mother retreated into bitterness that Bridie refused to tolerate.

Six years and thousands of trail miles later, she stood on this high bank with sixteen dogs in harness, a team of such perfectly matched canine souls, she had no doubt of her shot in this year's Iditarod, which began in just four days. Zorba, Moody, Watch, Spy, Frodo, Sandy, Alder, Chook, Stella, Boone, Jester, Jock, Murphy, Shy, Sheba, and Zeus. Just mouthing their names made her buzz, and she tried to stifle the adrenaline rush that came in spite of her fatigue. She slept only four hours a day now in preparation for the ten-day-long race, during which she would sleep very little. In most cases she'd use rest time for dog care and feeding, because without their good health, grace, and heart, there was no race.

She got off the sled and walked to the head of the team, encouraging each dog as she went. When she got to Zeus, she kneeled and submitted to a quick face-washing as she rubbed his chest.

"Ready?" she asked, and the blue eyes blared light as he crowhopped in place.

She returned to the sled and planted her boots on the runners, then yanked the snow hook. "Hike! Let's go home."

Zeus surged down the cut bank and onto river ice, his white shoulder fur slipping side to side as long forelegs stretched for good footing. The rest of the team scudded down behind him, rumps tucked, and finally came the sled, prow jutting into air before the weight of it tipped forward. As it dropped down the bank, she crouched on the runners, knees bent to take the shock.

Jim greeted her in the dog yard when she returned. He'd flown out from Fairbanks the week before to assume his duties as dog handler for the race. He would fly to certain checkpoints along the race route to help with the dogs and make sure the food drops and equipment were in order. This was what Jim chose to do on vacation. He and Gordon had known each other from their service in Vietnam. Jim would have chosen to race but for the fused vertebrae in his spine, an injury from the war.

"How's the trail?" he asked.

"Perfect."

"Flight's out in two hours. What's left to do?"

She gestured at the team. "Just taking care of these guys. Is Gordon around?"

Jim scuffed the dirty snow with his boot. "Think he had to grab something at the hardware store."

"He's that pissed?" she asked.

Jim's eyebrows twitched upward.

"I don't guess it would do any good to explain it to you?"

"Probably not."

Bridie sighed. "Guess it's a guy thing, then."

"Guess."

Bridie unhooked each dog and kenneled it, then dragged the sled to the lean-to. She folded the blue harness and stowed it in a canvas bag that had her name and address stenciled on it.

"Everything's packed and ready in the shed," she said. "There shouldn't be any confusion."

"You pack that .357 we got you?"

Bridie had planned to leave it behind. A lot of racers didn't carry guns and had no trouble. Sure, there were arguments in favor of packing a weapon. Things happened. Parts of the trail wound through prime moose habitat, which at that time of year, included cow moose with calves. Even the most well-trained dogs rarely resisted that kind of temptation. You used the gun to finish off a moose badly injured by the dogs, or vice versa. Either scenario was something she wouldn't give weight to by preparing for it. Maybe it was superstitious. Maybe just blind stubbornness. But as far as she was concerned, the .357 was deadweight that she'd just as soon have for extra dog snacks.

Jim huffed and kicked a divot in the snow. "Don't butt heads with him on this, Bridie. He's pissed enough as it is."

"Okay," she said.

"Okay what?"

"I'll put it in with my gear right now on one condition." Jim rolled his eyes. "What."

"Give me a ride up to the airstrip after I change and get my bag."

"Deal," he said. "Yell when you're ready."

Once she'd changed into what she referred to as her "city clothes," which were nothing but a cleaner version of her everyday clothes, she went back to the dog yard and said good-bye to the team, slipping each one a lard-and-fish Popsicle. Zeus smiled at her but didn't bother getting up. When not harnessed in lead, he could have been a porch dog.

"You old hound," she said, and scratched him behind the ears. "Guess I don't need to tell you to rest up." He rolled onto his side, stretched, and groaned. "Yeah. That's what I thought."

Jim drove her up to the airstrip on the back of the snow machine, her duffel wedged between them. The afternoon winds had kicked up, and the resulting ground blizzard made it hard to see five feet ahead. This was the kind of weather racers dreaded on the trail. To the dogs, it was all blizzard, even though the drivers could look above them and see markless blue sky.

After Jim dropped her off, she stood at the door of the tiny air service office and watched him pull away, the taillights blinking out of sight almost immediately. Inside, the room was overheated and crowded with people waiting for the afternoon flight into Anchorage.

Several people tapped her shoulder as she edged through the crowd, smiled, and said "good luck," thinking she was heading into Anchorage to prepare for the race start. She leaned against the wall next to an older woman, Glenna, who lived near Gordon and who prepared for Bridie the only food she took with her that was not made by Miranda.

"You got that dried salmon all shipped out?" Glenna asked.

"Sure do," Bridie said, and rested her arm across the tiny woman's shoulders. "It's kept me going more times than I can tell you."

"That's what salmon do," Glenna said. "Live and die so we can live and die, eh?" She grinned at Bridie. The few teeth she had left speckled her smile like Chiclets. But her smile faded as she looked past Bridie to the door. "Uh-oh. Here comes big pants."

Bridie knew she meant Gordon. He'd come to the small native village twenty-five years before to be a hunting guide, and built a small cabin upriver, where he spent the winters with dogs he'd bought from one of the pioneers of the Iditarod race, Herbie Nayokpuk. He'd intended to use them only for hauling wood and water, but Herbie passed the bug along, hidden in the rough fur of his dogs, and Gordon forgot all about guiding. Said he hated kowtowing to the idiots anyway.

Now his blond head weaved in and out of the sea of dark heads as he approached her.

"Burn up trail," Glenna said, and squeezed Bridie's elbow before she slipped away.

Gordon stood next to her, facing the window, his feet slightly apart, hands locked behind him in that at-ease pose he'd never shaken after the army.

"Jim said he dropped you off," Gordon said. "Shoulda made you walk for all the trouble you're causing."

Bridie said nothing.

"I retired three years ago, expecting somebody to carry the torch for me. I've put a lot into you. Did I screw up?"

"What do *you* think?" she asked, mostly because she knew he was going to tell her anyway.

"You're good, Bridie. You've got the knack with the dogs. Got the stamina. Got the drive. Unfortunately, you've got a woman's heart, and that's a weakness you can't overcome."

She knew he was baiting her, the old coach trick, but could not help her stomach tightening. A few years ago, her response would have blistered his face, but the racing had taught her to control herself. If you succumbed out there to frustration and anger, you might as well scratch.

"I'm ready, the dogs are ready, everything's organized. Nothing but an act of God will hurt me in this race. And if it's time for that, even a man's heart won't help."

"You're breaking training, concentration, the works."

"Today would have been their last hard day anyway," she said. "They're on a light schedule, and Jim can handle that fine. You know I like them hot out of the chute." She tried smiling at him to test the depth of his disapproval—and got her answer when he refused even to meet her gaze. She tried another tack.

"Look. I know taking on a 'woman's heart' has been difficult for you. I imagine you caught more shit for that than I do for being a woman. But I haven't disappointed you. I know that for a fact."

"You're disappointing me now," he said.

"Because you choose to be," she said. "There's no merit in it."

He cut his eyes at her. "Look at you, all of thirty, is it—?"

"Thirty-two," she said. If he was going to berate her, he might as well have the facts.

"—thirty-two. And what the hell do you know about merit? This girl's not even family, for Christ's sake. I wouldn't do it even if it was family."

She caught his eye for the breath of a second, thought of trying to explain that she probably wouldn't do it for family either. She remembered the moment she'd chosen Miranda as someone she trusted absolutely. She watched her fair-weather college friends troop into and out of the hospital room, their eyes falling away from her when she couldn't come up with the old razzle-dazzle. She'd wanted to yell at them, *I'm here. I'm still here,* but something steadied her each time she felt compelled to shout. Miranda knew she was there. And in all the time she'd spent later at the vineyard with Miranda, Bridie saw what others would fail to see in her friend, a woman whose limitless belief made you impervious to agony or weakness. How could Bridie possibly explain that to Gordon?

Gordon was still fuming. "You're not going to save anybody by going down there now."

"I don't expect to," she said.

"Then why are you cutting your throat?"

She scanned his face, which was scarlet with heat and anger, and she knew why he was beating this to death. When he retired from racing, he'd said he was over it. There wasn't enough challenge in it when he could win so easily. But he hadn't stopped wanting a challenge. So he'd got one. Her. And he was losing this race.

"It's not my throat you're worried about, is it," she said, her voice barely audible above the din around them.

"What do you mean?" he said.

The pilot posted himself at the door and began herding passengers onto the tarmac toward the plane.

Bridie looked away. "Nothing," she said. "You won't be disappointed, but that'll only be a pleasant by-product."

"What?"

"Even a woman's heart is capable of selfishness," she said.

"Last call!" the pilot shouted, and Bridie stepped into the swirl of snow on the tarmac.

She buckled herself in, careful not to scrunch the square of stiff paper in her coat pocket. She'd taken the photograph from her album to give to Ruben. It was the finish line of the first big race Bridie had won. She had the distinction of also being the first woman to take it. Five hundred miles of vicious weather, ice, streams, and rivers to cross. In the four days it took her to win it, she had slept only four hours. That was the trick. As long as the dogs are rested and fed and happy, all you have to do is stay awake and keep going. Never lose the momentum.

2

Once the sun beat back a morning mist, Petra saw them fade into view, row by row, acre to acre, scabrous trunks and cordons spreading skyward. Ruby Throat's vineyard manager, Luis Ruiz, and his crew crept up and down the rows, pruning vines. The men were easy to spot in bright yellow coveralls, clothing that would litter the aisles like molted skin after an hour more of the unseasonable warmth. Not bad for late February in Oregon, she thought, and decided then to have the service outside.

Ruby Throat's vineyards were demarcated on the downhill side by a dark line of trees, hazelnuts, still a big cash crop in the Willamette Valley. Beyond these trees lay the one hundred and twenty-five acres of Perry Hill, twenty-five of them planted to grapes. While Ruby Throat's vineyard yielded queenly fruit, it was the Perry Hill crop, sold exclusively to her winery for the past twenty-four years, that accounted for Petra's premier vintages. Perry Hill was Carter Perry's land, and it was Carter Perry's death the community would honor that afternoon.

A horse appeared from an old grove of cherry and hazelnut at the western edge of the vineyard, its rump a rounded bauble of white against its otherwise penny-colored coat. One of the crew waved, and the horse contracted in a bunchy squat. The rider covered the horse's knobby poll with his free hand, then stroked the crest of its neck until it relaxed and squared up. Petra smiled.

Duncan Fletcher, her winemaker, was as eccentric as winemakers were purported to be. In Australia, he'd made assistant winemaker at one of the large, corporate wineries in the Barossa Valley, where he learned to hate the recipe-style winemaking they endorsed, and went to France. He was only able to get on as a cellar rat at a lesser *domaine,* but it was in the Côte d'Or, and that was something. He scrubbed vats, steamed barrels, and swabbed cellars, smelling, tasting, listening, until he'd soaked up as much as he was going to, given the fact he would never be able to do more. The industry there was, as he liked to say, locked up tighter than a nun's ass.

A dog loped from the trees until it caught up to the horse, which it followed closely but slightly to the side as a proper stock dog would. Duncan had brought it with him from Australia to France and then to America. That said something, though Petra wasn't sure exactly what.

With the tip of one crook-boned finger against the picture window, she traced his progress to the house, leaving a map on the glass in unctuous, human oil. Madrita, Luis's wife, chastised her about it but the maps returned to the window.

Petra had leisure now to vex Madrita, but she'd done her time in the yellow coveralls, hands scarred and twisty from so many years of the work. She'd been able to cut back once Ruby Throat had finally made its mark, in spite of those who'd said it couldn't be done here, that pinot noir could not be grown this far north, not in Oregon. Her husband, Ernest, had been the grape's archangel all those years ago, and he'd been right.

She hadn't cut back in time to stave off the arthritis that had begun to plague her. She looked at her hands again. Once she thought that at age sixty she'd be jogging, learning to play tennis, getting back to the piano she'd loved as a girl. But she'd married a fledgling winemaker instead, one whose dreams entailed huge expenditures of capital they didn't have, which required in turn that they leach what they did have—their bodies and hearts—into the enterprise.

They'd come to Oregon's Willamette Valley in '62, looking for the soil and climate that resembled the great vineyards of Burgundy in France, where pinot noir flourished. They'd tested earth in cross sections as they hiked over the rough red crumble of the Dundee Hills. As they tested an eighty-acre parcel that was for sale, they wandered onto the downhill cherry orchards of the man who was selling the land.

Carter Perry hadn't blinked when he shook Ernest's hand, didn't disclose then that he was the seller, but patiently fielded the barrage of questions about soil, microclimate, prevailing winds, pests—all elements that contributed to the quality of the fruit and which the French summed up neatly in the word *terroir*. Carter was skeptical but not without interest in their endeavor. Grapes were fruit, and he had grown plenty of that. But the market for Oregon cherries had flattened once Michigan got into the fray, and he'd had a hard time giving away the fruit that had been his mainstay crop for so many years.

When Ernest talked to him about growing grapes on Carter's land, as well—a crop Ernest would contract for purchase—Carter said sure, why not, and hogged out an experimental acre to accommodate the vines Ernest kept at a nursery outside of Portland, vines it was rumored he'd smuggled in from France. It had taken Ernest two more years to get his own new acreage cleared and terraformed to his liking, where he then planted the remainder of the plants. Three years later, he'd completed his first crush from Carter's grapes, and he had been amazed. Not only had Carter a natural hand with the vines, but the grapes also had remarkable intensity, even in youth. When Ernest and Petra's first crop came in, it was good, but it never compared to Carter's. Not then or since.

Petra remembered the feel of Carter's hands at the hospital five days ago, their surfaces rough and raspy still, his grasp as strong as if he'd meant to bind himself to the world.

Madrita's voice drifted to her, a surprising soprano from one who grumbled so, reminding Duncan to take off his boots, and Duncan's rough bass in response, *Claro que sí,* and then Madrita scolding about his pitiful accent and how she wished he wouldn't desecrate her tongue in such a way. It was well-traveled territory between them. Madrita was openly distrustful of him when he came to Ruby Throat five years ago to turn his obsession into something solid. She said there was too much fire in his belly, which Petra translated as "too passionate." This was a good thing in a wine-maker, as long as the fire was aimed in the proper direction. Ernest knew it, and hired him as assistant winemaker, said Duncan had more passion for the grape than for the life of his own heart. When Ernest died three years ago, Petra had appointed Duncan wine-maker and given him a twenty percent interest in the business. Ernest would have done the same eventually. "Morning," she said without turning. "Coffee?"

"Maddy's got it." The nicknames. Another thing Madrita dis-liked.

"Have a seat," she said, though he had already lowered himself to a chair across the table.

The coffee appeared, along with slices of Madrita's lemon bread, a mound of goat cheese, and a small pitcher of warmed raspberry syrup. He spread the bread thickly with cheese, pooled the syrup in a coffer he made in the white crumble with his thumb, and ate, al-ternating with sips of black coffee, strong. He nodded his pleasure, eyes closed.

"I haven't had a chance to talk to her yet," Petra said. "She and the boy drove in yesterday, and her friend flew in last night."

The grape green of his eyes touched her face a minute before he turned to watch the men move up and down the rows, looking on with a blend of satisfaction and anxiety. He'd never seen Carter Perry's daughter in person, only pictures Petra flashed at him. She'd visited once in the five years Duncan had been at Ruby Throat, but he'd managed to miss her, he couldn't remember why.

As implacable as Carter had been, the one thing that got him going was the girl. Duncan wished he'd minded the situation more closely, because Carter was gone now, and he'd left Perry Hill to the daughter. Ruby Throat bought grapes from several vineyards in the area to increase its output, but Perry Hill consistently gave the best fruit, better even than Ruby Throat's own vineyard. Now the source hung on the fingertips of a ghost, and worry caught in his throat like dust.

"Miranda's had a hard time, but she can take a lot of pressure." Petra thought of the way the girl looked when Petra went to the hospital in San Francisco after Ruben was born. She'd found her asleep in a rocking chair in the neonatal unit, Ruben on her chest like a tiny, shriveled raisin. Petra could see the burned hollows grief had carved in her face even in sleep.

"I've seen her through most of her life," Petra continued. "She'll do the right thing."

"We could lease the vines from her," Duncan said.

"If we had the money," Petra said.

Ernest's medical care had put a strain on their finances. She'd refused to hospitalize him when she was no longer able to care for him on her own. The cancer had fought harder to kill him than most, and in-home nursing care had cost them the bundle that insurance didn't cover. She'd taken out a hefty loan against the business.

"Besides, it's not just the crop that needs retaining," Petra said.

"What else is there?" Duncan asked.

Petra shook her head. He was like a racehorse in blinders.

Through the window they watched the dog crawl through the grass in stealthy pursuit of something only it could see.

"What's she after?" Petra asked.

"Gopher. Bird. Anything that moves. She's bored," Duncan said.

"Teach her to work vines. That'll keep her busy."

He grinned, an unusual show of humor.

Distant activity at Perry Hill caught Petra's eye. Carter's old farmhouse, its white clapboards blinding against dark earth, belched forth a child and his mother after him. A faint blare of horn brought another woman leaping down the porch steps to the car, where she collapsed herself with the careless confidence of an athlete into the passenger's seat of the old blue Toyota. They were coming to help Petra set up for the service.

"They're on their way," she said, and gestured down the hill.

Duncan stood too quickly, catching the table across the thick meat of his thighs. She almost laughed at the consternation on his face as he tried to swipe spilled coffee from the rubbed wood surface. He amazed her still, this big, raw fellow from South Australia with his passion for winemaking, a minimum of social acuity, and an artist's sense for the delicacy of the pinot noir grape. He continued to swab until she took the napkin from his hand and spread it over the remaining mess. "It's all right," she said. "Madrita will get it."

"That's what I'm afraid of," he said.

"The memorial service is from three to five."

"I know," he said.

"I just want to make sure you're there. It's important."

"The girl doesn't even know me, and I've got four hundred barrels to monitor."

Petra twined her fingers into a platform on which she rested her chin. "Just show up," she said. "Pay your respects. That's all I ask."

He pressed his lips into a thin line and looked out the window once more before turning away.

"And her name's Miranda. Can you remember that?"

He raised his hand at her but did not stop his progress to the foyer.

She waited until she saw him ride down to the winery before she rose, easing herself slowly from the chair. Mornings were the worst. She meant to start the medication today, but decided to wait until tomorrow. It would be one more day she'd have to fend off age, pain, time.

Miranda tried to get Ruben to eat the rest of his sandwich before they headed up to Ruby Throat. He stood on the chair, his voice shrill, chanting an old Beatles song they'd heard on the oldies station.

Miranda stroked his hair. "You need to eat a little before the party."

Bridie returned from her run, shirt sagged and dark with perspiration, thick auburn hair braided tight as rope. Miranda set it swinging across her back as Bridie passed, got the usual snort in response. The hair was Bridie's big concession to gender. Otherwise it was jeans and flannel shirts and dogs.

Ruben bolted off the chair and ran to her, singing louder. "She's got a chicken to ride. . . ."

"She what?" Bridie asked, bent low to his face.

"Beatles song," Miranda said. "He heard it on the radio yesterday."

"It's a oldie, Aunt Bridie," Ruben said.

"Why does he call me that?" Bridie asked Miranda.

"What do you want him to call you, 'Godmother Bridie'?"

"How about just Bridie?"

"It's disrespectful. I want him to have manners."

"Yes, ma'am, thank you, say please," Ruben said.

"Ruben, two more bites," Miranda said.

"I wanna chicken to ride," he said, and ricocheted around the kitchen.

"I'll deal with this little monster while you get ready," Bridie said. She sprawled across a kitchen chair, practically obscuring it, and wrestled Ruben onto her lap. "Now you're gonna eat this stuff or I'll eat it for you." She took a big bite of his sandwich and moaned with her eyes closed while she chewed. "Apples and cheddar," she said. "I'd give anything to have a sandwich like this on the trail."

Ruben tried to take it from her, but she held it up higher than he could reach.

"Aunt Bridie," he said, staring at the sandwich in her outstretched hand.

"Oh, so now that I want it, you want it?"

"It's mine," Ruben said, but softer now, as if Bridie had transferred to him some kind of magical calm. Bridie always had a way with jittery creatures. She would have been a good vet.

But six years ago, she'd called Miranda from Alaska, where she'd spent the summer as a vet tech and told Miranda that she was going to take up sled-dog racing. She'd got hooked by one of the vet's clients, a four-time champion of the Iditarod sled-dog race. Bridie had run one Iditarod since then and finished third; a remarkable feat for a rookie was what the magazines said. She would run her second Iditarod in four days, but she looked ready now, Miranda thought, watching tendons slither like live things across her hands and arms.

Though she'd never seen Bridie race, Miranda followed it in the news. Westerners had a jones for all things Alaskan, and the Iditarod was the epitome of the state's character, eleven hundred miles by dogsled through country as bereft of human influence as country could be in the twenty-first century. It was a challenge that fitted Bridie as neatly as her own skin.

Even now, twelve years into a friendship that had continued since their sophomore year at Reed, Miranda wondered why Bridget Marie McLewan, woman about campus, had befriended little taciturn Miranda Perry. When Ruben's father, Dario, was killed, Miranda had just found out she was pregnant. It was Bridie who stayed and saw her through the pregnancy, though she'd had to delay taking the vet tech job in Anchorage to do it. It was Bridie who'd stood at the end of days that were like walking through fire. And three days ago, all Miranda had to do was dial the phone, say *Papa's gone. Will you come?* It was a lot to ask with the race only days away, but there had been no hesitation in Bridie's response. *Be right with you.*

Upstairs, Miranda shimmied into a navy blue wool dress Petra had left for her with a note. *Just in case you didn't have time to get something.* Petra had always mothered her, thought a young girl couldn't receive proper care from a mere father, no matter how kindly he was. Papa had never required Miranda to wear a dress; he himself would never attend a function for which anything but work clothes were necessary.

She smiled at the thought of his face if he could see her now. The expression wouldn't much change but for a tiny crimp at the corners of his mouth. The soft-spoken *Well* would acknowledge something not quite understood.

Bridie's voice floated up. "Time to go."

When Miranda came downstairs, Bridie looked her up and

down, choked back a laugh. "Well, good god, I didn't realize I'd need my ball gown for this."

"Petra" was all Miranda had to say, and Bridie nodded.

The crowd in Petra's garden was sizable. Miranda knew most of the people there, had grown up among them, but she had no idea what to do. *Make yourself available,* Petra had told her. Did that mean she should walk around or wait for people to come to her? So she stood with her back to the rose trellis, her spine rigid, flinching when the dress licked at her legs in the breeze and made her skin crawl.

People approached her, offered memories of her father, then wandered away to browse the tables that she and Bridie had helped set up earlier and covered with the yellow smocked linens Petra used for special vineyard dinners. The overhangs, which featured the Ruby Throat insignia, luffed in the breeze. Ruby Throat's "Perry Hill" bottling jeweled the globed, ten-ounce glasses; condolences floated to Miranda on its familiar mineral and blackberry smell. She eyed the expanse of Perry Hill vines creeping up the hill. Papa's vines.

A figure jutted obliquely into her field of vision, and she put out her hand before she realized who it was. Bridie took it anyway, laughing.

"Hell of a thing to come home for," Bridie said.

Miranda's eyes crinkled, but her mouth would not follow suit. Bridie pressed Miranda's head to her shoulder and ruffled her short, dark hair.

Petra disentangled herself from a knot of people and headed toward them. Iris-colored eyes flickered across Miranda's face.

Petra frowned and tried to straighten Miranda's hair, unable to resist the urge to spit-polish.

Ruben spurted out of the crowd and grabbed Bridie's hand. "There's a dog. Let's go see the dog."

Bridie floated away, attached to Ruben's hand like a human kite.

Petra glanced over her shoulder, and Miranda heard a voice, its accent as thick now as when she was a child. Jean-Paul Gagnon had come to America from Burgundy to make his mark with pinot noir as he had been unable to do in France. Because there, no matter how much talent one had, one had no chance of getting into the business without the proper family and legal connections. Miranda had watched him make the rounds, black and silver hair lacquered into a discreet ponytail. He stood before her now, the stem of his wineglass pinched expertly between thumb and two fingers.

"Not a perfect occasion to see you again," he said, and bowed over her hand, lips not quite touching skin.

"You're still into that Frenchie routine?" Miranda asked.

He thumped a fist to his chest. "You are as bad as your father. Sacrilege, blasphemy, and bullshit." He turned to Petra. "You must teach this young lady her graces."

"The child refuses to charm on demand," Petra said.

"*Alors,* American women. Cowboys, every one."

"Are we insulted?" Miranda asked Petra.

"We'll allow him a moment more if he has anything gracious to say," Petra said.

"Ah, but I do," he said. "I raise a glass of this marvelous elixir to a man I admired. Who helped us all when our skins were shiny and new and asked for nothing in return. We welcome home the part of him that remains."

Miranda was unprepared for the twist in her throat. She looked down, squeezed her eyes shut. A warm hand draped across the back of her neck as Petra asked Jean Paul about the small development that now abutted his vineyard.

Gagnon hissed. "My God, these people. They want the country they see in magazines but cannot manage the reality of it." He screwed up his face and squeaked his vocal cords together. " 'The deer eat my flowers. There is dirt on the ground. Manure smells like shit!' "

"I don't know why they had to move the line so soon," Petra said, shaking her head.

"What line?" Miranda asked.

"It's part of the state's stellar land-use vision," Petra said. "There's an Urban Growth Boundary line around Portland. Inside the circle, residential development is allowed but strictly regulated. Outside the line, our country character is to remain intact—that is, until the circle fills up. Three years ago, they expanded the line to include us. As long as we continue what we're doing, we still get agricultural status. Anything not in ag use will be rezoned residential, and property value skyrockets."

Papa had told Miranda about the development abutting Gagnon's vineyard, built on land farmed by an old friend. When he'd got too old to work the place, the developers had swooped on his children, all living elsewhere with lives of their own. Like Miranda, they had no idea about the Urban Growth Development line, or that it might be moved one day to include the farm. But developers knew, and they scalped the property for next to nothing.

Gagnon hunched his shoulders, spread his hands in the air. "Houses next to farms. It is no good."

"This doesn't happen in France?" Miranda asked.

"Of course. But Euros still know where food comes from. Here, people think it grows in plastic."

"The way most people treat soil, it pretty much does," Petra said.

"But that is another beef," he said. "Between zoning and all these corporations taking over the wine industry, we quiver like rabbits. But I must leave you ladies now, sad as you will be without me."

Petra smiled, revealing the blank slit between her two front teeth, knocked there when she'd rolled a tractor back when she and Ernest first moved to Oregon.

Petra sat next to Miranda on a wrought-iron bench.

"I love this time of year," she said. "There were years, of course, when I couldn't take the time to enjoy it." She looked at the misshapen hands spread across her thighs.

"What did Jean-Paul mean about corporate takeovers?"

"It's like the Blob," Petra said. "Big beverage corporations sweeping up little wineries to add to their cachet . . . industry mergers are nothing new—I just never foresaw it happening in this business."

"But we're too small for that, aren't we?" Miranda asked.

"They're gobbling wineries in Australia, California. They look for big producers to anchor their line, then snap up small, premium producers as a showcase. It puts independents like us at a huge disadvantage when it comes to marketing. These big companies can afford to swamp consumers with mediocre wine, demand the best spots in grocery and liquor stores, and demand that those stores buy huge lots, leaving the rest of us—"

"On the bottom shelf," Miranda finished.

Petra listened to the muted noise of the crowd behind them. Most of the valley's top wineries were represented there today. She'd felt the heat of curious eyes all afternoon. Many of them had gathered at Ernest's graveside two years ago, most of them harboring the same questions about Petra and the future of Ruby Throat as they no doubt harbored now about Miranda and Perry Hill.

"Now I know how elk feel in the fall," Petra said.

"How's that?"

"Fresh meat," Petra said, nodding her head at the crowd. "When Ernest died, the speculation was that I'd either sell Ruby Throat or marry someone who would run it for me."

"Now they know better," Miranda said.

"Indeed they do," Petra said. "But they don't know about you."

"Me?"

"You're a single female who's inherited a vineyard most of these people would prune an arm for. But they don't expect to have to go to such lengths. They figure you've been gone a long time, you have a profession of your own, and you'll let it go to the highest bidder. That's what absentee relatives do." Petra felt her cheek sting where the girl's eyes raked it.

"Don't take it personally, sweetie. This community is a good one, a strong one, but no one could resist this fantasy," she said, waved her hand in an arc around them. "Everyone and his brother wants in on a vineyard—attorneys, doctors, movie producers with too much money. . . . Working land is the most honorable profession in the world. There hasn't been a time somebody didn't approach Carter to sell, or at least to lure his crop away from Ruby Throat. It's just business. We always understood that. Everyone wants a 'jewel in the hills.' "

"Like Perry Hill," Miranda said.

"You grew up on that phrase."

"Yes."

"Well, it's your jewel now."

Petra watched the realization take shape in the girl's eyes. Of course she wouldn't have thought of it yet. She'd probably kept herself focused on what was to be done, minute to minute. The immediacy of caring for a child would have seen to that, but she had that Perry focus also that wouldn't allow her mind to stretch far into the future. That would have been impractical, too close to daydreaming for comfort. Carter would have told her so. She stared hard at the girl's profile, the high cliff of her forehead just like the old man's, but all the rest of her—size, coloring—like her mother.

It was Petra's role now to outline a soothing and practical course of action. She tried to push words past the cramp in her throat but failed, hearing Carter's voice instead: *Watch out for her. You always wanted to anyway. She'll do the right thing. That's why I'm leaving it for her and the boy,* but was confused by the echo in her head of Ernest's voice, of her hands in his, the smell of his dying so strong she thought she would vomit: *We've made something here, haven't we? It's for you. Don't let go.*

Petra pulled her cheeks taut against the desire to blurt everything she could foresee and tell. But here was Duncan's solid bulk moving toward them, the dog a gray speckled shadow behind him.

"Miranda, this is Duncan Fletcher."

"Pleasure," Duncan said to Miranda, and shook her hand, which looked like a bit of bleached cloth caught in the stained shell of his palm.

"What winery are you with?" Miranda asked.

Duncan looked at Petra.

"Honey, Duncan is Ruby Throat's winemaker. You remember how I told you he reminds me of Ernest but with an accent?"

"English?" Miranda asked.

"Australian," Petra said, then rolled her eyes. "But he does speak English, so I don't know why I'm answering for him."

"It's because you do it so much better," he said. Then, to Miranda, "Sorry so late. Busy time of year. But I don't need to explain that to you."

"No," Miranda said.

"We'll miss the old man . . . your father," he corrected himself and worked his neck against the confines of the collar he'd buttoned all the way to his throat. "He could taste a grape and gauge the sugar level exactly as a meter. He really knew his business. No doubt you'll carry on the tradition."

Petra could tell he'd rehearsed the minimal speech countless times.

Miranda shook her head. "I don't know anything about this except that if you do it, it's your whole life."

Duncan looked at Petra as if he had a sinking boat to bail out and nothing but his hands to do it with. He tugged at his collar, eyes pleading to be released. Petra jerked her head toward the winery. At least he could get some work done.

"Well, I'll get back to the winery," he said, already turning away. "If there's anything I can do . . ."

Petra sighed once he'd got out of earshot.

"He's a natural with animals and wine. Not so great with people. I wish I could let him have his way, leave him to the winery. He's really got the touch, more so than Ernest. But people want access to the winemaker. Part of the charm. And when he puts his mind to it, he can be quite charming."

"He seemed all right," Miranda said. "He talked to me."

Petra laughed. "If you can call that talk. Actually, he's better with strangers, at the tastings and such."

"I'm a stranger."

"No. You're Carter Perry's daughter."

The juice rested darkly in row after row of French oak barrels. Lot twelve. It was a contract from a vineyard Duncan hadn't tried before. He'd surveyed it last spring, had a good feeling about the place. The owner was a member of the LIVE program, which was as close to organic certification as you could get, and that was the most chemical manipulation Ruby Throat allowed. When Duncan looked over the crop that fall, he liked what he saw. He already knew the sugars were good. He'd checked it himself before he'd let the man harvest.

In the cellar, the rough oak staves seemed to eat up the light, leaving a perpetual dimness that Duncan liked. His belly temperature rose, saliva glands ached tartly as he climbed steel steps to the catwalk that ran along the third tier of barrels, lot twelve. When he'd crushed the grapes that fall, he'd left the juice on skins and stems for quite a while, was unsure how much stuffing they'd have. Skin contact was crucial. Yeasts, color, body, all came from the thin skin of the pinot noir grape.

The primary fermentation had gone off without a hitch, and he'd started the batch on its secondary fermentation, the malolactic, in late November. This was the process that caused his anxiety to spike off the meter, and he monitored the barrels daily, sipping, casting for off odors—nail polish remover, vinegar, rotten eggs, rubber—Fresno Boot, they called it here. That always gave him a laugh. So far, he'd smelled nothing off on his daily rounds, and there was good fruit on the palate from this new batch. It was one relief in a long, long line of things to wait for and worry about. He sucked a jigger of wine from one of the barrels with the glass-tubed thief and rolled it around his mouth. Lean, he thought. Top heavy. In the next couple of weeks it ought to bloom, balance a little. He prayed it would.

He moved down to the farthest bowels of the cellar, hand drifting along the tops of the barrels as familiar to him as children, until he came to the Perry Hill lot, which he always saved for last. These he treated in the old Burgundian way, barreled them before the primary was quite finished so there was still a little CO_2 to protect them through the malolactic fermentation. That way, no sulfite had to be added until they were bottled, and then only the bare minimum. The Perry Hill grapes responded like queens. He tasted a mouthful from a couple of the barrels, just to reassure himself, and felt the beginnings of the silky elegance that made the Perry Hill label the pride of Ruby Throat. The balance would come later. It always did.

He thought of the big, overwrought California wines and smirked. All balls and no elegance. There was too much sun, too much heat. Oregon's climate pushed the vines to the limits of weather, and the pinot noir grape liked to be on the edge. It rose to risk, like artists whose work was sublime when stretched to their utmost.

And then the winemaker had to learn to leave it alone as much as possible. He and Ernest had planned a gravity-feed winery, one that allowed the different processes to be performed at different levels. When the wine had to be transferred from vat to vat or vat to barrel, the juice would trickle down by its own weight instead of being forced through pumps. Pinot did not like to be handled.

He had lucked out coming here, surprising considering the unkind past. When his father lost their vineyard over a ridiculous title technicality, he'd been lucky enough to get on as an assistant at Henning's in the Barossa, but unlucky enough to realize he had a knack for winemaking and that what Henning's did was not winemaking so much as production. Then there was France, the Côte d'Or with all the attached romance along with the unpleasant ramifications of a snot-beleaguered industry. And then he'd found Ruby Throat, a mentor, room to do with each crop only what it was capable of doing. And bloody hell, were these vineyards capable. To have made an international mark as winemaker at forty-one was dream stuff. But the ground had begun to shift again. Subdivisions, corporate takeovers, daughters of untried character. It made him sour as hell.

He rinsed the thief and returned it to its resting place before he turned off the lights. He needed to eat, get a little rest before piling into another long day. The Perry Hill runneled still in the crevices of his tongue, berry and leather coasting on a slick of hazelnut and a hint of oak.

He walked down the hill to the small cottage nestled on the edge of the property. Ernest and Petra had built it when they'd first arrived and lived there for fifteen years until they'd been able to build their dream house up the hill, close to the winery.

Upon reaching the front door, Duncan realized the dog was not at his side. He turned and chirped into the darkness, called "Fluke!" then saw the yellow prisms of her eyes in the porch light as she came on in that smooth, low-headed trot. "Here, Fluke," he said, and saw in the darkness the white tip of her tail flash left and right.

He tucked her face into his cupping hands. "Long day, eh?" She butted the flat top of her head against his chest.

He walked in first, waited inside for the dog to come in after him. She would not pass an entrance unless he had gone first. Herd dog thing, he figured. Always bring up the rear.

She lay on the thin, plucked carpet, watching him fill her dish with lean ground lamb mixed with high-grade kibble and chicken broth. While she ate, he prepared his own meal: leftover roasted beets and carrots along with an elk steak seared in a rolling of mustard and blackberry jam. Madrita made the blackberry jam just the way he liked it, low sugar so as not to overpower the berry, and mostly sieved of the bothersome seeds. He drank down a glass of water which was achingly cold and full of minerals from three hundred feet down.

Finally he stretched himself onto the swayed double bed, able to close his eyes for a while. In the dark, he summoned again the feel of the fermenting juice in his mouth and nose, was amazed still at Ernest's acuity in finding the *terroir*. Soils and acclimation like that were rare, and while Ruby Throat's vineyards were exceptional, he'd known that the soil lower down the mountain had more magic, the air currents a gentler caress, that the cold, when it came, would not sit so cruelly there. And who knew. The trial vineyard could be another jewel in the hills.

He shifted deeper into the swale of the mattress. The dog moaned once at the side of the bed. "Hup," he said, and she sprang up, sowing herself into the furrow of his legs like a long, brindled seed.

⁓❦⁓

Miranda sat crossways on her old twin bed, reading to Ruben. She was exhausted by a fatigue that was more stressful than anything she'd experienced in the restaurant. At least there she knew what was expected of her, knew what to expect.

A photograph appeared in Ruben's hands. He held it close to his face, talked softly to it.

"What's that, Ru?" she asked.

"Zeus," he said.

"Who?"

"Aunt Bridie's dog," Ruben said.

"Let me see."

He passed it to her. It was a picture of Bridie kneeling with one of her dogs at the finish line of a race.

"Did Bridie give this to you, honey?"

"Yeah. 'Cause I want a dog like Zeus."

Bridie appeared at the door. "Zeus is my lead dog. He's the man, right, Ru?"

"Aunt Bridie's gonna get me a puppy."

"Is that so?" Miranda said, and gave Bridie a thanks-a-lot look.

"I told him we'd have to discuss it with you, first," Bridie said. "Right, Ru?"

"Uh-uh," Ruben said.

"He just doesn't remember," Bridie said.

Ruben's eyes glowed owlishly at her.

Miranda patted his leg and handed the picture to him, which he tucked under his pillow. "You've got to get some sleep."

Ruben scowled at her, then smiled. "Love you, Mom."

"Love you, baby."

She and Bridie stepped onto the balcony, where she'd held Ruben that morning. Miranda lowered herself cautiously onto the frayed webbing of the aluminum lawn chair Papa kept there.

Bridie gave a low whistle. "It really hits you from up here. We used to sit on this balcony at night and feel like we were in the void. Now there are houses everywhere."

"Everybody's nervous about it," Miranda said.

"Folks I met at the party today looked as if they were about to jump out of their skins. What's up with that?"

"Some of them are worried that I'll sell. Some are praying I will."

Bridie perched on the low railing in front of Miranda.

"That wood's kind of rotten," Miranda said.

Bridie resettled herself cross-legged on the deck.

"Will you?"

"What?"

"Sell."

Miranda knotted her fingers in her lap. "That's not what Papa had in mind."

"What did *you* have in mind?"

"The world with Papa in it."

Silence draped over them like wet wool. Miranda rolled her eyes in sockets that had grown sore and dry. Bridie was the only one who would not tiptoe around the Perry stubborn streak, *that suck-it-up pioneer shit*. Miranda thought if she was quiet and still, Bridie might not draw her out, might be too preoccupied with her own worries, and when Bridie sighed and stood up, Miranda thought she'd escaped.

Then Bridie said, "What are you going to do?"

"I've got one week to figure it out. That's all Eric would give me."

"The prick in the high hat," Bridie said. "He'd slip a shiv between your ribs before you could think to gasp."

"He's a perfectionist, Bridie. Not a ghoul."

"He's a man who had a couple of shots of brilliance. Now his shine has palled, he uses you to cover."

Miranda kept her mouth shut.

"What about those suits with the cash for your new restaurant?" Bridie asked.

"I haven't had a chance to contact them."

"Do you have a contract with them?"

"The backers? No. Why?"

"If you decide to stay, it would be easier not to have to break a contract."

"I can't stay, Bridie. I've got too much going on there."

"So sell it, then. You could afford to set up your own restaurant instead of relying on a bunch of fickle suits."

"Those vines represent thirty years of hard work. They are the lifeblood of Petra's business. She can't afford to lease the vines, not after what she went through with Ernest's medical care. And I can't sell the land. It's Papa's legacy to me, and to Ruben."

"Rock and a hard place," Bridie said.

"You have no idea what it takes to keep a vineyard up and running. A farm takes everything you've got."

"Sounds a lot like the restaurant business," Bridie said.

"Bingo," Miranda said.

"There are restaurants in Portland, you know."

"I don't have any connections there," Miranda said.

"Can't you hire somebody to run this while you do the food thing in Portland?"

"It would be like starting all over again."

"Well, what about Ruben?"

"Ruben?"

"This is a great place to raise a kid."

"I don't know, Bridie. San Francisco's home as far as he knows."

"He was happier than a pig in shit today," Bridie said. "He'd get used to this home pretty fast."

"So you're saying we should move here because he'd be happier?"

"Maybe. But I wonder if you wouldn't be happy here, too."

"What do you mean?"

"Sometimes people get tied to places by sadness as much as by happiness. What have you got in San Francisco but a bunch of Goodwill furniture in a dinky apartment and a headstone that reminds you of something that no longer exists? There's life here. It becomes you. And Ruben."

Miranda felt as if she were suspended in the glare of light. Just beyond its frigid edge she knew there was Bridie with her in the small apartment on Clement Street, beside her at Dario's funeral, then helping her with Ruben when he was born six weeks premature. Miranda hadn't decided on a name, so Bridie helped her decide. Ruben Salazar, a journalist famous for his relentless exposure of labor injustice, had been Dario's hero.

Bridie squeezed Miranda's knee just above the joint. "Ever seen a horse eat corn?" The knee responded unbidden to the pinched pressure points. Miranda flicked away Bridie's hand with a coarse cluck of her tongue.

"I'm sorry," Bridie said. "Always good to inject a little humor into a tense discussion."

"I am well aware of your approach to discussion," Miranda said.

"I'm just trying to make sure you've got everything on the table. Certain information tends to get stuck on that gooey little stubborn streak of yours."

"Speaking of stubborn streak, what about your folks? Do they even know about the race?"

"Dad really wanted to come out for the start this year, but with his knees gone south and the company fighting him on disability, Mom won't hardly let him make a phone call, much less pay for a plane ticket. He wanted to drive out, but he can't be gone that long. Besides, his knees wouldn't let him."

"Doesn't he get worker's comp or something?"

"Workman's comp benefits the company, not the worker."

"Papa was lucky that way. He never got sick. Never got hurt." Miranda stood up. "Want to take a walk? I've got Papa's ashes. He wanted to stay in the vineyard."

"Why not," Bridie said. "I'm on my low-sleep regimen."

In the distance, a truck whipsawed onto Miranda's road and howled toward the house, carburetor gasping for air.

"Somebody's in a white-hot hurry," Bridie said.

"Traffic really picked up around here the past few years. Families, teenagers . . . It made Papa crazy." She paused as the truck skidded through the ess curve, then roared past the house, slinging gravel against the already pocked white fence.

"Good thing the yard's fenced," Bridie said. "It's all set up for when you get a dog."

"Bridie."

"Don't mind my badgering," Bridie said. "Whatever you do or don't do or can't or won't do, I'm with you. I know it'll be fine. I know *you'll* be fine. You're just a fine kinda gal, and I'll love you any way it works out."

Miranda smiled in the dark.

"I brought Ruben a video," Bridie said. "I left it on his bed so he'll find it when he wakes up. *Old Yeller.* You're gonna love it."

Miranda sighed. Another video she would have to listen to over and over. "Naturally, the star has four legs," Miranda said.

"Naturally. What would life be without a little torture?" Bridie said, and squeezed her shoulder. "Enjoy."

"I will, and you will too next time we see you, because I'll make sure Ruben knows it's your favorite movie to watch."

"It was. Twenty years ago."

Miranda slit open the box and removed the heavy plastic sack, which she carried now across the yard. The dew was so heavy, their shoes were soaked by the time she and Bridie reached the vineyard gate. They dipped the soles of their shoes in the chlorine solution Papa kept in a pan there before they passed through the gate. It was one small way to keep the vines free of the phylloxera virus that could kill a vineyard in a few years' time. California vineyards had had a bad time of it, and Oregon vineyards that had not prepared by planting resistant rootstock were bowing to the tiny louse that spread the disease. Luis and Papa had anticipated the encroachment, insisted they prepare by interplanting resistant rootstock, and then watched as other vineyards were decimated by the virus.

"Been a long time," Bridie said. "Is it three years since you've been here?"

"Yes."

"Last time I was here was before Ruben was born. It was harvest, wasn't it?"

"Yes. I wish it were harvest now. Papa lived for that time of year."

Bridie followed Miranda up the end lane several rows before she turned down an aisle and stopped. It was part of the original acre Papa planted for Ernest, so the vines were as old as she was. Papa had named the section after her, Miranda's block.

The sack was heavy, like it might have been full of buckshot instead of Carter Perry's grainy remains. He always said he wouldn't take up good growing ground with his rotting body. Always the economist.

She tried to think of something to say while she spread the ashes, but it seemed superfluous considering the conversation they had in life consisted of what was necessary, what had to be done, and what remained to do. The work was hard, but there was never any doubt in it, never any doubt in him. As long as he'd been alive, she knew the world would go round, and she would go with it.

She flung the bag in a wide arc around her, listened to Papa's ashes rattling the leaves like sand, and was satisfied with the simplicity of it as he would have been.

Back in the house, Bridie refused to go to bed and insisted on sitting upstairs with Miranda while she lay down. Bridie dragged in the aluminum chair and sat by the bed with the lamp on, thumbing an old farm journal. It was the only reading material in the house.

Miranda lay with her arm across her forehead, remembering what Petra had told her about finding Carter. She couldn't help seeing her father slump from the tractor, his eyes opened only slightly wider than usual, amazed at the crush of pain in his chest. Petra said he'd hit his head on the step pedal of the old Deere and bled so heavily they thought at first that was the problem. But the head injury was second fiddle after all. You can live without your wits, not without your heart.

Petra had ridden with him in the ambulance, clutching his foot, which was just about the only part of him the paramedics ignored. At the hospital he'd held on long enough for her to get an attorney there to execute his will. Petra was surprised he hadn't prepared for this, but not Miranda. It wasn't like him to think ahead into darkness.

She tried to think of the space she'd located for her restaurant, instead of her father's hands in Petra's and her own hands clenched and damp on her belly. She curled onto her side and pressed the pillow to her face. She felt Bridie's hand on her back, patting a gentle rhythm, and she thought of Petra's and Madrita's hands smoothing on fresh sheets when they cleaned the house yesterday, talking softly about things that seemed to matter only when nothing else did.

3

Bridie left for the airport before dawn, so Miranda was more than awake when Luis tapped on the kitchen door at seven. She brought him coffee, noticed how much more salt there was in the pepper black of his hair, and tried to remember his age. Sixty? His work clothes hung more loosely now, though he still looked as square and strong as she remembered.

He'd crossed into the United States as a boy, followed the agricultural industry according to season—winter grapefruit in Texas, spring asparagus in California, summer hazelnuts in Oregon, fall apples in Washington. He met Madrita on a truck crossing from California to Oregon one summer and hadn't crossed another state line since.

His genius was in the vineyard, as if he had been plant matter in another life. Luis was the only man Carter Perry had listened to when it came to farming. He seemed to know just how much stress a vine could take before human intervention became necessary, tinkered with the genetics of rootstocks, created remedies out of thin air.

Ernest had seen the mark on Luis quick enough and made him Ruby Throat's vineyard manager inside of a year. But Ernest hadn't been the only one to see Luis's genius, and soon enough the offers of better jobs squeaked in. So Ernest had not hesitated to make Luis a partner to the tune of a thirty percent share of the winery. Papa always said it wouldn't have mattered. Luis would have stayed. He was that way. Just like Papa.

She hooked Luis at the elbow and pulled him close, had a flash of evenings when Luis and Papa would sit on the patio, talking, pipe smoke curling into dusk while she played jacks on the cool bricks at their feet.

"How is everybody?" she asked.

Luis grinned, his yellowed teeth marching like old dice across his mouth. "They are everywhere," he said. "Christina and Isadora are in Mexico, taking care of my mother. Paulina, she has a hair shop. The boys . . . They are everywhere." He smiled again, then said, "We are sorry without your father, but happy you are here."

He signed a cross over his chest with a blunted thumb, a punctuation to prayer against weather, disease, death.

"You think about land now. Hire manager I will choose," Luis was saying.

She smiled at his English. It had never come easily to him. But then he teased her about her Spanish, even though she was close to fluent. She'd spent a lot of time with Luis and Madrita and their kids.

Miranda sat on the couch, Luis next to her. The faint must of cumin emanated from the folds of his clothes.

"There's a lot to think about," she said.

"Put one foot ahead. Things get done. That's what Carter say."

"It was never like that."

"For him, yes."

She curled her hands to her jaws and tried to loosen the clutch of muscle there.

"Mira," he said. "I will help you."

"You don't have time for that, Luis. And besides, I can't afford you."

"You lived here all your life, no?"

Here it comes, she thought. The life lesson. Whenever Luis was about to teach her something, he started out with a question so obvious, it made her brain ache. She knew there was nothing for it but to answer the question—correctly, of course—and let him go on.

"Yes," she said. "All but the last twelve years."

"So you know how we do things."

"Yes," she said. "But you can't manage Perry Hill and Ruby Throat, too."

"You will manage. I will consult."

"I can't manage a vineyard from San Francisco."

"San Francisco?"

"Yes. I have only one week off. Ruben's missing school, and I'm about to start my own restaurant, Luis. Didn't Papa tell you?"

Luis sucked his lips over his teeth and scraped the gristle that had already begun to sprout on his chin.

"He didn't tell you?"

"He tell me, but we are different now."

"I can't just drop my life. Or Ruben's."

"There are schools here," he said.

"I have commitments, too. People are counting on me."

"There are no other cooks in California?" he asked.

"Luis, you know what I mean."

"This is commitment also. Or do you think of—?"

"No," she said, and stretched out her hand to him. "No, I won't sell it. I would never do that. But we can hire a manager to run the crew. He could report to you or something. I could rent the house. . . ."

"Where will you stay when you come home?"

"I won't be able to come often. Not for a while."

"And Ruben?"

She squinted at him. "Have you been talking to Bridie?"

"I see her yesterday. We say hello. That is all. I am thinking to myself, and Madrita also, of how happy it is for Ruben here."

"He's been fine in San Francisco."

"Cities are not good for children. There is too much sickness. They are soft here," he said, touching his chest where his heart was.

Miranda stared at him. Ruben had just got over his third cold since he started kindergarten that fall. And he was a little skittish, but then that was probably her fault. She cautioned him constantly about not answering the phone or the door, and she grilled him about backup plans everywhere she took him so he'd know what to do if separated from her. There never seemed to be enough backup plans. She had never been sick as a child as far as she remembered. Was she nervous? She didn't recall ever being frightened. She could go wherever she wanted.

She shook her head. She made a good living, and she was good at it. She did the best she could for Ruben, and what parent ever thought that was enough?

And then, as if Luis had willed it to happen, she heard Ruben scuffing down the hall.

"Mom?"

She braced herself for his usual morning crankiness. "Good morning sleepyhead. Hungry?"

He scraped his eyes, smiled when he saw Luis, and crawled into his lap. Luis wrapped his arms around the boy and rested his chin on the slick of dark hair.

"Ay, mi hijito, como te quiero."

Ruben giggled and plucked at the hard calluses on Luis's hand. Miranda had imagined this scene many times, only it was Dario holding Ruben. *Oh, my son, I love you so.* She stood up and moved unsteadily into the kitchen.

"Honey, I'm going to squeeze you some juice, okay?" she called.

"Okay," Ruben said. His voice was different, soft and buttery, and she knew exactly what was happening to her son. She had always been drawn to Luis that way, thought as a child that his affection had been hers alone until she realized he held everyone in the same warm web. That realization had bloomed into respect.

"Luis, how many crew did Papa have?" she called from the kitchen.

"Ten. But that is not enough now."

"What contractor did he use?"

"He does not use contractor. He find his own people."

"How?"

"Here and there. In town. He find them over the year. When someone don't come back, he find another one or two. He know what to say, what to ask. He know when they work out. We are pruning now."

"I used to help Papa, remember? I don't think I could do it now," she said.

She heard Ruben saying something to Luis, then Luis's voice crooning back a response. Orange oil released into the air as she clamped rinds to the old juicer. She breathed in the heavy tang of it and closed her eyes, told herself it was the citrus that made them burn and water.

Luis carried Ruben to the kitchen and set him down on the table.

"Ruben say he will come with old Luis this afternoon," Luis said. "But I say we will ask his mother first if that is okay."

"Are you sure?"

"*Claro*. We will see Madrita for lunch. You will have time to see Petra when she come back from Seattle."

"Seattle?"

"She is there with Duncan this morning for sales thing."

"When do they come?" she asked.

"Who?"

"The crew."

He frowned, looked at his watch. "Now, they should be. They will take advantage a little without manager. I will talk with them this afternoon."

"Should I talk to them?"

"I will go first. Then you will, later."

"Thank you, Luis. You're the next best thing to Papa."

She hugged him to her, as much to hide her eyes as to anchor herself.

His face turned blank for a moment before the crinkles returned to the corners of his eyes. "I will come back at noon for the boy. We will have lunch with Madrita, and then I will do business with my fine young helper." He ruffled Ruben's hair and made a buzzing noise.

"He'll be ready."

Luis let the screen door bang shut after him just as everybody had let it slam ever since she could remember. She shut the inner door against the cool air that sifted in and pulled her sweater tight around her.

"Ruben, it's pretty chilly today. Why don't you get dressed while I make breakfast."

His bare feet whispered away over the old linoleum. She cleaned off the table and started to mix pancake batter when she caught sight of someone at the kitchen door, made out a man's apologetic face and the curious face of a young boy next to him.

He introduced himself as Paul Trimble, a friend of her father's. "And this is Sonny," he said, pointing his chin at the boy. She gestured toward the kitchen table, and Paul galumphed in.

"We just moved down the road a few years ago. Petra said you were home since . . . We're real sorry about your father. He was a great guy."

She remembered Papa mentioning the Trimbles every now and then. Paul had helped with repairs on the house and barn when necessary. Papa had been a hell of a farmer, but was never much on the home upkeep. Papa said the Trimbles were good folk, and she knew her father had an unerring eye for character.

Paul said he was a cabinetmaker and worked out of a shop he had set up in an old barn on their property. She knew the place, one of the smaller farms in the area. His wife, Dianna, worked for the post office as a rural mail carrier. "Since she's gone most of the day, I usually perform social and baby-sitting duties. Sonny's got the day off from school, right, kid?"

Sonny nodded.

"Hi," Ruben called from the living room.

Sonny looked at Ruben, said hi in the smallest voice imaginable.

"Ruben, come in and meet Sonny and his dad, please."

Ruben stuck out his hand to Paul.

"I just squeezed some oranges. How about some juice, Sonny?" Miranda said.

Ruben carried Sonny's juice over with both hands and set it on the table. Sonny's eyes followed him.

"We were just about to make pancakes, Sonny. Would you like some?" But she looked to Paul for the answer.

Paul nodded. "Sure. Sonny loves pancakes more than he loves me—right, son?"

Sonny looked up at his dad to see if he was serious.

"How old are you, Sonny?" Miranda asked.

"Seven," Paul said.

"Is that true, Sonny?" she asked. "That means you're a whole year older than Ruben."

"I'm gonna get a dog," Ruben said.

"I like dogs," Sonny said.

"My dog's gonna pull me through the snow."

Miranda smiled at Paul. "My best friend races sled dogs in Alaska. Ruben's crazy about it."

"Wow," Paul said. "What's his name?"

"Her name is Bridie McLewan."

He nodded. "We've been following her," he said. "She's looking very good for this year's race."

"She was just here for the . . . service," Miranda said.

"Wish I'd known. We could have met her. But Dianna and Sonny and I are sure glad you're here," he said quickly. "When we heard the news about Carter, we thought uh-oh, there goes the neighborhood. Dianna's people are from around here. We lived up in Washington for a while, where I'm from, but we got pushed out by development, taxes, and toxics."

"Toxics?" Miranda said.

Paul grinned. "Computer components. They're just deadly as hell, beg pardon," he said. "Dianna was just itching to get home anyway, so that was the clincher. She's into all this organic stuff and grows most of our food. Yuppies and development were great for the woodworking business, but not so great for quality of life. So when we heard about Carter, we thought for sure the land would be sold. Now that you're here, we aren't worried about it." He pointed at Ruben, who was watching Sonny eat his pancake. "And there's a bonus friend in the bargain."

Miranda started to explain to him that she wasn't staying, but she didn't feel like going through it for the second time that morning. She just smiled and dipped maple syrup onto the steaming pancakes she'd set on the table.

Paul pinched a hunk of his son's pancake and hummed in appreciation. "They're kinda custardy. How'd you do that?"

"I use applesauce and buttermilk for the liquid. Would you like some?"

Paul grinned. "Well, I shouldn't, but I will."

Miranda griddled three cakes and set them in front of Paul, who ate them before she could return with the butter and syrup.

"Don't need accompaniment with these babies. They're a solo act."

He rose and rinsed his dishes in the sink.

"How's about Ruben comes down to our place for a little while? We have a state-of-the-art slam-dunker of a jungle gym setup that I built myself. The boys could get to know each other a bit."

She hesitated. In the city, she'd never let her son go off with someone she'd just met, but if Paul Trimble passed the Papa test, he had to be all right. "What do you think, Ru?" Miranda said.

"Yeah. Okay. Are you coming?"

"You want me to?"

Ruben looked at Sonny, then Paul. "No, that's okay."

"I'll pick him up at eleven," she said to Paul. "He's been promised elsewhere for the afternoon."

"Good enough," Paul said, and stood up. "Like I said. Welcome home, and we're real sorry about your father."

The screen door slammed shut, and she pushed the big door closed again.

She sat at the table with a fresh cup of coffee, feeling like she'd been to a long, exhausting party. She rarely had people over in the city—hadn't really gotten to know anyone other than her coworkers, and they tended to be young and not exactly in parent mode. She hadn't thought about it being any different. It was just the way their lives were.

In the dead quiet of the house, she heard her cell phone twittering upstairs. She twitched involuntarily, but then didn't get up. It was probably her sous, anyway. He'd leave a message. She wanted to sit still a minute in the silence that asked nothing of her and required no response.

Petra hated crossing the Columbia. Though Seattle was only a three-hour drive, once they were in Washington, it felt like another world. This spring meeting with the sales representatives of her top distributor in Seattle did nothing to improve her outlook. The sales reps believed in her wine and made a point of letting their contacts know it. They were the army that conquered the retail world for her and made sure Ruby Throat's wines got on the shelves.

But today there would be questions that didn't exactly pertain to the new vintages they were there to introduce. The sales reps would want to know the status of Perry Hill since the old man died. They would ask her to foresee the future, and she would have to deliver a forecast that would make them comfortable. She'd thought of bringing Miranda with her today, a living emblem of her rosy forecast, but after talking to Luis that morning, she decided it would be best to wait and talk to the girl that afternoon, to see just how quaky the ground was.

One thing was certain; she needed someone to take over. She could hire a marketing person, train them, bring them along, but that would be the next step toward letting Ruby Throat go. She wanted someone in her place whose blood was in the soil as surely as was hers and Ernest's and Carter's. Duncan was the right component in his place, but he could not do the dance that she did, could not sell the wine as she could. Without a front person, it didn't matter how good your wine was; it would not get on the shelf. It was the same in any business.

And the business was at that point again where it needed something new, something to add to its charm and cachet and keep it at the forefront. She didn't want to go so far as to increase their production. They weren't ready for that yet. The new gravity-feed winery would have been just the thing, but they couldn't afford that now.

She'd thought of adding a tasting room to bring in the tourists like other valley wineries. There would be the limo people to contend with: folks who jetted up from California, rented a limousine to tour the wineries, and generally drank a lot more than they bought. It was a status game, like buying labels. It was Napa and Sonoma all over again, and she didn't feel like playing Simon Says.

If she brought people to Ruby Throat, she meant them to take the wine seriously in a setting that encouraged thoughtful consumption. But you couldn't get tourists to hold on a minute in a tasting room. There were other wineries to move on to. So she'd put a lid on the idea. Still, they needed something, something she had not been able to come up with yet.

She could have used a big announcement of that sort for the reps at the meeting. Instead, she had what they could always count on: superlative wine. So today she would have to employ charm and verve that used to come naturally to her but that were now a huge expenditure of energy. Her joints plagued her so, it made her cranky and the pain let her sleep only in fits. She dropped the seat back as far as it would go and let Duncan do the driving. She didn't much care for the I-5 anyway. She cracked her window a touch. The cold, moist air would be hell on her hair, but she didn't care just then. In three hours she would care, but not right now. When her head lolled to the side, she braced it with the heel of her hand and fell asleep.

Duncan had to tap her awake after he parked and turned off the engine. Normally she chattered like a magpie to prep him for the ordeal. Still, she had performed as usual during the session, fielding questions, flashing percentages, statistics, and portraits with a rosy slash of her tongue, which left him to do his usual: walk the line, pour this or that vintage, offer convenient buzzwords the reps could work into a sales pitch. Petra said they loved his accent, that he could have said a vintage was as smooth as a loaded nappy and they would titter agreeably. But it was always Petra who delivered the goods.

When Petra told him Ernest named the winery, Duncan had assumed it was after the hummingbird, which hadn't made sense; the ruby throat wasn't native to the American West. But once Duncan saw how Petra worked a crowd, he knew it was her throat Ernest referred to, not the bird's.

The session went well, the distributor seemed confident in the strength of the winery, and he and Petra were ready to load and roll home when a rep stopped them in the hall to ask what they thought about the Ettinger merger in California. Petra had not lost her gleam, but he could see in the slowed, dry blink of her eyes that she was stunned.

Of course, neither of them had heard that BevCorp, the international beverage giant headquartered in Australia, had bought one of the big production wineries in California.

Yeah, the rep said, *deal was done yesterday, and word has it BevCorp's got an eye on Oregon. Anybody approached you?*

Petra laughed and said it would be like trying to rob a convent and let it go at that, but now she sat, chewing her nails, while they crept through Seattle's afternoon traffic, compliments of the Boeing Corporation, whose workers streamed out of the plants like termites.

"What would you think about leaving the wine on oak a little longer?" Petra asked. "Give it a little more vanilla."

He jerked a look at her and nearly veered out of his lane. After all their talk about holding the line in this market-crazed industry, he couldn't believe she would suggest dipping their feet in the muck.

"I'm just thinking," she said. "We need a little edge of some kind. A little bow to the average consumer wouldn't be so bad, would it?"

"You could just move to California," he said.

She made a face at him. "I'm just saying it might be appropriate at this point."

"Right," he said. "And then you'll suggest we muscle 'em up, give 'em more balls like California wines."

"Don't be so dramatic," she said. "And leave the personal equipment out of it."

"It's the girl, isn't it?"

"Miranda?"

"You *are* worried."

"There's no chink in our armor," she said. "It's business as usual."

He gave her a quick sideways look.

"Don't give me that look," she said. "We're fine."

"Didn't seem apples when Luis talked to her this morning."

Petra sighed. "Carter left it to her because he knew she would keep it. He knew she would do whatever it takes to keep it."

"Let's hope so," he said.

"She'll figure out a way to make it work. *We'll* figure out a way. We're all in this together, honey. It's a family thing."

It still made him feel unreasonably goofy when she said things like that. It was what he admired most in her, this loyalty, this ability to aggregate satellites of the most disparate kinds and make them orbit in unison. Her magnet was so powerful, it seemed to him that the whole thing would evaporate without her.

"I'll tell you what gooses me," she continued, "is this niche marketing thing. They want single-vineyard releases, they want us to characterize a vineyard as if it were stamped in stone. Eola Hills pinots are ripe berry, Dundee Hills pinots are pepper and spice, Chehalem Ridge gives floral elegance. Wines are volatile, not Campbell's soup. These twitty little MBAs and their ideas. I'd like to thump them once or twice, get them out here in the trenches and the weather and then let them say one vineyard's production will always be thus and so."

They'd had this discussion more than once, and she knew it made his ears smoke. As a proper larrikin, he would do a lot more than thump them once or ten times. But today he opted for the smile instead of smoke.

"I'll bet Ruben would love to ride that horse of yours," she said suddenly.

"I'll just pop down later and give him a little spin, eh?" Duncan said.

"Yes," she said. "Good idea. Anything we can do to make their lives here . . . desirable. I'm just glad she's home."

Duncan swore a foul streak when the car in front of them refused to move aside.

"Easy, Mr. Outback," she said. "We'll get there when we get there."

And he thought, *Yeah, but I wouldn't mind getting there in this life,* so he punched the horn and moved up closer to the car in front of him as if he might remove the obstacle that lay between him and his winery, as if he thought that BevCorp might beat him home.

Petra picked up Miranda that afternoon, beeped twice just like she used to do when Miranda was a kid and Petra came to take her shopping in Portland. Miranda wanted to know where they were going, and Petra just said *not far* with that wispy smile she reserved for knowledge retained.

And Miranda should have known when she pulled up beside the bright red ice cream parlor in Dundee. The Problem-Solving Place. Her face got hot as if she'd been offered something she was afraid to ask for.

"Remember?" Petra said.

"Yes. Many times over," Miranda said. Whenever Miranda got stuck on something, Petra would bring her here. *I think we can solve this problem better with something smooth in our throats.* And off they'd go.

"I didn't think you'd mind, even if you are accustomed to whipping up confections of a more sophisticated kind than banana blitz boats."

"I don't do much in the way of desserts," Miranda said. "We have a pastry chef for that."

"Still, I bet you could fill in, in a pinch."

Petra led the way to the corner booth in the back and slid across the red vinyl seat to the window.

Miranda smiled. It had always been her favorite spot. She remembered crying one time when they'd come in and the place was so crowded, they'd had to sit on stools at the counter.

She peered at the menu but didn't know why she bothered. She would have a mint chocolate chip hot fudge sundae no matter how many times she read down the list of flavors and combinations.

"Hey, they've got something new," Miranda said. "What's a Blurry?"

"I don't know. I haven't been here since the last time I was here with you. Old ladies don't need much ice cream," she said, and patted her stomach. "Have you brought Ruben yet?"

"We came here with Papa three years ago, but he doesn't remember any of it. I was hoping he would."

"The place or Carter?"

"Papa. And the place."

"He'll remember everything now. I saw Luis riding him around on the tractor when I drove down to get you. Looked like he was having a ball."

The counter boy plunked down their orders and slid them over. Petra tucked her spoon into the cup but did not eat.

"I haven't had a chance to thank you for the party," Miranda said. "It was beautiful."

"Carter wouldn't have approved," Petra said.

"He wasn't much for parties, was he?" Miranda said.

"He was for the day to day. It kept him sane, uncomplicated."

Miranda felt her eyes water and tucked a spoonful of syrupy ice cream into her mouth. "Things feel pretty complicated now," Miranda said.

"I suppose they do. Is there any way I can help you untangle?"

"How?" Miranda said. "I have a job, a reputation, and the possibility of having my own restaurant, finally. And now there's this." She waved her hand at hills she couldn't see. "When I talked to Luis this morning, he thought I was staying. I had to tell him I couldn't."

Petra moved her spoon around in the melting heap of toffee crunch.

Miranda continued. "He thought that meant I would sell the place, but I can't. I wouldn't. We could hire a manager, rent the house to offset the cost of the manager. Does that make sense?"

"Sure," Petra said.

"But you don't like the idea."

"It's not that," Petra said.

"What, then?"

"You can certainly give it a try," Petra said.

"But what?"

"Well, hiring a manger who can do everything Carter did, as well as be a manager for a top vineyard, requires a serious search and money. You have to trust this person with everything that your father built up. It's a tremendous burden, and you won't be here to oversee any of it."

"He could report to Luis," Miranda said.

"Luis is over the limit as it is. And he's not getting younger, as they say. None of us are."

"What does that mean?"

Petra shifted uncomfortably in her seat. "My arthritis is worse. I'm on medication now, and that helps a bit, but pretty soon I'm going to have to flee to warmer, drier climes in the winter. The dampness here is just hell on me, even with the drugs."

Miranda looked at her closely for the first time in years. In her mind, Petra was as fixed as the stars, as Papa had been. It had been Petra who visited her in San Francisco when she came down for big regional wine events. It was Petra who brought things for her and Ruben and the apartment. She always knew what to get, and she was always organized, never hurried or stressed even though what she did was as stressful as Miranda's job. Tastes were fickle, and at the end of the day, both their lives depended on the public palate.

"You never said anything about it."

Petra smiled. "There's nothing worse than old people whining about their pain. Besides, it wasn't that bad until recently. And it'll get worse yet."

"What will you do, hire a marketing person?"

"I could," Petra said. "Of course, whatever is done must be done by consensus with my partners. Luis and Duncan have as much say as I do."

"And what do they think?"

"We pretty much think the same thing."

"A marketing person?"

"No," Petra said. Her eyes held Miranda's for a moment.

"You're not—"

"Why wouldn't I? You're as close as a child to me. Closer, maybe. It was always our desire to have you here."

"You're kidding, right?"

"Icebergs," Petra said. "There's always more to them than you think."

"And nobody filled me in on these plans at a time I might have been able to deal with them?"

"Sweetie, there is never a good time until it's time."

"I'd argue that."

"And you would have then or before or any time. Actually, it was never a solid idea until Ernest died. We never really talked about it until then."

"But you've been holding this bag for three years."

"Look, sweetie, it's just an idea. You are perfectly within your rights to tell everyone, the living *and* the dead, to flip off. Whatever you do, we're behind you one hundred percent."

Petra bit her lip and watched ice cream melt from Miranda's suspended spoon.

"I know how much you need Perry Hill," Miranda said.

"I can't deny that," Petra said. "We buy from other vineyards to increase our output, but as far as grand cru quality, nothing holds a candle to Perry Hill fruit, or our own, for that matter."

"I won't let it go. It will be there for you. But I'll lose my job if I'm not back in a week. Eric's probably chewing over who to hire in my place already. But that won't be an issue when I have my own restaurant. I've got meetings scheduled with my backers next week to finalize plans on the space I'd like to lease, and if they sense there's one hair out of place, they'll bolt. Part of their attraction to my proposal in the first place is that I'm there, I'm organized, and I do what I say I'll do when I say it'll be done."

"Not to mention your talent," Petra said.

"I've worked hard for it, and I don't know the first thing about what you do, or what Papa did, for that matter. It would take years to get me up to speed."

"Certainly there would be ropes to climb, but you know a lot about this business purely by osmosis."

"I know food. And I know the scene in San Francisco. There's nothing going on here."

"You haven't lived here for years," Petra said. "There's more going on here than you think."

"Even if that's true, it's nothing like San Francisco. I make a good living, and I want a good life for Ruben."

Petra flattened her hands across the red Formica. "I will do whatever I can to help you in that endeavor," Petra said.

"Thank you. I need a manager for Perry Hill, and I need to get the house packed up so I can rent it. I only have four days."

"Let's get to work, then," Petra said, and pushed herself up from the booth.

"You didn't even touch your ice cream," Miranda said.

"Like I said, those kinds of calories are not high on the nutritional agenda."

Bridie had all her gear spread out in the Harrimans' heated garage, except one item, which Mr. Harriman had discreetly secreted in the family safe after making a crack about Dirty Harry. She laughed at the reference, but only because she was sure that, as president of a local bank, his taste in safes was dependable.

Harriman had tried to convince the bank to sponsor Bridie's race bid, but she was still a rookie in their minds, not to mention a girl, so the Harrimans had sponsored Bridie privately and given up their guest quarters to her. It was a great boon for racers who never had enough money and couldn't afford hotels, certainly not at Anchorage rates, plus they let her keep Zeus with her. He was so mellow, it wasn't an issue, and the Harrimans' kids chalked up plenty of popularity points when she took Zeus to their school for show-and-tell the day before the race.

The children's questions always amazed her. Inevitably one of the little girls wanted to know how she went to the bathroom if there *were* no bathrooms. Bridie made the mistake once of explaining that she wore men's snowsuits that allowed certain access so she could use a device developed for people who were physically unable to sit down or squat. When the wind was howling at thirty below, you really didn't want to expose your behind. The teacher had shaken her head in dismay halfway through the explanation, so the next time Bridie got the question, she just said, *We manage,* and smiled.

Gordon and Jim stayed with friends in Wasilla, where they could stake the dogs out in the woods without fear of neighborhood reprisal at the noise and smell. She'd felt a little left out last year in the arrangement, but when she saw their condition each morning she drove to Wasilla to work with the team, she decided she was better off at the Harrimans' who only tossed back the odd glass of wine of an evening. She always brought them a bottle of Perry Hill, compliments of Miranda.

She had very cozy digs in their garage apartment, which meant she could pace and worry and stay up and check and recheck her gear without bothering anyone. She had the dogs' harness spread out once again, testing every stitch for damage and weakness. But the harness had not changed one iota since she'd checked it that morning after the light run she'd given the dogs. She rolled it carefully and replaced it in the canvas bag. She ran her hands over every inch of the lightweight racing sled, feeling for sprains, feathered wood, loose bindings or screws, and then tipped it on its side. She had replaced the plastic shoes on the runners before she left the village, and the brief outings since then had caused no particular wear.

She straightened and sighed. It was always like this the night before. She almost wished she weren't so scrupulous with her gear and that just once she would discover a major repair that would keep her occupied through the night. It was only midnight, six hours until she'd meet Gordon and Jim in downtown Anchorage, where the race began. She had nothing to do but sleep, and she knew for a fact that would not come. She looked at Zeus where he lay sleeping on the pallet she'd brought for him and wished she felt as nonchalant as he.

"Wanna go out with me?" she asked him, but he only raised his head and looked at her briefly before groaning and stretching onto his side.

"I should have known," she said.

She shouldered on her parka, pulled the hood up, and went outside.

Anchorage glittered in a huge bowl of white below her. She stood for a while at the foot of the driveway and tried to pick out Front Street, where volunteers were setting up for tomorrow, bringing in truckloads of snow to cover the streets of the route out of town. It was warm here, a balmy twenty degrees, which meant the trucked-in snow would be mealy, almost like sand. Racers hated it because they knew it could mean tendon injuries as the dogs, well rested and crazy to run, tore through the slop.

She went back in the garage and gave Zeus a good-night scratch before heading upstairs. The Harrimans had given her permission to use the phone, and she used it now. It was the last chance she'd get to talk to Miranda before she finished the race. Her dad had called earlier. He'd been as pumped as she was, but her mother had refused to get on the phone. Bridie could hear her in the background, reminding her father at thirty-second intervals how expensive the call was. She didn't want that to be the last conversation she had before the race.

"I know you're asleep," she said when Miranda answered.

"I wasn't."

"Why?"

"A lot on my mind," Miranda said.

"Like what?"

"Never mind. We'll talk about it when you get back. Why are *you* up?"

"I never sleep the night before. You know that."

"Are you scared?"

"Nervous. Anxious. Maybe that's scared, I don't know. I'm fifth out of the chute," Bridie said.

"That's good, isn't it?"

"Yes and no. If the trail's crappy, it's a disadvantage. If the trail's good, it could mean we'll fly, and my strategy is to get as much 'first to' money as possible."

"What's that?"

"Awards for being the first to someplace. You get three grand in gold nuggets for being the first to Cripple."

"Cripple sounds creepy."

"That's the halfway checkpoint. And by then, you pretty much feel crippled, you're so tired, but it's not so bad if you're first and you get the three grand."

"But you'll be first to Nome. That's what matters."

"Yeah, but it's nice to have a little money in the bag in case something happens."

"But nothing's going to happen. You've done this before."

"That's right," Bridie said. "Smooth sailing all the way."

"And we'll be with you. I've got the route map you left us. Ruben's all over it."

"Tell him I love him. Tell him I'll call him first when I get to Nome."

"And me second."

"Naturally."

"Bridie?"

"Yeah?"

"Don't forget to feed yourself as well as you do the dogs. The stuff I sent you will keep you going."

"I know it will. It always has. I'll talk to you soon, okay?"

"Ten days, right?"

"Right," Bridie said. "And not a moment later."

4

In the morning, Miranda woke up disoriented. She'd moved the old bed against another wall. It was the only way she'd been able to sleep there. But the smell of him haunted her still when she opened the closet where she'd pushed her father's clothes to one end to make way for the few things she had.

The day after the memorial service, she'd packed his clothes into boxes. The shirts were hardly usable, many-times mended and worn to tissue, even though he could well afford to buy replacements. Papa wouldn't refuse Miranda anything, yet he'd done nothing for himself outside of what was necessary. As far as she knew, he'd never left the vineyard but for trips to the farm or hardware store.

She took the boxes to Goodwill, but when she saw them stacked on the cement apron behind the store, she changed her mind and brought them back home instead. She'd just have to do it later.

She hadn't finished dressing when she heard Ruben yell, the quavery pitch to it that made her belly rise in her throat. She yanked a shirt over her head and ran downstairs to find Ruben in front of the television, the picture on with no sound, waiting for an Iditarod race report.

"The news isn't on yet, Ru."

"But I wanna see Zeus."

When he started to cry, she picked him up and held him to her, something she didn't normally do anymore because he hated it.

"Let's get some breakfast," she said, stroking his hair. "Aren't you hungry?"

"I wanna see Aunt Bridie."

"The race just started this morning. There won't be any reports till later. We'll check tonight, sweetie. I promise."

She spread out the map of the race route on the kitchen table. Ruben liked to follow the bold line with his fingertip. She sliced fruit into a bowl of homemade yogurt, drizzled honey over it, and thought of the paperwork she had to go through that morning. She'd been home four days and still hadn't been able to go into the back bedroom Papa used as an office. But she'd have to go over the records and bank statements to familiarize herself with a part of Perry Hill she knew nothing about.

"I'll call the Trimbles and see if Sonny can come down after school today."

"Okay," he said, and his face brightened a little before his eyes darted to the window and he scrambled off his chair and ran for the door. By the time she got there, he was already standing next to the horse, practically underneath it. A gray speckled dog sat at his knee.

"Ruben," she said, her voice sharp with fear.

"He's fine," Duncan said. "They're used to each other by now—eh, Ru?"

Ruben rubbed the horse's leg with one hand and held on to Duncan's boot with the other.

"Besides, Fluke keeps an eye out. We had a little ride yesterday after the Seattle gig, didn't we, mate?"

"He was riding that horse?"

Duncan looked at Ruben and then back at her. "Petra seemed to think it was okay."

"Ah," Miranda said, nodding. "Well if everybody thinks it's all right, I guess that means it's all right."

"I ride him with me. It's not like he goes alone."

An arctic jay screamed from the old hickory in the backyard, and the mare danced sideways, tossed her head. Miranda touched her throat. Duncan's hand slid down the mare's neck, his fingers as thick and swollen as Petra's.

"She's careful," he said. "See how she sidled away from the kid?"

"Yeah," Miranda said. "I saw."

"Petra said you were a fair horseman in your day, but if you don't want him to ride, s'no bother."

"Mom," Ruben said, his eyes on her like hot pokers.

"I didn't say no." She looked at Duncan.

"Care for a spin?" he asked.

"I've got way too much to do in there," she said.

"Just a spin," Duncan said. "Show the nipper the old mum's still got some spank."

"Moms don't ride horses," Ruben said to Duncan. "They're too old."

"That does it," she said to Duncan. "Please step away from the vehicle."

Duncan swung down and held the mare's head with one hand while cupping the other to leg her up. She was surprised at how familiar it felt when she settled lightly in the warm saddle.

"I'll just run those stirrups up a notch or two," he said.

"Don't bother," she said. "Stirrups are for wimps and old people."

The mare pivoted around Duncan as he held her head. Miranda gathered the reins and nodded, and he let her go. The mare hopped sideways a little but responded when Miranda gave her leg pressure on the opposite side and stood still.

"You've got her attention now," Duncan said.

"She's well trained to leg commands," Miranda said. "Did you do that?"

"In person," he said.

She pushed the mare into a mincing trot toward the vineyard gate. There she eased the mare sideways so she could open the gate without dismounting, and was surprised again at how responsive she was. Once in the vineyard, she slacked the reins a little and squeezed the horse to a canter. She followed the end aisle all the way up the hill before reining the horse down to a walk. She hadn't ridden in, what, fifteen years? It felt good to be in the vineyard this way. Even this slight elevation gave her a different perspective on things.

And then she realized what Duncan had done, how easily she'd played into it. She turned the mare and let her trot back down to the gate. The three of them, man, boy, and dog sat, waiting for her.

She pulled the mare to a stop and dismounted before Duncan had a chance to grab the bridle. "Well, that was nice," she said without looking at him.

"Looked as if you enjoyed the ride," he said.

"It was nice," she repeated.

Ruben grabbed her hand. "Mom, you ride good. Will you teach me how?"

She bent and gave him a hug. "Sometime, I will, but you can go with Duncan now." She looked up at Duncan. "Just no running or anything, okay?"

"Not on the agenda," he said.

Duncan swung onto the mare's back, then flicked the boy up behind him as if he were a dry stick. At least he had the good sense to ride the child behind him instead of in front as people often did, thinking it was safer. Ruben clamped himself to Duncan like a barnacle.

"You look great, honey," she said.

"We'll just poke around the vineyard. Back in a bit," Duncan said, and reined the mare around.

Miranda watched the mare's white rump swing away, Ruben swaying from side to side.

She'd thought the week away would be quality time spent with Ruben. When she was working, the pace was unrelenting and she often ended up seeing him for only two or three hours a day. While it seemed she saw him even less here, she didn't feel that sharp pinch of guilt at being away from him, because he was happy and excited when they found each other again. Horses, tractors, friends . . . It was all new to him. She remembered what Luis had said: this was what life should be like for a child. But she couldn't jump tracks now. There was too much at stake.

She forced herself back to the small bedroom that Papa used as his office. It was piled high with farm journals, old newspapers, junk she knew he didn't think he could part with. She bagged and boxed everything that didn't look important and hauled it to the end of the driveway for garbage pickup. She separated the mail—junk to the left, openers on the right. Fortunately, the junk pile was bigger. She'd just box it and set it out for recycling with the rest of the stuff.

She sighed and looked around her. Three more days, and she hadn't made a dent in the house. If she didn't deal with it now, she didn't know when she could get back to take care of the rest of it, and she'd need to rent the house to help defray the cost of the manager. She'd spent most of her life here, and Papa had lived here always, like his father before him. It was hard to see the place as if she were an outsider, as if she were someone who cared about worn linoleum and superficial imperfections. The thought of other eyes on the place, judging it, made her bristle.

She heard Ruben calling her, so she closed the door to the office and went to meet him. He'd be excited and full of stories about his big adventure, just as he'd been since they got here.

Familiar smells on warm air made her knees weak when she opened the door to the *taquería* in Dundee. Luis had taken Ruben across the street to the hardware store, so she ordered for them and waited at one of the orange Formica tables. She could put her head down right now and catch ten minutes. Instead, she forced her back straight and waited.

Day six, and they still had no manager and no extra crew. She'd managed to clear up only half the house. The crew was behind on the pruning, and Luis didn't like to risk letting the vines go through a warm spell before they'd been cleaned of unnecessary old growth and canes. Papa had been the same way. She would have to tell Eric she needed just a few more days to take care of things. He would hit the roof, but she'd explain that if she didn't get everything settled now, she would have to take time off later. As for the backers, she'd have to postpone the meeting a few days.

A man was circulating from table to table, a faded red-and-white cap pressed to his chest, his Carhartt coat so worn, it was almost white and showed through to the lining in places. A boy followed him closely. They stopped and moved in unison like a Marx Brothers routine. The boy looked about ten, though she knew that the children of migrant workers tended to be older than their size might suggest. The boy's shoes were several sizes too big, and the cap he wore hid the top half of his face.

The waitress placed a tray of food in front of her. Miranda mumbled *gracias* but did not pick up her fork.

The pair drew closer until she could make out the thin line of the child's mouth, the lips gray and cracked from weather. They stopped at the table next to her, and she heard the man asking for work.

The diners shook their heads, said they heard there might be something at Tree of Life.

She shivered at the name. The nursery industry was huge in Oregon, and Tree of Life was the biggest of them. They started out with landscaping trees and now included shrubs, perennials, annuals. Insiders lost no breath making fun of the corporation's name, because they had a record of worker abuse as long as the OSHA inspector's arm. Agribusiness was a convenient shield for labor abuse, all for the sake of profit, all of it etched into the boy's cracked lips and hands that were strangely elegant in spite of scars and scabs.

The man started to move past her.

"*Con permiso,*" she said, still staring at the boy.

The man stopped and took a step backward, which caused the boy to pile into him. The man caught the edge of the table and steadied himself.

"*Buenas,*" she said. "You're looking for work?"

"Yes," he said. "Me and my son." He gestured with his cap over his shoulder at the boy who had raised his chin slightly, the better to see the steaming plates of food.

"I might have some work," she said. "*Sientace.*" She kicked out a chair with the toe of her shoe. The man sat next to Miranda, and she gestured at the boy to sit down also. She looked closely at the man's face and took in the bitter smell of his skin, the off, ashy color of it. He didn't look healthy, that was for sure. Probably he hadn't had work in a long time and was struggling to feed a large family.

As she talked to the man, she pushed her plate across the table to the boy. The boy looked at the man, moved the plate toward him.

She smiled at the boy and pushed the plate back. "No, no. *Come.*" Then she pushed another plate at the man, but he shook his head. *"No, gracias."*

The boy picked up the empanada and stuffed a corner into his mouth. The stretched skin of his lips began to bleed, but he seemed not to notice and licked away the food that gathered there along with the blood. The man watched him eat.

"Señor," she said, and when he turned to her, she thought she saw envy in the gray, pinched corners of his eyes. "If you are looking for work, I need some pruners in my vineyard. My name's Miranda."

He said his name was Corio, and he had worked in vineyards before. Knew the pruning pretty well.

"How many vines a minute?" she asked.

"Ten. Twelve. *Mas o menos.*"

"How is the boy called?"

"Tito."

"What will you do with Tito?" she asked.

"He is sixteen," Corio said. "He will work also."

"No," she said. "I need only you. But bring Tito with you. It's okay. When can you start?"

"Ahora," he said.

She drew a map on a napkin and handed it to him. "You can follow me there if you'd like."

He ran a finger across the bottom of his nose, a brisk gesture, and shook his head.

"I see," she said. "Ride up with me in a little while. You can arrange for a ride tomorrow with the crew."

"We will wait outside." He stood and pulled the boy up from the chair, shuffled him out the door. Through the picture window she watched how the man positioned the child between himself and the wall, using his body as a windbreak. When he doubled over in a fit of coughing, he tucked his face into the coat. The child turned away.

Miranda and Dario had met at a soup kitchen where they both

volunteered. When they moved in together, she was surprised to find that he brought home families with children who had no place to go when the shelters were full. Dario told her a Nobel Prize winner once said there should have been an eleventh command- ment: *Thou shalt not stand idly by.*

Luis would be angry with her for picking up a loner; if he was sick or in trouble, he might draw suspicion. But it was worth it to get the extra help, and for the boy.

Miranda and Ruben had watched the race coverage on the news that morning. Day five of the race, and Bridie was out front with a solid lead.

When Miranda bathed Ruben at night, she could not help thinking of Tito. For the past three days, she watched from the kitchen as the men arrived in the morning. Corio would climb out of the back of a pickup and walk away, not bothering to help the boy. Tito negotiated the tailgate to the bumper and then to the ground, his movements slow and purposeful, as if his bones might shatter at the slightest jolt.

She waited this morning, eyeing the vineyard through misting rain until she heard Petra's *beep-beep* out front; she'd promised Ruben a spin to McMinnville. Miranda took her son's chunky hand at the door, kneeled, and kissed him but let go of his hand before she walked him out. Already he was opposed to blatant Mom con- tact in front of other people. As they drove away, he refused to look at her as she raised a hand, and she thought how strange it was that a child could echo your own past so utterly.

A rain squall passed through, and she shucked up the hood of her coat, meaning to head to the vineyard, but she stood a while longer. Luis told her that she needed to speak with the crew each morning to let them know somebody was there and expecting a certain amount of work to be done that day, *Just until we get a manager,* he'd been careful to add.

She dreaded the ritual. How was she supposed to check up on work she knew nothing about? In her kitchen at the restaurant, she knew every nick in the worktable. There wasn't a leaf of parsley in the house that she had not personally ordered and inspected on its arrival. But for the last three days since she'd hired Corio, she looked forward to the morning update because it meant she could check on the boy.

She didn't know how long she'd been standing there when she heard the gravel crunch in the driveway behind her. She did not recognize the car, a ratty Suburban that was well past better days.

A man got out of the car and approached her. He was tall for a Latino. A thicket of black hair roughed his scalp, his teeth displayed white and even as piano keys. His cheeks were pressed flat, his skin the color of copper earth. Mayan heritage maybe. Shadow pooled in the pocks of old acne scars as a smile inched his mouth wider.

"Can I help you?" she asked.

"I think I'm here to help you," he said.

His English was clean and precise; he was probably born in the States.

It occurred to her then that Luis had sent him—possible manager material.

"Come inside, and we'll talk about the job," she said.

His pupils shrank in the dark amber stain of his eyes. He moved closer, took her surprised hand, and shook it. "I should introduce myself," he said. "Dr. Ayudar. You should call me Beto. I work at the Buenavista clinic in Salem."

"Miranda Perry," she said, and slipped her hand into her coat pocket. "I'm sorry," she said. "We're looking for a manager. I just thought—"

"Understandable, considering my ethnicity."

She didn't know what to say, so she just pinched her lips shut and let the thoughts pile up behind them.

He made a motion as if to wipe the air clean between them. "I do outreach on the side," he said. "It's hard to get workers into clinics. Half of them are illegal; the other half tend to be suspicious—and superstitious. If I take it on the road, see them in their territory, I can accomplish a little. At least that's the idea. I'd like to get another clinic established up here with a full-time traveler. They're doing it elsewhere." He shoved his hands into his pockets, causing the silver filigreed belt buckle to sag forward.

"Do you have some identification?" she asked.

Again his eyes narrowed at her; then he smiled. "I'm not INS, if that's what you're thinking. And besides, I'm sure you run a clean operation."

Four days ago, it would have been true, but now she could not say.

"Look, I hope this isn't going to turn into a hair-pull or something," he said.

"You've got more hair than I do," she said. "It wouldn't be much of a contest."

He laughed. "So do you mind if I talk to your crew? Do a little basic diagnostic?"

"Sure," she said. "I'll go up first. Break the ice a little."

"Sounds like a plan," he said.

"Would you like to wait inside, where it's warm?"

"No thanks. I'm plenty warm."

Sodden air clung to her as she moved up the hill, looking for splashes of yellow among the vines. When she saw Hector toward the end of the row, she turned down it, the loose tops of her rubber boots slapping the backs of her legs like hand claps. He stopped working when she was halfway to him, and slid his pruning knife into the pocket of his slicker.

Hector was young yet, but Luis had his eye on him, said he was sharp and fast and had a hand for the vines. *Good enough for manager material?* she'd asked. Luis just shook his head and smiled. *Maybe later.*

She scanned the vines for Corio but did not see him or the boy. She talked with Hector a minute, her eyes on the pruned canes at her feet that littered the aisles. They would be picked up later and chopped for mulch between the vines. Hector said that things were well, that they might finish in time.

"So Corio's working out?" she asked him in Spanish.

Hector's eyes flickered away.

"What is it?" she asked.

"He is not here."

"But I saw him come with you this morning."

"Yes."

"He left?"

"I think so, yes. He said he had to take a piss, but that was fifteen minutes ago."

"What about the boy?"

"I don't know," he said. "I am working."

"I just thought you might have noticed something. It's all right." She told him about the doctor and asked if Hector would mind if he talked to the crew. Hector looked up and down the row he'd been pruning, then shook his head.

"I'll bring him up, then," she said, and walked back to the house.

Dr. Ayudar was leaning against the Suburban, his legs crossed at the ankle as if it were a fine spring day instead of a gray, squally mess.

"It's okay," she said. "Do you mind walking up?"

"No problem," he said. "I could stomp around here all day."

Not if you had to, she thought.

She looked for Tito as they went, but she did not see him.

She pointed at the end cap. "Wait here. I'll get the rest of the guys."

She felt his eyes on her back as she moved away.

Once they had the crew together, Beto stepped up and introduced himself in Spanish. "Nobody sent me here," he said. "I do this on my own time. I'd like to talk to each of you about any problems you have, any sickness. Also, if you know of anyone who's sick and needs help, you can tell me and I'll go to him. I have some medicines with me in the truck, and I don't charge anything. This is completely free." He flashed his perfect teeth again. The men scuffed their boots and looked around.

"I know you feel uncomfortable with the lady boss," he continued. "But she doesn't mind. I know it must be hard for you, working with a woman." Some of the crew smiled then; a few actually tittered. He misinterpreted their smiles and continued. "I understand how you feel. My boss is a lady also, and it drives me a little crazy, eh? They can be difficult, no?"

The crew's smiles widened, and some of them laughed outright now, looked back and forth between him and Miranda, amazed at this man's unfortunate mistake.

Miranda leaned against the trellis anchor, determined to let him dig on, until Hector finally asked her in Spanish how long this was going to take and would their pay be docked for it.

Dr. Ayudar did not turn, but she could see the red creep quickly across the back of his neck when she answered in Spanish, "Of course not. This is a paid break. You should speak with Dr. Ayudar as long as you like. He's very good-hearted to give us his time like this."

She stepped up behind him. "I'll be down at the house. Stop in when you're finished. I'll put some coffee on." She headed down the hill, her step lighter than it had been in days.

Back at the house, Beto wrapped his hands around the warm coffee cup and stared at the table. "I hope you realize what I was doing back there, you know, with my 'approach.' "

"You might have thought of another way around it," she said.

"But it worked," he said. "They loosened up, let me talk to them. The other way takes so much time, and I don't have a lot of that."

"It doesn't matter what I think," she said. "You came here for them. I appreciate that."

His eyes roved the kitchen, took in the peeling linoleum, the sagging screen door with only enough paint left on it to suggest that it once was painted, the refrigerator pocked with rust.

"What?" she said.

He smiled and shook his head. "I don't know. I guess I thought . . . Well, a lot of these vineyards have quite the digs for housing. Rich people coming in to play with the earth because they think it's easy."

"You thought I had some green."

His coppery skin darkened. "You have to admit you're young to have a vineyard like this."

She sipped her coffee, couldn't help smiling at the way he refused to be put off, just like Bridie.

"What's so funny?" he asked.

"I have a friend who's a lot like you," she said.

"Well I hope you're not as cryptic with him."

"I'm not, but only because she doesn't allow it."

"Oh," he said. "I see."

She smiled again. "You probably don't. She's my best friend. She races dogs in Alaska, and nothing scares her, not even people."

"Oh," he said. "That race is on now, isn't it?"

"The Iditarod, yes. She's in it. She's going to win."

"I heard something about it on the radio on the way over here."

"What was it?"

He held up his hands. "Sorry. Had I known I needed to pay attention, I would have."

"We'll just have to wait for the evening news."

"We?"

"My son, Ruben."

He put his fingers to his lips as if to button them, but his eyes asked the question anyway.

"My father died twelve days ago. That's why we're here. He left the vineyard to me, but we're going back to San Francisco as soon as I get everything squared away here."

"Does your son's father have any say in this?" Beto asked.

"Ruben's father is dead," she said, and marveled at how easily the words she had avoided saying for six years floated into air.

He watched her steadily but said nothing until she looked away. "Truth is, I didn't just stop by on a whim. I'm tracking somebody."

She looked at him sharply, but he held up a hand.

"No, I'm *not* INS, like I said. I'm tracking somebody medically. The grapevine tells me he was in Dundee, and that he talked to a woman there at the *taquería*. I thought maybe it was you."

"What do you mean, tracking him medically?"

"He's got TB. He started the treatment at my clinic in Salem, but never finished the medication. That means the virus will become resistant and he'll probably die. Meanwhile, he's a Typhoid Mary, and he's got a kid with him."

Miranda's thoughts corkscrewed through the sequence of events,

Corio's ashy skin, the way he'd coughed into his coat outside the *taquería*. She'd thought it was just a cold and poor nutrition.

"I saw him and his father last week in Dundee. Corio was looking for work. I needed somebody. Mostly I was worried about the kid."

"I can see why," he said.

"They were here this morning, but when I went up to tell the crew you were here, he was gone."

"He might have seen my truck," Beto said. "He knows I'm looking for him. The grapevine works both ways."

"Is the boy sick?" she asked.

"It's possible he's not infected."

"What about the crew? Should they be tested?"

He smiled at her, and there was a hint of sadness to the stretch of his mouth.

"TB's endemic to the migrant population now. There's a good chance many of them would test positive as carriers but they don't show symptoms. The disease is only infectious when symptoms show. If you tested the crew and some of them are positive, you wouldn't know if it was because of exposure to Corio or not."

Miranda stared at him. "Should Ruben and I get tested?"

He twirled his spoon a few times around the cup. "You weren't exposed to him very long. Did he cough while he was near you?"

"No, not until he was outside."

"I wouldn't worry about it, then. Beto took his cup to the sink, rinsed it, and set it on the counter. "If you see Corio, let me know." He flipped a card on the table. "Don't think of it as ratting. I'm not going to report him. He thinks that's what's going to happen but I'm just trying to keep this from spreading. If it does, public health will get into it, and that's the next step to the INS."

She picked up the card, turned it over and back to front again. His cell phone number was handwritten on the back, and she wondered if he did that to all his cards or whether he'd scribbled it there before he came in for coffee.

❧

That evening she sat with Ruben in her lap, waiting for the news to come on. He was exhausted from his day out and had fallen asleep an hour ago while he was telling her everything he'd done. Petra had taken him to lunch at Niko's, and Niko himself had made him a special plate and brought him a fresh baked tarte tartin with a candle in it. *Like it was my birthday and everything,* Ruben said. Then Petra had taken him to the farm store and bought him a little Carhartt coat; she'd told him it was exactly like what his grandpa wore every day in the vineyard.

He'd played with Sonny again that afternoon, and Paul had let the boys sand wood in his shop after they were tired of the jungle gym. Then Paul's wife, Dianna, had come home and baked fresh cookies. *They were real, Mom. Just like yours. Cherries and big chocolate chunks.* Dianna had sent some home with Ruben, and Miranda had to admit they were as good as she'd have made. They had sheep and goats, too, and Ruben loved playing with the goats. *Dianna makes cheese from the goats,* Ruben told her, and that got Miranda's attention. If the woman was making artisanal cheeses right down the road, that was something, and she'd made a note to herself to swing down there and meet this infamous Dianna who made chef-quality cookies and goat cheese to boot.

When the news came on, she waited through the main stories and the weather before she roused Ruben. They always ran Iditarod news in the sports segment toward the end of the half hour. She slid him off her lap and went to wash up. They were due at Luis and Madrita's for dinner, for the treat of Madrita's cooking—puffy handmade tortillas that melted in your mouth rather than the tough machine-made rounds you got in the store. And Miranda had especially requested Madrita's mole sauce. She remembered tasting it for the first time as a child, how it lay on her tongue like spiced chocolate velvet.

She heard Ruben squeal in the living room, "Mom."

She tried to dry her hands, but the phone rang and she ground her jaw so hard she thought her teeth might shatter, but then realized it was Papa's phone ringing and it might be Petra or Luis.

The man's voice in her ear sounded tinny and distant. "This is Gordon James, Bridie's trainer."

79

"Mom!" Ruben called, "you're missing it."

She held out her hand to Ruben, one finger raised. "I'm sorry, I missed that," she said to the man.

"I'm Gordon James. Bridie trains with me."

"Yes, I'm sorry. Go ahead."

There was a weird echo and delay on the line that made her feel as if she were talking to someone on the moon.

"Bridie's hurt. We're here at the hospital in Anchorage."

Ruben stood in front of her. "Mom, there was a heelachopper. You missed it."

"What?" she said into the phone.

"She's in surgery. Something with her back," Gordon said.

"Her back? Is it—?"

"I don't know," he said. "The doc said something about the lower back, and that was better than middle or upper. Said he was worried about the spinal cord. They'll know more after the surgery."

"How long ago did they take her in?"

"Half hour, maybe. She asked me to call you. Knew your number by heart. She never remembers numbers."

Her eyes stung, and she turned away from Ruben. "Listen, I've got to make some arrangements here. If you talk to her before I get there, tell her I'll be there as soon as I can."

"You want me to pick you up at the airport or something?"

"I'll get a car. Thanks."

He gave her his cell phone number, and she hung up. She didn't know they had cell phones in Alaska.

She put her hand on top of Ruben's head, and when she realized her fingers were trembling she pulled it away and kneeled in front of him.

"There was a picture of Aunt Bridie, Mom," Ruben said. "There was a heelachopper. Did she win?"

"No, sweetie. I need you to watch the TV for me for a minute." She handed him a bowl of yogurt with fruit cut into it. "I just have to make a phone call, okay?"

He wiped his nose on his sleeve and took the bowl from her.

She stretched the phone cord onto the porch out of Ruben's earshot, and called Luis to explain what had happened.

"Luis, it's just a couple of days. Would you check on the guys when you can?"

"This is not the only thing," he said.

"What do you mean?"

"We are behind, you see? We are not making enough progress."

"Who told you that?"

He sighed. "I have eyes," he said. "I am doing this for long time."

"Are you talking to Hector?" she asked.

"Which is that?" he asked, and she knew his voice well enough to know that he had talked to Hector, probably every day.

"I know we're behind schedule," she said. "We lost a crewman today, but I'll find somebody else when I get back."

He paused, and she could hear dishes clinking in the background.

"*Dios,*" he said. "I am talking to a ghost."

"What are you talking about?" she asked.

"Nothing," he said. "I will take care of things."

"Thank you. Please tell Madrita I'm sorry. Tell her to save the mole for me."

He sighed. "We will save it, and we will help with Ruben, also."

"I don't think you'll have a choice," she said. "He's in love with you and that tractor. I'm sure that's how you wanted it." She could practically see his wily smile as she hung up the phone.

Duncan had come around the corner on the horse so quietly she hadn't heard him. "You in bother?" he asked.

"Bridie," she said, her voice sounded like a recording.

Duncan stepped off the horse and wound the reins around the porch railing. "The dog racer?" he asked.

"Yes. She's been hurt in the race. She's in surgery." She paused a minute. "I'll call Petra."

"She just ran down to Dundee, be back in a bit. Pack the nipper. I'll get the truck and take him up, explain the situation."

"Mom?" Ruben stood at the screen door. "Can I ride?"

"Later, sweetie, but right now we need to have a little talk."

She led him to his bedroom and tried to explain what had happened to Bridie while she packed his suitcase, her anxiety mounting as she picked out words she hoped wouldn't frighten him.

She turned on the porch light when Duncan rumbled up in the truck, the dog silhouetted next to him on the seat. She was relieved when she saw the dog. Ruben would be happy.

Duncan listened to Miranda's instructions patiently about what he would and would not eat. "No worries," he'd said. "Petra will know what to do."

Though it was March, Miranda bundled the boy in his winter coat, mittens dangling from the clips of his sleeves.

"Weather's apples," Duncan pointed out. "He won't need that."

"It might turn," she said without looking at him.

"Honey, Petra's going to take care of you while I help Bridie," she explained to Ruben.

"Why can't I go?"

"Bridie's sick, honey, and Momma's got to go help her, okay?"

"I'll help," he said. His voice quavered. "I'll take care of Zeus."

She hadn't even asked Gordon about the dogs. "Duncan's going to need some help with his dog, Ru. You think you can do that?"

"Fluke!" Ruben said. His face brightened.

"I'll be back as soon as I can," Miranda said.

"Aunt Bridie comin'?"

"I don't know, honey. We'll have to see what she wants."

She lifted him into the truck and felt that peculiar twist in her belly when she let go of his hand. "Mind Duncan, Ru. Do exactly what he says."

"He'll be fine," Duncan said.

His eyes were green as new grapes. She hadn't noticed that before.

She watched the taillights weave up the hill in the dusk while she booked the flight. She would have just enough time to get to Portland for the shuttle to Seattle, and from there a four-hour flight to Anchorage.

5

When asked to be apprised of Bridie's status, the doctors had been fairly forthcoming. The neurosurgeon had even searched her out that morning in the cafeteria, where she slumped over a cup of scalded coffee and a bowl of something that was supposed to be oatmeal.

"Ms. Perry?"

She glanced up, a spoon of mush halfway between the bowl and her unwilling mouth.

He extended a hand. "Dr. Lindall. I operated on your friend last night."

She had expected someone grizzled, wearing at least a flannel shirt under the whites. But he was as clean shaved and trim as you would expect of a surgeon in a big city hospital anywhere, and she was so tired she'd said, "You're not what I expected."

He tilted his head at her, glasses going white in the fluorescent glare. Only then did she realize his hand was still outstretched; she let the spoon plop into the mush and performed the obligatory shake.

He stitched his arms across the perfectly starched front of his coat. "MRI didn't look good, so we went in. Multilevel unstable fractures, L1 through 4, but from what I could see, the cord wasn't transected. We pinned the rami at all four sites and got out. Without complications, she could recover."

"Completely?"

"Hard to say."

"But it's probable?"

"I'd say possible. I've seen worse. It's a tough race. Big, strapping men come in here beat to a pulp."

In all her talk about the racing, Bridie had never mentioned that people got hurt, and Miranda felt like an idiot for not thinking of it.

Miranda stared at the gruel. A sickly gray film had formed over the surface. She pushed it away. The idea of Bridie not on her feet, all six feet of her, was impossible. Her brain functioned as well as her body, but Bridie lived in her body, not in her mind.

"How close are you?"

Miranda looked at him, uncomprehending.

"I just wondered who would be the most appropriate person to break the news when she comes to," he said.

Miranda wondered if anyone had called Bridie's parents. Bridie always laughed off her mother's disapproval of Bridie's lifestyle, but now Miranda felt as if she'd failed Bridie, that if she'd expressed concern, advocated caution . . .

"Ms. Perry?" The doctor stared at her.

"This'll be hard," Miranda said. "She was an athlete, you know?"

He granted her a tight little smile. "I'll say she's an athlete. She's a Gordon James protégée, running his dogs. I hear Gordon's around, but I haven't seen him." He cocked one foot on its heel, regarded the toe of his shoe. "Well, page me when she starts to come around. It could be any time."

When she got back to Bridie's room, a man's body was spread across the chair in the corner. His head hung off the back of his neck, cramping nasal passages that complained rudely in the quiet room. Bits of straw hung from the quilted flannel shirt. His boots, unlaced and gaping, rested in little puddles of melted snow. She hadn't expected Gordon to look like that. He could pass for forty or sixty.

Since he occupied the only chair in the room, she stood by the bed and held Bridie's hand until the man finally reached the as-

phyxiation level and jolted awake with a groan. The pouches under
his eyes looked chalky. Poor diet, no doubt. He blinked and seemed
about to say something unpleasant, as if she had got in the wrong
room and it was now his duty to send her on her way.

"Gordon?" she said.

"Naw, I'm Jim," he said, and yawned so wide she thought his jaw
would break. "And you would be—?"

"Miranda Perry."

"Oh, yeah. Bridie showed me pictures. Cute kid."

"Ruben," she said. "That would be Ruben."

"Okay. Ruben." When he yawned again, she looked away.

"Has anyone called her parents?" Miranda asked.

"I dunno," he said. "Gordon's checking the dogs in the truck.
He'll be back in a minute."

She looked down and realized she was standing in a little puddle of white-crusted water.

An attractive blond nurse came in and introduced herself as Jill.
She went over Bridie's chart with Miranda until her attention
shifted to something over Miranda's shoulder.

"Hi, Gordon," Jill said. "Don't forget you promised me an auto-
graph."

Gordon. If it hadn't been for him, Bridie probably wouldn't have
got into dog racing to begin with. The oatmeal she'd choked down
tried to make a comeback, and Miranda thought for a moment she
might be sick.

Bridie knew it was pain, but it hovered at the edge, a shape-
changing mass that interfaced sometimes with the other thing she
knew. Sometimes she thought she was touching snow, her hands
opening and closing on it, but this snow had neither temperature
nor texture. Forms surged within the thing that she knew. She could
almost make them out, a taut curve, tufted planes. Round surfaces
glinted and winked with alluring regularity, but she could not blink
back.

Now there was something new, a shapeless presence that was

bright and that she sensed was good. Details bloomed in the dark, then receded. If she could grasp the thing that was good, then she would have something to hold on to when the other shapes came too close. It went on like that, interminable, frustrating, like swimming in glue.

Synapses sparked. She began to discern something tonal, something she could hear in snatches and strings. With great effort, she broke free, felt her feet come clear, and then the rush and pull of air sucking her up and up and up, her arms pressed tightly to her sides, until she broke the surface into blinding light that almost collapsed her eyes. They fluttered, unwilling to close themselves against the thing she was trying to see. And when finally they slowed enough to blink, she saw between the shuttered flashes a figure so welcome that tears eked from the corners of eyes now cramped in the effort to smile.

"She's coming up," Miranda said, and pointed to Bridie's fingers where they squirmed and twisted in her hand, then said to Jim, "Tell the nurse to page Lindall."

"Who?"

"Dr. Lindall. The surgeon."

Jim's boots squeaked away down the hall.

She said Bridie's name. Auditory response is the last thing to go and the first to return. She said Bridie's name again, forcing brightness into her voice, and saw the eyelids twitch in response. "It's Ran, Bridie. I'm here."

Bridie moved her lips.

"Hello, sweetie," Miranda said.

Jim's boots squeaked to the doorway. "Doc's on his way."

When Bridie tried to ease onto her side, pain came from her in a low, sucking hiss. "I can't move my legs."

Miranda stroked Bridie's knotty hair. "You hurt your back. That's why you can't move your legs right now."

And then Lindall was at the foot of the bed. "Ms. McLewan. I'm Dr. Lindall, the surgeon who put you together last night."

"Put me together?" Bridie looked at Miranda.

"Doc-speak, honey. Relax."

"*Relax?* I can't feel my *legs.*"

Gordon reached across the bed to shake Lindall's hand. "Gordon James," he said.

Lindall beamed like a little kid who'd just been granted an audience with a king. "Mr. James," he said. "We've followed every one of your races."

Miranda was appalled by their little testosterone display and barely resisted the urge to slap them both. "Bridie, Dr. Lindall's going to explain the surgery now," Miranda said, her voice jacked up so loud, even Bridie flinched.

Lindall cleared his throat. "Four of your lower lumbar were fractured, so we pinned them. The spinal cord was badly bruised but intact. It's not unusual in these cases for temporary impairment to occur. We'll have to see where we stand once the swelling subsides."

See where we *stand?* Miranda couldn't believe the guy was so tactless.

"Zeus pulled a muscle getting out of that mess before the Burn," Bridie said. "I had him in the sled bag. Gordon?" Bridie's eyes clung to him.

Gordon fidgeted mindlessly with the change in his pocket. "Zeus is at the vet. It doesn't look good."

Bridie's face contorted. "Miranda?"

"Don't worry about Zeus. I'll make sure he's okay."

Miranda caught Lindall's eye and gestured at the morphine bag. He nodded and opened the valve. Bridie's face softened, and she sighed. Her eyes shifted, then closed. Miranda asked Lindall if he'd be around later.

"Yes. I'm on all day. There's a good breakfast place on Spenard. Gwynnie's. Reindeer sausage, classic atmosphere." He looked at Gordon. "But you probably know the place."

The dimples squirmed. "Been there a few times."

Lindall clapped a hand across Gordon's back and guided him into the hall, chattered about signing something for his wife.

Miranda looked at Jim slumped in the chair. "Had breakfast yet?" she asked.

"No," Jim grumbled. "And I'm just shy of starved."

"If we can get your pal away from his fans . . ."

"It's always like that," Jim said.

They sat in silence while Jim hoovered down the Klondike Klassic— a tall stack of blueberry pancakes, three eggs over easy, three reindeer sausage, and a separate plate mounded with home fries—in less time than it took Miranda to eat two pieces of toast, which Jim then watched her eat as if hoping she'd up and die before she finished it. Afterward, she ordered a carafe of coffee that she drank black while he and Gordon whitened and sweetened theirs with four packets of sugar.

"Holy mackerel" was all she could think to say as Jim stirred the sugar in and probed his teeth for leftovers. He grunted and peeled off layers of flannel.

"Would somebody mind filling me in now?" Miranda asked.

"Nobody saw it," Jim said. "The next racer was hours behind her in the checkpoint. The plan was Bridie would do one of her mandatory eight-hour layovers and time it so she could hit the next leg in daylight. It's one of the worst stretches of trail in the race." Jim stopped and looked at Gordon. "Maybe you should tell it."

"If she'd have taken the eight-hour like we planned, it would have been daylight," Gordon said. "But it was still dark by the time she got up on the Burn, and top that off with the storm coming in."

"What's the Burn?" Miranda said.

"The Farewell Burn, site of Alaska's largest forest fire, in '78," Gordon said. "Millions of acres fried to a crisp, and the trail goes right through it. It's full of burnt half-stumps and clumps of willow growing back in. The stumps get hidden under drifting snow so you can't always see them. BLM and trail crew cleared up a lot of the mess. It used to be worse. Plenty of accidents.

"It had to be blowing forty out in the open. In the dark with snow in your eyes like sand. With the wind in their faces, the dogs must have smelled it for miles. They were probably hellin' for it right down the trail."

"For what?"

"Moose. They're dog magnets. You can't stop them when they get tearing after one, especially when they're fresh and you got a big team. She still had fifteen dogs in harness—minus Zeus, who was in the sled—and that's pretty much a pack of wild animals with strings on. Dogs probably tear-assed off the trail, whiplashed the sled and her and everything into one of those stumps, is what I figure. Dogs piled into that moose like a train wreck, tangling harness and all right under its belly. It stomped seven dogs dead. Pulverized them. Two were tore up so bad, they put 'em down right on the trail. Six came out a little bunged up, but okay." He sighed and crossed his arms on the table.

"And then there's Zeus," Gordon said, his eyes on the table.

Miranda thought of the picture Ruben kept under his pillow.

"The dog gave her too much confidence. He took a hell of a beating, which is odd, considering he wasn't even in harness. When the next racer found them, Zeus was right next to Bridie, just this side of alive. They were going to put him down, but she wouldn't let go of him. When the chopper came, she wouldn't let them go without Zeus. Made the medics load him in next to her."

"Where is he now?"

Jim looked at Gordon.

"At the vet," Gordon said.

"What vet?"

"Bascomb. The best around."

"She's the one Bridie did her internship with," Miranda said. "Where she met you."

"Yeah. If anyone can get the dog through, it would be Bascomb."

"He was in bad shape," Jim said.

"We've already established that," Miranda said.

"Jim is the best handler in the business. That's why I sent him with Bridie. He's worked hard, held the line in this fiasco," Gordon said.

Miranda's hands were curled and hot in her lap. *Fiasco*.

"I don't doubt Jim's skills or Bridie's," she said. "If Bridie thought she needed to keep going without taking the layover, then that's what was best. When she's ready to tell us what happened, we'll know the whole story."

"People at the checkpoint said she was nervous about the guy on her tail. Said that was why she took off. But he was hours behind her, and he hadn't taken his first eight-hour, either. It would have evened out across the race. There's a lot of strategy involved, and you have to stick with the plan. She was distracted," Gordon said.

"By what?" Miranda asked.

Gordon fiddled with a paper napkin, twisting it into smaller and smaller knots. "Her concentration was shot before she ever started. That's why she screwed up."

"What do you mean? She was ready as she's ever been. I could tell when I saw her."

"That's what I mean," Gordon said, and he looked straight at her. "It was the sidetrip got her out of whack."

"She shoulda packed that .357 like I said," Jim said.

"And you were responsible for making sure she did," Gordon said to Jim.

"Now hold the hell up a minute," Jim said.

"I'm thinking of those dogs dead in the snow when all she'd a had to do was point and shoot that fucking moose. She could have saved most of them. But it didn't start there. If she'd a done what she was supposed to do in the first place, the gun wouldn't have been an issue."

Jim excused himself to take a piss.

Miranda set her coffee cup down hard on the table, oblivious of the hot liquid spilling over her fingers. If anyone was to blame for this, it was Gordon and his damned dogs and his champion dreams egging Bridie on. He'd known from experience how dangerous it was, and he'd never discouraged Bridie from it. But when the steam was about to hiss from her mouth, something else tugged at her. She rose from her chair, then sat down again and pushed the thought away.

Gordon dropped his chin to his chest. Finally, he cleared his throat and looked up at her with miserable, red-hatched eyes. "She would have won this race. I shit you not. She had an instinct for it, you know? That's why I took her on. But she is tough and soft in equal proportion. She cancels herself out."

Miranda clamped her hands to the edge of the table to keep the room from dipping this way and that. From the years they'd shared an apartment in college, Miranda knew how Bridie buttered her toast, folded her shirts, and what she looked like coming out of a shower. Bridie ate carrots raw, never cooked. She loved coffee, drank it so black and strong she joked it could eat metal. She didn't wear makeup, mess with her nails, or primp her hair. When she went to bed at night, she rubbed her feet rhythmically across the sheets until she fell asleep. She was Ruben's godmother, his idol, Miranda's chosen sister and the finest of friends. Gordon had known Bridie for only a few years and only as a mentor. How had he seen something in her that Miranda had not?

Tears crept down her face, but she didn't wipe them away.

Gordon sighed and flipped his fork back and forth on the empty plate until Jim returned, eyeing them cautiously.

"We should get back to the truck and check on the dogs," Jim said. "They're still a little freaked."

Miranda meant to return to the hospital, but she decided then to swing by the vet and check on Zeus in the hope of good news. Bridie would need a little carrot.

When Miranda asked to see Dr. Bascomb about Zeus, the receptionist perked up and asked her to wait.

Thumbing through that month's issue of *Alaska* magazine, which featured rundowns on the race hopefuls, she was looking for Bridie's name when she heard a woman's voice behind her. "Can I help you?"

Miranda stood. "I'd like to see Dr. Bascomb about Bridie McLewan's dog, Zeus."

"I'm Dr. Bascomb," the woman said.

"Miranda Perry," Miranda said. "Bridie's friend."

"Oh," Bascomb said. "Oregon, right?"

Miranda started to say *California,* then said, "Yes, that's right."

"It's a shame about Bridie," Bascomb said. "She should have been close to Nome by now. What's her status?"

"The surgeon repaired some lumbar vertebrae, but the cord wasn't cut. He said she'll recover."

Bascomb peered at Miranda. "He said she'd recover?"

"Possibly," Miranda said. "But if you know Bridie, then you know that she'll recover. How is the dog?"

"Zeus," Bascomb waved a small hand in irritation. "Multiple rib fractures; spleen was shot, so we removed that; liver lacerated, which we repaired. Diaphragm punctured. Internal bleeding. Broken jaw . . . You want more?"

Miranda shook her head.

"Do you know anything about these dogs?" Bascomb asked.

Miranda thought she should have been able to say *Yes, of course I do,* but the more she thought she knew things, the less she was able to say with any certainty.

"They're working dogs," Bascomb said. "They get to do what they're meant to do. People complain that they're ill treated, forced to run against their wills. Nothing could be further from the truth. They're treated like athletes, like the sentient creatures they are. Their hearts are completely wrapped up in what they do. If Zeus survives this, his quality of life will be severely affected. He may live, but he won't be alive. The dog should have been put down. Bridie should know better, but that's why she quit. She couldn't put down dogs that needed it, even when it was a kindness. She argued every single injection to the point where she made my work miserable. I was glad she quit. She's a great gal, don't get me wrong, but she was not cut out for this job." Bascomb took in Miranda's numb stare. "She didn't tell you she quit, did she?"

Miranda shook her head.

"I'm not surprised," Bascomb said. "It pissed her off."

Miranda swiped at her forehead as if there were something on it. "I'd like to see the dog, if you don't mind," she said.

"All right. But you may not enter the cage, nor should you attempt to touch him through the wire."

Bascomb led her through a swinging door off the reception area and then through another door until they turned down a long cement run. There was the underlying smell of antiseptic, bleach, and the noxious chemical smell of medicine, but there was above that the smell of feces, urine, open flesh. She swallowed down the knot in her throat and continued to follow Bascomb's white coat until they reached a cage. The other dogs howled, or yipped hoarsely. The noise was not threatening so much as anguished.

Bascomb shouted at her, "Remember. Don't reach into the cage," then retreated down the hall, her figure leaned permanently forward as if she were born hurrying.

Miranda peered into the cage. Zeus lay on his side, legs extended to the edge of the pallet, his head closest to her. He had been shaved bare except for his tail, the silver skin in stark relief to the ventral sutures that ran from slow-heaving chest to belly. His forelegs were bandaged. When the platform darkened with liquid around the black tail, she thought she saw something in his face, disgust, disdain that he had been reduced to this barely living mess of pins and plates, lying in a puddle of his own urine.

She kneeled, unaware of the sound and stench, on a plane now where the dog's one mizzled eye could see her clearly without having to move his head. His face, raw and gray without its customary silk of fur, was more agonizing than the suture wounds. But when she saw herself in the pool of the dog's eye, she saw something that Bridie hadn't been able to let go, something that had waited with her for whatever it sensed was inevitable. She felt herself dissolve, felt she knew for certain the depth of the soul, the stretch of the will against all that pain.

When she got back to the front desk, she scribbled out her contact information in Oregon and California and paid whatever charges had accrued so far, then asked to see the doctor again. She stood by a plant in the waiting area, idly stroking dust from the surface of its seared leaves. They were obviously preoccupied with fauna here, not flora. The door swished open behind her.

Miranda turned to face Dr. Bascomb. "I've made arrangements with the receptionist for future billing, and paid for all services to date," Miranda said.

Bascomb's hair was pulled back so tightly, her face appeared almost featureless.

"I'll be in touch on a regular basis. When he's recovered enough to travel, we'll take it from there."

Bascomb smiled. "I'm sorry if I was a little curt before. It's just that for someone with so much energy and smarts, Bridie ought to have more sense."

"The dog's alive because he wants to be," Miranda said. "Bridie knows that."

"All right," Bascomb said, took the criticism unwavering, and Miranda saw a glimmer of why Bridie thought so much of her. "Is she conscious yet?" Bascomb asked. "Have you spoken with her?"

"Yes. But only for a minute. She was . . . upset."

"It's when they don't react at all that you know you have a problem," Bascomb said. "So upset's good."

"Let's hope so," Miranda said, and walked into the snow-blinding glare of afternoon.

First thing learned, first thing remembered: The dogs are everything. Never let go of the sled, because if you lose the dogs, so will you be lost.

Bridie tried to move her hands, feel for the handlebar of the sled, but all she could feel was snow. All she could breathe was snow.

When she came up this time, it was immediate, but pain surfaced with her thoughts, and she couldn't help the mealy sound that came from her mouth. "Where's Miranda?"

The nurse finished scanning the monitors and noting their levels on a chart. "I'll check at the desk. Be back in a jiff."

Bridie closed her eyes and wasn't sure how much time had passed when she heard the familiar voice from far away. Maybe she had imagined it. "Ran?"

"It's me, sweetie."

It seemed as if her eyes had been open before she saw anything. But there was Miranda, stroking her hand. "Jesus, it hurts," Bridie said. Her voice sounded like a squeak.

"I know," Miranda said, and stroked her hand as if it were the thinnest of tissue.

"Sorry," Bridie said.

"Don't be," Miranda said. "Besides, you got me to Alaska, didn't you?"

"Alaska from a hospital wouldn't have been my first choice."

When Miranda rose and stretched her back, Bridie followed her movements with her eyes, but said nothing.

Miranda buzzed the nurse.

"What's wrong?" Bridie asked.

"Saline bag's almost empty."

Bridie rolled her eyes at it. "No wonder my bladder's about to pop."

"That's good," Miranda said.

"Easy to say when you can make it to a bathroom," Bridie said.

"No, I mean it's great you can feel that."

"I'd rather feel my legs than my bladder."

"They'll come around," Miranda said.

"That's not what the surgeon said."

"He's just being cautious, Bridie. They're always like that."

"Where is everybody?" Bridie asked.

Miranda tried to keep her feelings below Bridie's radar. "Gordon and Jim are at the hotel. Has anyone called your folks?"

"I did."

"And?"

"I told them it was just a sprain. No need to panic."

Miranda said nothing.

"I can't have my dad trying to borrow money to get out here. I'll be fine."

"Okay," Miranda said.

"What about the dogs?" Bridie asked.

"Seven of them are okay," Miranda said.

"Zeus?" she said.

"He's at the vet. I saw him yesterday," Miranda said.

"And?"

"He was awake when I saw him. He asked about you." Miranda hoped she wouldn't ask for details.

"What did Bascomb say?"

"He's lucky to be alive," Miranda said. "She said to say hello."

Bridie turned her face to the wall.

"Do you remember what happened?" Miranda asked.

Bridie thought of Zeus lying in the stinking kennel, sewed and stitched and bandaged. She had felt his life flutter under her hand and later when they'd cut off her clothes, most of the blood on them had been his, not hers. Her sweat stank with the certainty that she had screwed up. She could tell by the way people talked to her, and didn't.

The nurse arrived to hang a fresh bag of saline, and Miranda helped her position Bridie on the bedpan. Bridie made no protest, only kept her eyes shut against the pain.

When the nurse left, Miranda sat on the edge of the bed, watching Bridie's ribs rise and fall under the sheet.

"Do you remember what happened?"

"No." Bridie rolled her eyes toward the window.

Miranda followed her gaze and saw blunted white mountains through a thin veil of falling snow. Bridie should be out there, dogs arrayed before her, licking errant flakes from her mouth instead of tears.

Miranda yanked a tissue from the bedside table and pressed it to Bridie's face. "We need to make a plan," Miranda said. "You're supposed to go into a skilled nursing facility for rehab, but I don't think it should be here."

"You think I should go home?"

"Is that what you want to do?" Miranda asked.

Bridie looked at her as if she'd sprouted a third eye.

"I didn't think so," Miranda said. "So I'll come back and get you when the doc says you're ready."

"That's brilliant," Bridie said. "Saddle yourself with a crippled chick and a child in San Francisco. Your apartment is a two-floor walk-up. Thanks but no thanks. I'll stay here."

"There's nobody here for you."

"Zeus is here."

"We'll bring him home, too. I talked to Dr. Bascomb about it."

"Like I said: San Franciso, two-floor walk-up. Christ, you're never home as it is."

"We'll get somebody. We'll get help."

Her words were like arrows of light that disappeared with a despondent sizzle when they reached Bridie's face.

"When are you going back?" Bridie asked.

"Tonight," Miranda said. "I know it's soon, but I've left Ruben with Petra, and Eric . . ."

"I know. The prick in the high hat."

Miranda hesitated. Bridie didn't need to hear about Eric's threats. *I've been there,* he'd said. *But I hired you so I didn't have to be there anymore, and now I'm here chopping parsley like a freaking rookie because your sous is useless and I'm about to fire him, too.* Still, he'd given her three more days.

When the phone rang, Miranda answered it, then covered the receiver and mouthed the word "mother."

Bridie closed her eyes.

"You want me to tell her you're asleep?"

"It's okay," Bridie said.

"I'll tell her," Miranda said.

"No," Bridie said. "I mean it's okay for you to go home."

Bridie clicked the morphine drip twice. Miranda watched her face slump, leaned quickly to her ear. "I'll see you soon," she whispered, and hoped Bridie could still hear her.

6

Duncan checked the refrigerator in the banquet room first thing and was relieved to find they'd turned it on in advance. The last two tastings he had arrived to find the door open and the damn thing unplugged. They'd had to set up bins filled with ice and water in order to chill the wine in time. Petra never teased him about coming early after that.

The monthly wine tastings in Portland had been Petra's idea, a way to get local wine buffs and beginners together and expose them to the industry sprouting in their own backyards. Wine was easily relegated to a rarefied place in people's minds, Petra said. They needed to show people that it was hard work, farming, and the more consumers met the people in the trenches, the more they'd build a positive perception.

Duncan knew it was a good idea, good for business, but he fucking well hated the social grind. Petra didn't understand why he reared away from it; as she so aptly noted, he could turn on the charm like a well-greased spout. But she didn't know how much it took from him, how after one of these gigs he felt as if he'd been blood-sucked to a fare-thee-well, complete with splitting headache. Not even the binges from his larrikin days in Melbourne before his dad moved them out to the vineyard had delivered headaches to match.

He could feel the shadow of it lurking in his cranium now, and he knew that as Petra's health worsened, so would his headaches.

He filled the fridge with wine, rearranged tables, and then polished the stemware with the flour-sack dish towels he brought himself. He scanned the room again. Each of the hundred glasses sparkled like girls in a chorus line. It looked good. Appetizing. That was the point.

He sashed the shades to the top of the long windows overlooking downtown and the sluggish crawl of the Willamette River. By the time the tasting started, the westering sun would make it all look like a gilt painting.

Paul, the restaurant's day manager, stuck his head in the door. "That fridge cold enough for ya?"

"Brilliant," Duncan said. "You have the list?"

Paul fluttered the papers bunched in his hand. "Right here."

Duncan took the chef's notes and went over the ingredient list she'd made. He knew it pissed her off, but it wasn't the chef he worried about so much as some sous chef taking it upon himself to add a little balsamic vinegar that would turn his big wines flabby, or use something fruity that would clash with the fruit in the wine.

"Everything okay?" Paul asked.

"Long as the tasties come out on schedule."

"Beg your pardon?"

"Tasties, snacks, hors d'oeuvres," he said.

"Oooohhh. Right," the manager said, with a laugh. "You Brits have the most colorful expressions."

"Australian," Duncan said.

"Same thing."

"No," Duncan said. He crossed the pale carpeted expanse of room and duffed Paul's arm with the side of his fist. "Different thing entirely." Then flashed the elusive smile, turning himself momentarily into a person a fellow thought he could joke with.

"How come you don't say g'day and all that?"

"No use wearing it out, eh?"

"No," Paul said. "Guess not. Well, if everything's okay, I'm outta here. Jeremy's here for the evening shift. Need anything, he's your man."

"Right," Duncan said.

He had an hour to spare. Plenty of time to hustle down to Oscar's and slurp back a dozen of those sweet little Yaquina Bay oysters.

He cut over to Ankeny and dropped down to First, hugging the curb to avoid the sidewalk crowd. Ankeny Square was full of vendors hawking all kinds of gook for the Rose City Festival. He'd toured the booths exactly once when he first came to Portland.

He ducked gratefully into the steamed glass door of the oyster bar and squeezed past a clot of people arguing over how many were in their party. He caught John's eye where he stood behind the bar, his massive white apron smeared gray with shell grit.

"How's the wine biz?" John had no trouble projecting his ample voice over the din.

"No worries," Duncan said, hand partly raised and pointing to the back.

"Yeah, find a spot. I'll send Betty," John said. He scrunched one eye tight and leered like a pirate.

"Thanks a lot," Duncan said.

He weaved through the crowd and slid into a small, dark-paneled booth in the middle of the restaurant. Duncan liked the cupping dimness here, like the ship's hold it was meant to imitate. He did not bother to flip open one of the paperboard menus cut in the shape of an oyster shell.

Betty appeared suddenly by the table. "Well, don't you look spiff. Mommy dress you, or what?" Her usual lack of cheer oozed from the yellowed line of her outdated hairdo.

"Something like that, Betty. Nice of you to notice."

His throat squirmed against the soft green flannel collar. The buttoned brown tweed coat shifted across his belly, so he unbuttoned it.

Sharp, Petra would say, snapping her fingers. *Sophisticated.*

And why not, since she'd bought the stuff. Much as he thought he would, he didn't mind her doing it. She treated it as the business transaction it was. He represented the winery at these social gigs, and as long as he had to do them, he might as well do it right. He wiggled his toes in the comfortable brogans—plebian but acceptable here in the Northwest of America—and thanked God Petra hadn't insisted on something poofy, like loafers. What the hell. Long as he didn't have to wear the rope, he'd suffer it; he hated ties with a passion normally reserved for clumsy wine.

"What's it today?" Betty asked.

"Coupla dozen Yaqs,"

"Drink?"

"Sauv blanc."

She shook her head, rubbery lips pressed out straight. "Do you good to drink a beer every now and then. We got all the fancy stuff."

"Gotta keep up with the business, Betty. Know what I mean?"

"Nope." She slid the order pad into her apron and disappeared.

When she plunked the huge cork-bottomed tray in front of him, he thanked her in spite of his urge to say something outrageous and squeezed lemon in lessening circles over the shells. He forked a little horseradish onto each glistening ruffle of meat, then slurped them down, not minding the occasional gnash of grit on his teeth.

It took him all of seven minutes to empty two dozen shells, but he lingered over the wine for at least fifteen. It was an affordable Pouilly-Fumé he had convinced John to stock, made entirely of sauvignon blanc grapes instead of the insipid blend of sémillon. Mondavi had nurtured sauvignon blanc in California, where it was called fumé blanc, but it had too much body for that style of wine, too long a finish. He preferred the acidic herbaceousness of a true sauv blanc, so he stuck with the French. And there was no better finish to oysters, as far as he was concerned. His palate tart and refreshed, he headed up to the register.

John waved him over. The usual toothpick rolled from side to side as he talked, a habit he'd picked up when he quit smoking. "Hate to mix business with your pleasure," John said, winking, "but we need a few more cases of your pinot gris. Sells like crazy come summer."

White wine was the mass market beverage of choice, and since Oregon didn't do well with chardonnay, the marketing coup of the last decade, they'd had to come up with something to pit against it.

Pinot gris was the answer, and the crowds loved it. He promised John delivery of the desired cases before he left, then walked slowly back to the banquet room.

In the bathroom there, he smoothed his hair down with a little water and emptied his bladder in preparation for the siege. He stopped cold in the doorway of the banquet room, thought for a minute he'd got the wrong place. But there were his wine bottles, only on tables that were not as he'd left them. The chafing dishes and hors d'oeuvres tray were set up, but he hadn't given the okay sign for them to be brought out yet. The pressure began to build against the top of his skull.

"You remember I have to go to that wine tasting tonight with Duncan," Miranda said to Ruben.

He looked at her, annoyed that she'd stopped the tape.

Miranda had to borrow a video machine from Petra so that he could watch it, and she thought of some way to rib Bridie for it every time she cued up the tape. She sat next to him on the couch so she could fast-forward through the parts that frightened him; he still couldn't get through the scene where Yeller fought with the bear and saved Travis's life. When she got back from Alaska, he'd asked about Zeus. She told him that Zeus was very sick, just like Yeller was when he fought the bear.

In the two days since she'd returned, Miranda called Bridie twice a day and reported Ruben's antics, the spring buds exploding on the vines, everything but what worried her most. She could save that for later, because she'd already made up her mind that Bridie would come home with her. It was the only way. She had one more week in the hospital before she'd have to go into a rehab facility, and Miranda wasn't about to let her stay there.

"I just wanted to remind you," Miranda continued, "because you're going over to Luis and Madrita's for dinner, like we were going to do before I had to go see Aunt Bridie."

He perked up. "Can I go to Dianna's?"

"We just got back from the Trimbles', Ru. Luis and Madrita

would like to see you, too." She handed him the remote. "Call me if you get scared."

She went upstairs to change for the wine tasting, thinking she wouldn't mind going back to the Trimbles' herself. She'd met Dianna, finally, when she'd gone to pick up Ruben that afternoon. She'd meant to make it a high-speed pass, but when she shook Dianna's hand, she remembered again the taste and texture of the cookies Dianna sent home with Ruben, and something about the chicory blue of her eyes made Miranda want to keep hold of her hand.

When Miranda praised the cookies, Dianna clucked and wagged her head. *It's all in the components,* she said. *Start with the right ingredients, let them do the talking, and you can hardly screw up.*

Goats blatted from somewhere behind the house, and Dianna led her back to the little spring house where she made her goat cheese. They toured the gardens, surprise after delight of herbs, edible flowers, vegetables. Miranda pinched, rubbed, and tasted everything.

She cupped her hands to her face now, which still smelled of lemon balm, oregano, verbena. She'd not have time to go back to Dianna's again, not if she was going back to San Francisco tomorrow. And though she still had to finish packing, when Petra called her that morning, her voice barely audible from laryngitis, Miranda could hardly refuse to take her place at the wine tasting.

"One of the cellar workers will drive Duncan in early. He likes to make sure everything's set up," Petra'd said. "Just meet him in the banquet room, pour some wine, say nice things, *true* things about your wine, then drive him back here. I'd let Duncan go it alone, but he works better with a foil." Miranda had to admit she was probably right. The tasting wouldn't be difficult. It was the hour drive back that she dreaded. Between Duncan's reticence and her diffidence, there'd be a whole lot of blank space between them.

Petra had asked her to wear something nice, so she changed into the dress she'd worn to Papa's memorial service. She smoothed her hair and strapped a watch around the thin, white skin of her wrist, and remembered the brown twig of the boy's wrist as he gobbled down her lunch at the *taquería* in Dundee.

All the way into Portland, she thought of him. She'd asked Hector if he'd seen Corio or the boy, but Hector just shook his head. When she'd asked him to let her know if he saw them, he'd looked at her sideways. *I am worried for the boy,* she said. *The father is sick.*

It is not your worry, Hector said.

And she'd thought how differently Dario would have seen it. *Thou shalt not stand idly by.* Every time she looked at Ruben and saw how healthy he was, she thought he was that way only because she'd neglected something else.

When she arrived at the banquet room at the restaurant, she clucked her tongue. The staff obviously had no concept of how to circulate people through a room, make them feel comfortable, hungry. She set about reworking the setup, and it gave her mind something to hide behind.

"Looks good, doesn't it?"

The woman's voice came from the doorway. Duncan should have known. Some nosy fucking waitress had taken it upon herself to rearrange his setup. He shucked off his jacket to help vent the steam he felt gushing from every pore and draped it carefully over one arm before turning, had it on his tongue to say, *I don't care how many staff you have to pull to get this room the way I want it, but it had better be done by six o'clock sharp,* only said nothing when he saw Miranda there looking exactly as she had the day he met her at Carter's memorial service. He'd forgotten she'd been commandeered to take Petra's place.

He hooked a thumb around the room. "You do this?"

She dropped her chin so that her eyes seemed larger. "Yes. Better circulation this way. And I'd have done something better with your hors d'oeuvres, but I didn't have time."

"I've seen to them myself," he said.

She seemed to relent a little. "Yes, they're good," she said. "But . . . Well, it's what I'm good at. I do this for a living."

He nodded as if that were an explanation he could digest.

"Relax," she said. "It'll come out fine when you pour good wine."

He tilted his head at her.

"Papa used to say that."

"Papa?"

"Carter. My father."

The pores of his face extruded sweat. She plucked a napkin from a stack that had been carefully fanned and handed it to him as the first tasters swooped through the door and headed for the chafing dishes. The chow hounds. They always managed to arrive first. He swirled his jacket on, the better to hide the widening dampness on his shirtsleeves, and uncorked a few of the younger wines.

Miranda parked herself behind one of the tables and began to pour something for the early birds. Within minutes, the room flooded with people, and Duncan put himself in auto mode, fielding questions about the winery, trying to synthesize his job into something lay people could digest. As people accumulated about the tables, he tried to hear what Miranda said, but the general din of the room made it impossible to flesh out words.

An hour passed. With a mere thirty minutes to go, Duncan began to relax, letting himself move a bit on the balls of his feet. The smile became a little less automatic. He poured himself a glass of the '96 pinot reserve and moved out from behind the table to mingle a bit, something Petra usually did. He grazed the hors d'oeuvres table as he chatted, smoked salmon skewers, mousseline of duck, pheasant pâté . . . The fat and protein mixed with the tannins in the wine like silk. He'd have to check in with the kitchen staff to let them know they'd done a good job.

A small knot of people had gathered before Miranda, listening intently to a gentleman among them as he flashed the glass overhead with an expert tilt and swirl. He squinted at the light through the liquid while his free hand punctuated every word with a separate flourish. He used his entire face to speak, well-worked lines creasing as he frowned or smiled. Duncan watched the perfectly tailored tweed coat bunch and settle as the man moved about on the soles of what looked to be very pricey shoes. Probably some poof with more money than he knew what to do with, but if he was a wine critic Duncan didn't recognize, he wanted to know about it. As a rule, Ruby Throat did not submit its wines for critics' ratings. Ernest said it was absurd to rate something that changed constantly.

He drifted toward Miranda's table until he felt a hand on his shoulder, punched up the smile before turning.

"Hey, Duncan," Moore said. "Good crowd tonight."

"Yes, indeed," Duncan said, aware that the smile he'd intended had turned into something more crackly. Ken Moore was a staffer at the *Journal*. While the paper didn't report wine news on a regular basis, Moore had taken it upon himself to become the voice of vino. Trouble was, he wrote about it as if it were hard news, not wine, and he loved to focus on the vineyards' inner workings as if they were the cabinets of presidents. Reporters usually didn't show up at tastings unannounced, and Ken Moore was definitely unannounced.

"We breaking with tradition or something?" Duncan said.

"Oh, well," Moore said, waving his arm around. "We like to jump the gun every now and then. Keep people on their toes. How's it going for you folks? I heard about the old man." As if Moore hadn't been the one to print the brief statement Petra had given him, that Perry Hill would continue to operate under the ownership of Carter's daughter, and that the vineyard's crop would continue to be sold to Ruby Throat.

"He was a dab hand with the vines," Duncan said. "Best I ever saw."

Of course, Moore hadn't been able to resist beefing up the story with Carter's pioneer history, along with speculation about the re-zoning of the area and how much land was worth there now.

"You here to get some juice on the girl? That it?" Duncan asked.

Moore gave a dyspeptic belch and laughed. "Might make a nice sidebar."

"To what?"

Moore's eyes slithered to Miranda and back to Duncan like greased blue marbles. "Yeah, right," Moore said, with a quick slap to the shoulder. "I monitor the guest list at the Benson. That's how I knew he was in town. Figured he would show up here." Moore stared at Duncan's blank face. "Looks like I got there ahead of you, man."

"The hell are you babbling about?" Duncan asked.

"Charles Feering. Vice president in charge of acquisitions for BevCorp. He bought Ettinger last week," Moore said. "He's here." Moore jabbed a finger toward Miranda's table. "He's *there*."

Duncan took in the man he'd noticed before and tried not to let Moore smell his confusion.

"Any idea why he's here?" Moore asked.

"This isn't invitation only, y'know," Duncan said, heard his accent broadening and tried to check it.

"You're not about to say coincidence," Moore said.

"If some big wheel wants to sample our wine, I won't stand in his way," Duncan said, "and I hope I'm not preventing you from trying this new single vineyard I've got. It's balls and elegance on a knife edge, but I know you wouldn't print it up exactly like that." Duncan courted Moore to his weak spot, wine, put every bit of juice he had left into a smile.

"This a new vintage Perry Hill?"

"No. Let me get you a glass," Duncan said, "and mouth some of that pâté before you drink. It'll ride like a Cadillac."

Duncan filled a glass, tried to think how he should play this. Bloody hell but Petra picked a bad night to be sick. He brought the glass to Moore and twirled the stem before handing it to him as if Moore were a rookie. "Get a snoutful," he said.

Moore took a deep breath, sipped, and chewed the wine. "More elegance than balls, I'd say. A cut above the crowd. Very nice." He drank more. "So you really didn't know Feering was in town?" Moore asked.

"No," Duncan said. "I really didn't."

"Any particular reason you're pushing a new vineyard here?" Moore pointed his eyes at the glass he held.

Duncan looked at him. "Bet as a child you thought there were rabbits in every hat."

Moore laughed.

"Maybe," he said. "But there were always some hats that looked more hospitable than others." Moore's greasy eyes tracked away to Feering. "He sure is glued to her."

The night manager signaled him from the doorway, and Duncan nodded at him, then looked back at Moore. "Last call," he said. "Room's booked for a party after us. Mind if I pack up?"

Moore flourished his glass in acknowledgement and slopped wine onto his hand, which he carefully licked off.

Duncan smiled. "Now that's what I like to see. A man who can't let go of a drop."

By the time he'd finished packing his table, Feering and Moore were gone.

Miranda's car surfaced from the underground parking garage like a little blue cork in a sea of rain and traffic. Duncan sank into the passenger's seat and stared straight ahead through the dripping windscreen. The weather had gone to hell in a blink.

Miranda poked the little car through a slip in traffic and managed to get onto a side street, then zigzagged west and south, making a wide arc around downtown to get over to Barbour. From there she could backroad it without having to suffer through the bowels of Tigard in the company of a grumpy Australian.

Being alone in a car two feet from a stranger was definitely a situation that called for small talk, but there was something about his grunted responses to anything she said that made her give up finally and turn on the radio, which she kept on until she pulled up in front of his cottage and put on the parking brake. "Thanks for your help tonight," he said, unmoving.

Great, she thought. An hour of silence in the car, and now he wants to chat. She fumbled for something to bring up in return. "I really appreciate your riding with Ruben. He's not had much of that in the city."

"Good kid," he said.

He stared through the windshield at the mist curling around the cottage in the headlights. She mashed the clutch to the floor and messed with the gear shift.

"That bloke," he said, suddenly. "Did you talk to him?"

"Who?"

"Speechy bloke with the crowd at your table."

"You mean the English guy," she said.

"Right," he said, and she thought she saw a hint of smirk around his mouth.

"He's the head of some company, I forget what it was. He knew a lot about the industry here. Vintages, winemakers, production . . . He even knew about Perry Hill."

"What about it?"

"Knew that Ernest and Petra had bought Ruby Throat's land from Papa. Knew that Papa died."

Duncan didn't respond.

"I think his last name was Farthing," she continued. "Something like that. You know him?"

"No," he said, and continued to stare through the dripping windshield. "Did he ask anything else about the vineyard?"

"Ruby Throat or Perry Hill?"

Duncan hunched up his shoulders. "Either."

"Why? Think he's after your job?" she asked.

He drew a sharp breath as if to speak, hesitated, and then said, "I suppose you think me a bit of a mug."

"Excuse me?"

"Jerk. Nerd."

"Petra thinks the world of you, and you're nice to Ruben so you can't be all bad."

"Nice kid," he said, and seemed unaware that he'd already said that. "How's your friend doing?"

Miranda shifted into neutral and relaxed her feet on the floorboard. "Her chances of recovery are excellent. It's her head I'm worried about."

"She hurt her head in the accident?"

Miranda laughed. "Her state of mind," Miranda said. "Injuries like hers typically bring on depression even in couch potatoes. She was an athlete."

"You could tell that just by looking at her," he said.

"You met her?"

"Ruben introduced her to Fluke at the funeral. Nice girl."

Miranda didn't know which surprised her more, that Bridie didn't mention meeting Duncan or that he'd referred to her as a nice girl. The latter would surely make Bridie laugh.

Duncan popped his seat belt and opened the door. She squinted in the feeble aura of the dome light, noticed the pale pucker of a scar over his eyebrow. She pointed at it. "Bar fight?" she asked.

"Worked summers on my uncle's sheep station. Ranch, you'd call it out here. You get nicked up a bit."

"Is that where you learned to ride?" she asked, and thought of him drifting through the vineyards on the copper horse.

"Yeah," he said.

"How'd you get into wine?"

"Dad hated the woolies. Sold out to my uncle and bought land in the Barossa. Said grapes were the thing to get into. The industry would go riot, and we'd be there, ready for it."

"What happened?"

"Industry went riot, all right. Trouble is it takes so long to get established, you know, with the capital investment and all. Dad got caught off before he was ready, bad coupla years, learning curve . . . we lost the place to the bank."

"I'm sorry," she said.

"What for?" he asked.

"Losing your place."

"Probably a good thing, as it turns out. I started working in one of the big wineries in the Barossa. Learned a thing or two, mostly that it was what I was good at."

"Still, I'm sorry you lost your place," she said.

"No worries," he said.

And she thought, *My ass.*

"Fluke'll be pining for a romp," he said. "And the boss'll be waiting for my report."

"Petra?" Miranda said.

"Yes. She'll want the skinny on who was there, how much we sold."

Miranda smiled. "Tell her I said nice things about our wine."

"Beg pardon?"

"Never mind. I'll tell her myself. Tomorrow. Tell her I'll come by before we take off."

"Take off?"

"I'm going back to San Francisco tomorrow," she said.

He fixed his eyes on her.

"She didn't tell you?"

"None of my business," he said.

"It *is* your business."

"The winery," he said. "Not you."

She was taken aback by the curtness in his voice. Had she been less tired, she would have pursued it, but she let it go. She didn't really have any choice, after all, because he got out of the car and walked into the cottage.

Since the rain had let up, Duncan fed the mare and turned her out in the paddock, then fed the dog, waited restlessly for her to finish before he loaded her into the truck beside him, and drove to Petra's.

A black crew cab truck was parked outside, the Gagnon Winery insignia air-brushed on its doors. He hesitated after turning off the key and stared at the light gathered in the water beaded on the truck's perfectly waxed surface. Like Ernest, Duncan had no interest in clothes and perfectly waxed automobiles, but he liked Gagnon, after all. He was a dab hand with wine, and a decent fellow.

He tapped thick fingers on the steering wheel. Best to meet the thing head-on, is what his dad always said.

He let Fluke out of the truck so she could wander, then stepped up to the heavy oak door which swung in by way of Gagnon himself, dressed in his signature black suit and gray, collarless shirt.

"Monsieur Fletcher," he said, waving him in. "The mistress expects you."

"Jean-Paul," Duncan said, shaking his hand as he passed.

"She's not much for conversation tonight, I'll warn you. Bit of frog in her throat." He laughed. "Not a pun."

It never failed to amaze Duncan how bluntly the French referred to sex. Not that Aussies didn't think about it constantly; they just failed to bring it into every verbal exchange.

From the tiled foyer he saw Petra curled into the hulk of an oversize armchair by the fireplace, her blond hair gone bronze, boxy jaw softened by the light. She smiled and pointed to a chair close by. He was careful to remove his boots in deference to the growling Madrita.

"Gone crook on me, have you?" he asked Petra.

She nodded, miming a miserable face.

"Crook?" Gagnon said. "Now she's stealing?"

Petra rolled her eyes at Duncan.

"*Crook* means 'sick' in Australia," Duncan said.

Petra snapped her fingers to get Duncan's attention and gestured as if pouring something in her mouth, eyebrows raised. Gagnon stood. "The lady insists on something warm and nonalcoholic, hence, unhealthy. For us? We have a lovely Bordeaux quickly breathing its last. Join me?"

"Certainly," Duncan said, and took the proffered glass, poured to exactly the right mark. He held the glass before the fire, appreciated the deeper blood of the Bordeaux as opposed to the lighter berry of their pinot, then swirled the liquid, bringing the glass immediately to his face for a full hit of the aroma. It furled unctuously into his nose, agreeably complex, undoubtedly cabernet. He chewed a quick mouthful and held it on his tongue a moment before swallowing, then breathed in slowly, openmouthed. Gagnon had watched him through the process, an expectant smile curling the corners of his mouth.

"Ah?" he said now to Duncan.

"Big," Duncan said. "More like American cabs every day." And he smiled wickedly at Gagnon to see if he'd react to the gibe.

"Well, but it's Bordeaux. What can you say. Hard to screw up, unlike our fickle little grapes." Gagnon took a deep draft of the wine, eyes closed, and then swallowed. "So, how was your tasting tonight?"

Duncan looked at the glass he rested on his knee. "Coupla interesting characters on show tonight," Duncan said. "Miranda talked to one, Charles Feering from BevCorp. Ken Moore showed up, too, because he knew this bloke, Feering, was in town."

Gagnon peeled his lips back as if he'd drunk something unpleasant, tinked a fingernail lightly against his glass. "Charles Feering. He is Aussie, like yourself. You do not know him?"

"That's like saying an American ought to know somebody else just because they're American. Australia's a big fucking country."

"Well, you know *of* him, is what I mean," Gagnon said. "You know BevCorp bought Ettinger last week. He is a name we do not like to hear when business is in trouble," he said.

"We're not in trouble."

"Of course not," Gagnon said, pouring more wine into first his own and then Duncan's glass. "But when this man comes, *somebody* has trouble. I cannot think of the words for him here, but he is like shark, you see? He comes with blood."

Gagnon babbled on about some French insurance conglomerate that had picked off wine properties in the Bordeaux until they practically owned the region.

"But it's no different from the way it was before, really. For over a century Bordeaux was controlled by the Chartronnais, *les négociants*. They take up all the wine from the local producers, age and bottle, and sell it under their name. Producers make nothing. At least now they make something."

"Why's this bloke here?" Duncan asked, and tried to keep his voice from cracking.

"Why do you think? We are on the map here, you know. Even French drink Oregon pinot now." His smile was thin.

"We'd bloody well better find out why he's here."

Petra was at Duncan's side, her hand gripping the top of his shoulder so hard, she got his attention. She leaned close to him. "Relax, Dee. We're fine."

"I know *we* are," he said. "But what about Perry Hill? He made a point of talking to Miranda. Never came near me."

Gagnon laughed. "That is no wonder. You have no breasts."

Petra whispered, "Did he say anything to her about selling?"

"No. I don't know. She didn't say he did."

"I'll talk to her," she said.

"Better make it quick," Duncan said. "She's leaving tomorrow."

"I know. Keep cool."

Gagnon stood by the fireplace, braced against the mantel like a fashion photograph. "She is right," he said. "One phone call means nothing."

Petra shook her head at Gagnon, but Gagnon continued. "He is your partner. He must know."

But Duncan knew it then anyway. It all added up. Gagnon was right to compare the man to a shark, because Feering must have contacted Petra in one of his infamous probes, the way a shark brushes its prey to test its strength before the final attack. He wished now that he'd pressed Miranda for more information. Surely she would have said something had Feering asked her certain questions. But then, Duncan didn't know her from a blue 'roo, did he?

Petra was trying to get his attention, but he pushed his hand at her, palm out, until she sat back in her chair. Her eyes were more brown than blue in the shadow of the fire, but he could not read her expression. If she had planned to withhold the news of Feering's contact from him, he wasn't sure he wanted to know why. He shook his head as if a snake had dropped on it.

"It is no thing, Duncan," Gagnon said. "All is well here. Must not to worry, ah?"

Gagnon brushed a hand down the front of his jacket, the gesture as elegant as a dancer's but for the sound his callused palm made against the cloth. He grazed his lips across each of Petra's cheeks, then patted Duncan on the shoulder on his way to the door.

He seemed to take the air with him when he closed the door. Duncan's skin felt shriveled as dried fruit.

"I know what you'd say," Duncan said. "But I'm not sure I'd believe it."

Petra used the arms of the chair to lever herself up. "I love you like a son," she rasped. "But I'm more in need of a partner. Either way, you should trust me."

She'd done it again. Made him go all goofy. He rubbed his face between his palms. "All right," he said, and then again, "All right."

When he went outside, Fluke was crouched under the driver's side of the truck to get out of the rain that had resumed with a vengeance. He opened the door and signaled her in. She posed herself in the middle of the bench seat and stared as if to tell him to hurry. Couldn't he see it was raining? But he stood braced in the doorway, strapped into a morning twenty-two years ago when his father sat him at the table in the kitchen of the tiny prefab house he'd thrown up on the vineyard property. He'd put all his savings and loan money into getting good plants for the vineyard, never mind the house. They could build a fine house when the cash began to flow.

He saw his mother at the clothesline, pegging the wash to it as if each clothespin were a knife. Sheets snapped and furled around her body that was one minute a recognizable figure, the next a ghost.

So you see, lad, we've got no choice. It's all here in black-and-white, but Duncan hadn't been able to respond, could not take his eyes off his mother and the white, white sheets wrapping her legs like shrouds.

Fluke gave a short, sharp bark as if to remind him he was standing in the rain.

"All right, girl," he said. "Been a long day." He shook his head quickly from side to side to rid himself of the water in his hair before he slid in the truck, then smiled at the way Fluke looked at him. "We learn a thing or two from dogs, don't we?" he said, and draped an arm over her damp, steaming shoulders.

Miranda thought she'd go right to bed after Ruben fell asleep, but she was restless. She put on a sweater and raincoat and went outside. The weather had worsened again. She wandered to the barn to get out of the rain and walked slowly down the central aisle, dragging her hand along the dusty planks. The halogen light on the barnyard pole cast blue light through the shrunken siding. Papa used to keep a couple of milk cows here. Because she'd grown up on fresh milk, she had never been able to stomach the thin chemical taste of the stuff in supermarkets. In San Francisco, Miranda bought fresh milk for Ruben from the co-op.

She stumbled over a scrap of fallen wood in the aisle. The barn needed cleaning—it would have been a good draw for some upscale tenants who wanted to have horses—but she would hardly have time for that since they were leaving tomorrow.

She looked around at the jumble of wood and leaves and scraps that had accumulated over years of disuse. There was so much clutter, the boy could have been another coil of rope or crumpled paper bag but for the telltale flush of cheek, the arm pulled slowly closer to his body. She stepped back involuntarily, fell over something metal, then scrambled to her hands and knees and crawled to the boy where he lay curled in a stall. The pink of his cheek made her sure she'd feel heat when she lay her hand across his face, but his skin was as cool as if she'd touched metal instead.

She rocked back on her knees and lifted the child's torso to her so she could get her arms more fully around him before she heaved him to her shoulder. He was easily half Ruben's weight. In the kitchen, she laid him carefully on the table, peeled off the wet coat, and flung it on the floor. She looked over his face in the good light, then left him on the table and gathered a blanket, towels, and a thermometer she hoped still worked, and went back to the kitchen. She stuffed the towels loosely in the microwave and set it going, then struggled to remove the boy's jeans, which stuck to him wetly even though they were many sizes too big. Corio obviously didn't have a knack for sizing.

He mumbled and flung an arm across his chest, which she moved gently back to his side.

"It's okay, sweetie," she crooned. "You're going to be okay."

She got the hot towels from the microwave and wrapped his chest and legs with them, then pulled the blanket to his waist.

She unbuttoned his shirt halfway down to slip the thermometer in an armpit. She managed to wedge the glass tube in and pressed the boy's arm to his side with her free hand. And then she saw it, exposed now by the gapped shirtfront, the clearly pubescent breast, a small, pale circle within reddened flesh.

The child's eyes batted open and shut, then became frantic as she made sense of Miranda's face.

Miranda pulled the thermometer away and tried to manage the

windmill of limbs until the girl lay still, panting. Her eyes were like bottomless dark in the cool, blued skin of her face before they rolled out of sight like a drunk's. Miranda wrapped the girl in the blanket and carried her to the couch. She found the hot water bottles in a hall closet, filled them and packed them against the girl's torso, then rewarmed the towels and layered them under the blanket. Occasionally the girl came to and regarded her through half-open eyes.

"Como te llamas, nina?" Miranda asked.

And she thought the girl said something about a star, *estrella.*

"What does your father call you?"

"Me llamo Estrella."

"Where is your father?"

"Me dejo," the girl said.

"Gone? He left you?"

The girl shook her head and closed her eyes. Tears squeezed through her lashes like hot, plump peas.

Miranda's lips went numb as she said the word, *"Muerto?"*

The girl nodded once.

Miranda found her purse and rummaged through it until she found the card and dialed Dr. Ayudar's number.

After examining the girl, he'd praised Miranda's course of action, said she'd done all the right things. "She's dehydrated along with the hypothermia. We'll have to get some warm fluids on board, slowly at first, okay?"

Miranda's face radiated heat into the cool air.

"What are your plans for the child?" Beto asked.

"My plans?"

"Well, you're going back to San Francisco soon, no?"

"Tomorrow."

"There are foster programs," he said.

"To take care of her until she's well enough to be deported," Miranda said. "I know all about those. Dario did an exposé of the practice."

"Dario?"

"Ruben's father." She said it quickly, hoping the clutch in her head would go away. "The girl has no one," Miranda continued. "What would you do?"

"She's not contagious as long as she's not symptomatic, but we should test her for TB, first thing," he said. "Just a little skin puncture, and it'll show in forty-eight hours. Can you bring her to the clinic tomorrow?"

The clinic in Salem was south, on the way back to California. Miranda thought of her suitcase packed upstairs.

They heard Estrella moaning in the living room.

"I should check on her," Miranda said.

"Fluids when you can," he reminded her. "Keep her warm until she's up to speed. It may take a few hours."

"Thanks for coming out like this," she said.

"Nobody ever has an emergency during the day."

"I'll bring her tomorrow," she said. "For the test."

"Sure," he said. "We'll take it from there."

"What do you mean?"

"Find a place for her," he said. "If we can."

Estrella was sitting up on the couch, her knees pinned to her chest by arms that looked like smooth brown rope.

Miranda sat next to her, slipped a hand around the back of the girl's neck. Her skin was still quite cool.

"Qué pasa, nina?"

"Dolor de cabeza," the girl whispered.

No surprise the kid had a whopper of a headache. No food or water for God knows how long. Miranda took her glass to the kitchen and refilled it with warm water from the kettle.

She waited for the girl to drink it down before she ran a tub of hot water and coaxed Estrella into it. She floated Ruben's toys around her, but the girl had little interest. Miranda got her to lie back, and she sat cross-legged on the floor and angled the girl's head in her hand. She rested her own head on an outstretched arm, feet curled under her against the cold tile floor.

Papa had bathed her here. She tried to recall whether she'd had a worry, but could not remember it. What a privilege it was to never have a care.

Sometimes during the prep at the restaurant she daydreamed of being home, standing at the kitchen sink, careful not to catch a toe under the peeled flap of linoleum as she washed dishes, listening to the splash of water down the hall while Papa amused Ruben through his bath. He hated baths and cried when she washed his hair or sat trembling silently when she could manage to allay the tears. Papa would have been able to get him over it. He'd worked wonders on her. Sometimes it was Papa she heard talking to Ruben. Sometimes it was Dario.

The girl shifted and mumbled something. Miranda raised her head. *"Qué quieres?"*

The girl looked at her with woozy eyes. "My head."

"It'll go away in a little while. And then we'll get you something to eat."

Miranda got her out of the tub and dried her before wrapping her in an old bathrobe. She looked ghostly and nebulous as Miranda shepherded her back to the couch. Tomorrow she'd stop by the Goodwill and get Estrella some clothes. She tucked a hot-water bottle on the girl's chest before wrapping her in blankets, then smeared a little olive oil on the girl's cracked lips.

Estrella's eyes drooped and finally closed. When her breathing evened and slowed, Miranda got up and went down the hall to Ruben's room. He lay on his side in a jumble, his body so contorted she was amazed he could sleep. She didn't want to wake him, so she left the lights off while she took the old canvas cover off the daybed and made it up with fresh sheets and blankets. She didn't need the light anyway. She'd grown up in that room, where not one thing had changed since she left.

She stood between the beds and turned slowly about, her memory measuring the distance between every scuff and picture on the walls. Rain splashed inexorably from the broken gutter outside the window.

She padded into the kitchen. She was almost out of yogurt, so she lined a strainer with cheesecloth into which she poured whole milk and set it in the fridge over a bowl, then thought how ridiculous that was. They were leaving tomorrow.

She noticed the little package Ruben had brought home from the Trimbles'. It was a mound of Dianna's homemade goat cheese artfully wrapped in pickled grape leaves and tied off with brown twine. With it was a tiny jar of raspberry jam. She spread the cheese onto some sesame crackers and spread a little of Dianna's jam on each white crumble. The flavors were bright and musky and rich all at once, and she felt them spreading into her like a tonic. Her spine relaxed as she concentrated on the textures in her mouth. It was good to focus on something that was necessary and had no consequence.

7

One month ago, Bridie would have had to run ten miles to raise such a sweat, had to run dogs all day, not to mention do her kennel chores, to be this exhausted. Now, she had only to maneuver the wheelchair into the bathroom to urinate before her thighs sweat-glued to the cheap Naugahyde of the loaner chair. Medicaid had approved a new chair for her, but it had to be fitted and then ordered. The nurses said she'd be lucky to get it by Christmas.

Her hair hung in twisted pods. She went through the motions of personal care at the aide's urging, mostly at the aide's doing. The aide had appealed to the head nurse, Mason, but even he ceased to hound her about it after the first couple of passes. He had his hands full. Bridie referred to Mason as Nurse Ratched. Mason protested that Nurse Ratched was a woman with vengeance on her mind, and he was neither female nor vengeful. Bridie hadn't even expected him to get the reference.

In therapy, she never complained about the work, or the pain, just couldn't do what they asked her to do. She tried, thought she was trying, but to no more avail than a wringing sweat and fatigue that immobilized her.

Her eyes wandered to the window, something she had avoided doing, but recently they gravitated to it, unbidden. She knew the topography by heart. The city draped itself over the bowed head of

Cook inlet, semicircled on its backside by the Chugach Mountains and the Alaska Range. Her room faced away from the inlet, toward the Alaska Range. She could pick out Rainy Pass, the one through which the Iditarod trail coiled, through which she and the dogs had run.

She turned her chair away from the window, caught blurred sight of herself in the mirror as she swung around, the brief image sending a runner of pain through her that was worse than the physical injury. Her eyes felt bruised by it, so she closed them, unable to "visualize something positive" as the staff constantly remonstrated her to do. There was nothing positive that did not involve the past, and the future looked about as positive as the grave.

The results of the second MRI revealed damage to the cord, which meant that some recovery was probable, and anything more than that was "possible." It was the most hopeful word the surgeon was able to conjure. He'd told her she was lucky the cord hadn't been broken. She would have laughed at his use of the word *lucky* if she hadn't been so astonished at *possible,* particularly since she had begun to regain some sensation in ribbons of living flesh. Didn't that mean something?

Possibly.

Men had worshiped her legs, couldn't get enough of them. Like an Amazonian goddess, one of her boyfriends in college used to moan. When she looked at them now, she saw the future—two useless lengths of numb and diminishing flesh.

Her life had been a matter of doing things that she thought about, so what was there to do when all there was to do was think? What good was the mind without the body to follow through on one's thoughts? She couldn't imagine a use for herself without both. She thought she should be able to get out of the chair and walk, but she could not. In her therapy sessions, she thought she should be able to do what the therapists told her to do, but she could not. Her efforts only exhausted her to the point of dispassion. If she fell when trying to get in and out of the chair, she couldn't always get up. Mason had found her on the floor more than once.

She had tried sleeping in the bed, but there she slept more

deeply, helpless to shut out his arrival, tongue lolling, vapor-rich air streaming from his lungs. She could smell the warm, sour fur, see power in the drawn-tight tug lines. In sleep, she ground her fingers into her face, hoping her skin would split and bleed like overripe fruit.

She'd dreaded it, but Gordon had come to say good-bye before he flew the dogs back to the village. For ten minutes she tried to shrink into the sheets while he fought not to say what he wanted to say. After a protracted silence that he spent staring out the window, he'd finally ended up blurting, *What the hell were you thinking, Bridie? You had eight hours on that guy, plenty of time to wait. I can't have you risking my dogs because of your bad judgment. You won't race with me again, even if you could.*

Her first reaction was a surge of anger so bitter she tasted it on the back of her tongue, heavy and metallic. *Race with you?* she thought. *I'd give anything to be able to walk to the bathroom.* But then the true spite of it sank in.

If there was any daylight left in her heart at that moment, it was now as dark as her memory. *Your bad judgment.* The words pierced her like poisoned darts.

She had two more days before the hospital discharged her. Every time she talked to her parents, her mother made it absolutely clear that Bridie was to come home as soon as possible. If it was back to her parents in Michigan—to days spent reading the unspoken words behind her mother's every utterance, every look—if that was all, she'd just as soon slit her wrists.

And she would have had she been able to keep Miranda and Ruben out of her head. Miranda would never understand Bridie's leaving, would not allow it. But Bridie couldn't see being the lump of concrete at the end of the rope for Miranda, couldn't bear Ruben not seeing her as he had.

A hank of hair was stuck to the damp paste of her cheeks. She tried to brush it aside but it refused to come away, causing her to repeat the gesture again and again, each swipe of her hand more difficult than the one before. She wheeled herself to the drawer in the vanity, careful to avoid the mirror. Even this minimal effort raised a stinking sweat that soaked unctuously into the gaping neck of her shirt. She rested a few minutes before scrabbling through the drawer in search of her ditty bag.

When her hand reached its canvas folds, she pulled it out and set it in her lap, then wheeled herself into the middle of the room. She cocked her head at the familiar rubberized step at her door and flipped the pocket shut.

"Whatcha doing?" Mason asked.

"Nothing."

"Need anything, just give a holler."

"Okay."

She waited until his voice floated to her from the other end of the unit before removing the all-in-one tool. She'd never even used the scissor accessory, and she wasn't sure they'd work for what she had in mind. If they didn't, she'd use the knife because, what the hell, this was no fashion show.

But the scissors worked as well as anything, and with each snip, the strands felt so heavy she fancied they would plop like snakes when they hit the floor. She was disappointed when the clippings drifted noiselessly down, banking up around the chair like dark, moldy rope. She thought of what Miranda would say, but what did that matter? Miranda was in San Francisco by now. She'd never know.

It took her half an hour, resting her arm every few passes, until her head felt light again, until there was nothing left that could be out of place. She ran a hand over her skull. Shorter even than dog fur, she thought, and relaxed into her Naugahyde sling, neither waiting nor hopeful, merely existing in the shell of herself.

Miranda sat in the living room of Papa's house with Luis and Madrita, who had come to bring some things for Estrella. She had thought they wouldn't understand her taking in the girl, but they had not missed a beat, though she was certain they agreed with Petra when she'd said it wasn't her place to take on the child. She had tried to believe it, even intended to leave Estrella at the clinic but then they'd passed the giant tracts of nursery plants outside of McMinn-ville, where hundreds of workers bent to the ground in the rain.

Estrella had strained to the window, her hands wiping away the steam of her breath that collected there.

"What is it?" Miranda said.

"I do this," Estrella said, pointing at the workers. And Miranda noticed again the cicatrix of scars on the child's hands.

She had asked the girl then, just to be sure, "You have done this work?"

The girl nodded and shivered. "Many days."

The clinic had been jammed with patients. Beto had two emer-gencies on his hands, and they'd had to wait hours. Finally she'd stepped into the parking lot to call her sous at the restaurant, but Eric had answered instead.

Just tell me you'll be here by five P.M., and I'll hang up the phone, no questions asked, he'd said.

I can't say that.

Then take all the time you need. Take your whole life.

The nurse had signaled her from the window then, and she'd gone into the little exam room with Ruben and Estrella.

She was impressed by the doctor's way with them, even more impressed by the way he'd managed to find a place for Estrella.

It's temporary, he'd said, *but something may come up in the meantime.*

Something has already come up, Miranda said. *She's staying with us.*

So it's off to San Francisco with your brood?

No, she'd said. *We're going home.*

So she drove back the way she came, her hands curled numbly to the wheel, but her head as clear as it had ever been, as clear as it was now, watching Madrita teach Estrella a card game. Though she had raised seven children of her own, not to mention Miranda and others, Madrita approached every child as if it were her own, her first and only. Miranda watched Estrella respond to her, even though her guardedness still prevailed. Luis watched his wife smiling as he did when he was relaxed and happy, an expression he wore invari-ably when Madrita was close.

"We are happy you stay now," Luis said to Miranda.

"I thought you would be angry."

"It is no obvious we want you home?"

Miranda gestured at Estrella. "You were upset that I took on Corio in the first place."

"But that is different," he said. "Here is a child with nothing, no person to help her. She must be taken care of. This is what to do."

And she knew that was true. What she didn't understand was the frisson of relief that left her belly soft when she'd headed north from the clinic that day. Was this what she'd wanted all along, or was she hiding in the safety of a decision that had been made for her? She thought of Dario for whom decisions had not existed, for whom Luis's words were a credo.

Miranda nodded at Luis. "Thou shalt not stand idly by."

"What?"

"Something Dario used to say," Miranda said. When Luis and Madrita crossed themselves, Estrella crossed herself, also.

Madrita beamed at the girl. "You see? The Virgin is with this child. She is blessed."

Luis laughed. "The child is surrounded by perfection. That is all she needs."

It had taken a few days to get Ruben and Estrella into the little school down the hill. When she was a child, it had only been an elementary school, but they now offered kindergarten placement, as well. While she could not enroll Estrella formally, the principal took the girl in on Miranda's word that it was only a matter of time before her papers came through. She swallowed the lie without blinking while she watched him stamp Estrella's file TEMPORARY. The school already taught "bridge" classes for children who needed English language skills, so it wasn't as if Estrella was the only kid there whose family had no papers.

So she tried to settle them into a schedule, something she needed for herself more than anything. The interior walls of the old house had yellowed to parchment, and she set about painting them. She arranged for her landlady in California to send hers and

Ruben's clothing along with some of her favored kitchenware. The rest of Papa's belongings had to be sorted, organized, and packed away. And always, there was the daily call to Bridie.

She meant to tell Bridie everything that had happened but felt herself veer away from it the moment she heard Bridie's voice. The conversations were brief, strangely enervating, and again she saw her words as specks of light disappearing into darkness. She stuck to questions about Bridie's routine, her progress, questions Bridie answered flatly if at all. Still, she went to the phone each day, anticipating the past, thinking, *Today, she'll be there.*

That day Estrella came home with a tape recorder and English/Spanish tapes. Since Miranda wanted Ruben to start learning his second language, she set them up together in the living room and told Ruben Estrella would need help.

Then she felt safe melting into the kitchen. She had prepared the chickpeas earlier. Her fingers still smelled of butternut from squeezing the peas from their skins after cooking. Now she'd make falafel and a lemon tahini dipping sauce. Ruben loved the crusty baked patties. It was the closest he'd ever get to Chicken McNuggets as long as she had any say-so.

When her cell phone rang, she almost let it lie but picked up at the last minute. The man introduced himself as Mason, the head nurse's aide at Bridie's rehab facility.

"Sorry to bother you at home," Mason said. "But after what she did to her hair and all," Mason said.

"What about her hair?"

"She cut it. Real short. With an all-purpose tool."

Miranda squeezed the phone so tightly, her hand started to tingle.

Mason continued. "I keep thinking she'll come around, but she's way into depression at this point."

Miranda saw thick ropes of dark red hair carpeting the floor and knew that Bridie was disconnecting, even from herself. After that, the gap between her and oblivion could be bridged with a whisper. Miranda knew that bridge. Had Bridie not been there, had Ruben not been growing in her belly, she might have crossed it.

"Tell her I'm coming, Mason," Miranda said into the phone.

"Tell her to wait for me. I'm going to bring her home until she gets back on her feet." She trailed off, cringing at her choice of words, then thought no, that was exactly what she meant.

On her way to the vet, Miranda scanned the map at a red light to make sure she was on the right road. She'd left Oregon in April, where spring was well under way, but here in Anchorage, a snowstorm had delayed her arrival. Cars lumbered through the intersection in front of her, way too many cars, flinging goopy snow on her windshield. She sprayed on the windshield washer, relieved that she didn't have to live with this mess, wondering about the mental acuity of people who did.

When Miranda asked Bascomb if Zeus could take the flight, the same quizzical expression as before appeared on the woman's face. He'd need a few more days to gather his strength, she thought. Then he might be able to take it.

"He'll require constant care," Bascomb said. "He can stand on his own and walk a short distance to do his business. Anything more than that, and he needs a sling support. Stairs are definitely out for a couple of months yet. It's a lot of work. Is Bridie up to it?"

"She will be," Miranda said. "In the meantime, we'll take care of Zeus."

"We?" Bascomb asked.

"Me and the kids."

"He has to be hefted in a sling. Can a child do that?"

"We'll take care of him until Bridie's ready," Miranda said, and tried not to let her mind wander to the future. She had to stay where she was, right now, or she'd lose it.

"Just remember what I said about quality of life," Bascomb said. "He's functioning physically, more or less, but his mind's not there yet. When I visited Bridie, it seemed she was pretty much the same. Might not be good to have them together, two negatives colliding, as it were."

"But they can't be apart. Not like this. Bridie would never—"

"Forgive herself?"

"Exactly."

"She won't be able to forgive herself regardless. It's that soft thing."

Bascomb promised to keep her up to date on the dog's recovery and said she would see to his flight arrangements herself. Miranda thanked her, but when she started for the door, she heard Bascomb say, "Hang on a sec."

Miranda waited while Bascomb hurried away and then came leaning back through the door as if she'd pushed it open with her head.

Bascomb held out her hand; something dangled across her fingers. The nylon webbing had been bright blue, the color of harness she knew Bridie used on the dogs, but now the collar was stained dark. They must have cut it off the dog when they flew him in, because the Fastex buckle was still hooked, a few gray-black hairs stuck to the plastic with dried blood. The dog's name was written on the inside of the webbing in permanent marker, ZEUS.

"I was going to give it to Bridie," Bascomb said. "Just never had the heart."

"I'll keep it for her," Miranda said.

"Probably silly," Bascomb said with a flick of her tiny hand.

Miranda smiled and slipped the collar into her purse. The woman had a heartbeat after all.

Miranda hesitated in front of Bridie's closed door. A television blared a few rooms down. A door at the far end of the hall rattled as if to open, and without thinking, she turned the knob and stepped in, muffling the door closed behind her.

Her pupils expanded painfully in the tenebrous gloom. Then the voice, ragged, coarse: "Don't worry, Mason. I'm fine." Miranda saw the outline of Bridie's head against the lower half of the window, boyish now without the adornment of hair she'd kept exactly the same length ever since Miranda had met her.

"You don't have to stay."

Miranda should speak, tell her it was not Mason but her best friend, come to take her home. But she was paralyzed in the face of something she thought she had prepared herself to handle.

The fuzzed head silhouetted before her now was as familiar as her own child's, but as well as she knew Bridie, she didn't know how to deal with this. Didn't know if this was Bridie anymore.

She moved slowly toward the wheelchair, said her friend's name aloud, "Bridie," and sensed more than saw the muscles go rigid. She dragged a chair as close as she could wedge it, facing the pale profile. They sat in silence while the natural light faded and the synthetic light rose from the parking lot lamps. When Bridie turned to her, Miranda saw the damp streak on the one lighted cheek and felt as if she were choking, knew in that raw, open-eyed minute that all the things she'd prepared to say were for her own benefit, because to accept the agony she saw before her, even for a moment, was a burden of terrible proportion.

Miranda tried to take Bridie's hands, but she pulled them back and tucked them under crossed arms. "I'm taking you home," Miranda whispered. "Ruben's there. You can watch *Old Yeller* with him because I can't take it anymore."

Bridie's face dissolved, the features slumping on one another like wet canvas.

"I talked to your doctor," Miranda continued. "He won't express optimism because he's covering his ass, but I'm telling you there is a good chance of recovery. You refuse to see that because you're depressed and that makes everything seem insurmountable." She kept talking. "They're going to put you on a low dose of antidepressant that will help knock back the attitude and relieve some of the nerve pain. There's a woman right in Dundee who specializes in water therapy. I went to high school with her. She'll work with you, no charge." Bridie's hands loosened and settled along the rails of the chair. Before they could disappear again, Miranda took one, held it. The touch was important. "Will you come with me? Give it a try?"

The streetlight's halogen glow blued Bridie's skin, her face gone to angles made even sharper by the surreal light. Bridie blinked slowly, as if the effort to lower and raise her eyelids exhausted her.

"Dundee," Bridie said.

"Yes."

"Perry Hill."

Miranda knew what Bridie was thinking, that in the self-centric suck of her misery and guilt, everything was her fault. Miranda would have given anything to tell Bridie how she had watched the outlines of her own world disappear, silent as smoke, knew that she might cry if she tried to describe Eric's voice when she'd asked him for a few more days and he'd said, *Take all the days you want. Take your whole life.* But she pinched the desire back in her throat because Bridie had her own disappearance to contend with. Instead, Miranda convinced herself that Bridie would come back, and when that happened, all the lines would be redrawn.

"I must look like what you looked like when Dario died," Bridie said.

Miranda swallowed. It took more than she thought she had to skid away from the wreck of grief she was heading for. Had she been as cavalier in her attitude toward Dario's work as she had been with Bridie's lifestyle? If she had told Dario that his work was too dangerous, would he have been with her now instead of in the Tenderloin the night he was shot?

Bridie's hand turned hard in Miranda's and started to withdraw, but Miranda gripped it.

"It's not what you think."

"All I have to do is think, Miranda," Bridie said. "It was enough that I wrecked those dogs, Zeus, myself. Now I'm supposed to consciously wreck your life?"

"There's more to this decision than you know, Bridie. It's not all about you. You'll see when we get home. You'll understand."

"Even if that were true, what about Zeus? You saw him. Tell me that's not my fault."

Miranda thought of the dog's naked face. "He's coming home with us. He'll make it same as I did. Same as you will."

Bridie lowered her head, shook it side to side once. "It's not going to work."

Miranda forced her head up. "I didn't think it would work either. But you made it happen."

"What about Ruben?"

"What about him?"

Bridie's eyes flickered down to encompass herself in the chair.

"He knows about the accident. He knows you're going to get well."

"What if I don't?"

"You will."

The halogen lights made Bridie's tears look like sapphires. Miranda let go of her hand and rose.

"Let's get you on the bed so you can dress more easily."

"Miranda, that's the *only* way I can get dressed."

It took half an hour. Miranda was astonished at how difficult it was to do something as basic as putting on underwear, and how humiliating it must be to have somebody else do it for you.

When they got to the airport, it was all Miranda could do to get Bridie from the car into the chair. She slung one bag from her shoulder, piled the other in Bridie's lap, and pushed her into the terminal. The logistics of it were as complicated as traveling with a child. Once she checked them in and got rid of the luggage, she started for the snack bar until she spied the coffee cart and headed the wheelchair straight for it.

"You want a cup?" she asked Bridie, and got the first recognizably Bridie response she'd had since before the accident.

"Been so long, even that dishwater would put me through the roof."

People had always looked at her. What was it one of her boyfriends said? *Women wish they were you, and men had better not wish they were with you.* Now their eyes either covered her with politically correct briefness or clung to her as if she were a freak. As vendors dealt with them in the airport, she noticed how forcibly they kept their eyes on her face.

Her skin felt pale and cracked in the fluorescent airport lights. She wished she could stay in the car, where she looked like anyone else. But in an airport terminal, she was a freak show for all to surreptitiously, (or not), enjoy. She felt herself splitting in two as the Bridie who presented herself with great vigor fought with this new Bridie who was dank and shriveled and wished for a magic shell in which to hide. Every time she had to speak, she felt the words push up from under the new self with great effort, and every time the old Bridie surfaced, she saw Miranda's face brighten with hope, her vigilance slacken. How could she explain to this woman, who used to know her better than anyone alive, that she didn't know her anymore and wouldn't want to? Because now Bridie was not a friend, but another soul for Miranda to save, another piece of what Bridie used to call Miranda's Collection.

She was appalled that she had to be put on the plane before everyone else, deposited into her seat by two hostesses who didn't look strong enough to heft a cast-iron skillet, much less a large human body. They lost their grip toward the end, and she gasped at the pain that shot up her spine when her butt hit the cushion. She'd closed her eyes quickly, the better not to see the solicitous faces that accompanied the apologies. Miranda leaned over her, her lemony smell barely supplanting the powerful perfume worn by one of the women.

"You okay?" she whispered. "Mason gave me some pain pills for the trip."

Bridie gargled a laugh while nodding her desire for oblivion and quickly swallowed whatever it was Miranda palmed her.

The smell must have jiggered something in her head, and Bridie surfaced to find herself parked on the sidewalk outside the terminal, her duffel draped over her lap and the strap of a suitcase looped over a dangled wrist. Miranda was nowhere in sight. She didn't know what kind of drugs she'd been given, but if she'd blanked out so hard she didn't even remember getting off the plane, she would certainly request a few more of those babies.

She squinted against the morning light, breathing in as deeply as her chest would allow. It was good, that breath, full of moisture and the smell of green-laden April air she remembered from her years in school here. This air didn't scorch her lungs like the dry winter of the north had done for so many years. She was suddenly aware of how warm it was, especially since she was still bundled up like the Michelin man. At least she could take off her own freaking coat, but as she tried to twist out of it, the duffel tumbled from her lap and plopped heavily on the sidewalk at her feet. She stopped struggling, one arm still trapped in the coat.

Adrenaline stung limp, unwilling muscles, and with it the realization that her bladder was full to bursting. She scanned her surroundings, panic growing with the ache in her groin. She tried to bend forward and grab the duffel, but the pain stopped her. She straightened, her face and neck damp. She eyed the few stray persons in front of the terminal, looking for a likely target, but they were so far away, she would have to yell to get somebody's attention.

She maneuvered the chair sideways, awkwardly because she had to push the suitcase around with it, and finally reached the duffel by leaning to the side. Pulling it over the arm rail with one hand made her head spin, and she had to rest until the pain let up, but once it did, the urgency of her situation returned. Turning the chair to face the sliding doors, she tried to wheel inside, her progress insanely slow as she stopped to drag the suitcase forward, then struggled to force the chair forward again while the ends of the duffel that hung over the armrests dragged against the wheel tops. Her arms twitched uncontrollaby; sweat drooled down her face. She looked for a rest room, finally spotted one at the other end of the baggage area.

Acres of black-flecked linoleum rolled and pitched before her, an interminable stretch of open sea between her and the bathroom door. No amount of forcing her rubbery arms would get her there in time. Pain bloomed across her lower back. Her mind went blank while the warmth spread from her crotch to her pant legs, following the path of least resistance. She folded her arms slowly across the top of the duffel and felt as if she had been erased.

⁕

The wall against Miranda's back was still warm from the afternoon sun, though the sun had been down for a good hour already. The small back porch off the kitchen was her favorite place to sit after a long day, listening to the crickets tune up. If the wind was right, she could hear the Trimbles' goats blatting. Estrella's voice wafted through the screen as she chanted back to the English language tapes the school had given her.

Miranda thought about that morning at the airport. Since they were able to get a direct flight and wouldn't have to change planes, she'd doled out a liberal dose of pain meds. She thought Bridie was alert when she left her on the sidewalk with the bags because Bridie repeated everything back and seemed to understand that Miranda was going to get the car. When she'd finally found Bridie in the luggage area, smelled the urine as she approached, she'd felt as she had the night before when she'd stared at the back of Bridie's shorn head and thought that anything she said would sound hollow in the thin space between them. Not twenty-four hours into her watch and she'd screwed up.

She heard Ruben breathing at the door a long time before he said anything. "Mom," he stage-whispered.

"Yes, sweetie."

"Can I come out?"

"Please do," she answered, always amazed at the peculiar juxtaposition between her desire to be alone and pleasure at the fact that he wanted or required her presence.

The screen door opened, then barked shut and he squatted beside her.

"What's up?"

"When's Zeus comin'?"

"In a couple of days," she said, but had not been able to bring herself to tell him that Zeus would not look like the dog in the photograph.

"You okay?" she asked him.

"Yeah."

"What do you think about all this?" she asked.

"I dunno."

She gave it thirty seconds until he'd ask his question, but he'd taken only twenty.

"What's wrong with Aunt Bridie?"

"Remember how I explained to you about the accident? And how she hurt her back so bad she can't move her legs for a while?"

"Not that."

"What, then?"

"What's wrong with her face?"

"Well, she cut her hair. Everybody looks different when they cut their hair."

"Not that, Mom. Her face."

"There's nothing wrong with her face, Ru."

"It don't look like her." He plunked down next to her, his feet tucked underneath him, and ran a sleeve under his nose. "Mom?" he nudged her, the smell of his fresh-cherry breath washing over her face.

"Sometimes when people get hurt, it upsets them so much that they have to sort of turn off their feelings. Sometimes, that changes the way they look."

"But her body's hurt, not her feelings."

"The kind of hurt somebody has can really hurt their feelings, too. Bridie is a very active person, you know? Now she feels like that's all gone and she doesn't know how to be that Bridie anymore. It's going to take a while for her to figure this out, and while she does, she has to sort of put those feelings to sleep."

"Until she can be like she was?"

"Her kind of hurt is very complicated. Some people think she may not get all the way better. But I think she can get a lot better. Don't you?"

"I dunno."

"We both need to help her believe that, honey, until she can believe it for herself."

He leaned against the railing.

"Mind that railing, Ru. It's kinda loose. I'll ask Mr. Trimble if he can fix that for us when he's finished with the ramp."

"That ramp's cool. Sonny doesn't have a ramp at his house."

She smiled, a pleasure entirely between her and the dark. Ruben wanted a bike to ride on the smooth, plywood incline that had begun to take shape at the front door. She had hoped it might be done by the time she got back with Bridie, but Paul Trimble had run into a couple of snags.

Ruben hip-hopped on one leg around the porch, then stood silently at the screen door. She started counting.

"Mom?"

"Yeah?"

"Was your face like that when my dad died?"

"Yes," she said, the elision between question and answer as smooth as the milky night air. She rubbed her thumb across the tips of her fingers, remembering the familiar smell of garlic, herbs, fresh fruit.

"Mom?"

"Yes?"

"Brian says Estrella can't be my sister."

"Who's Brian?"

"Kid at school. He says your mom has to give you a sister. Like you got me."

"I think of Bridie as my sister, and she didn't come from Papa."

Ruben said nothing.

"Do you like Estrella?" Miranda asked.

"She doesn't talk much."

"But you know when you like someone or not, even if you don't talk, don't you?"

"Yeah, I like her."

"You'll need to watch out for her, Ru. She's probably very scared."

"Why?"

"Her father died just like Papa. And she doesn't speak English very well yet. Plus, she doesn't really know us. Wouldn't you be scared?"

"Yeah."

"So help her as much as you can, honey, and she'll help you, too, when she can."

"Mom?"

"What?"

"Are you scared that Papa's gone?"

Miranda hooked her fingers in the boy's pocket and pulled him to her. "Sometimes," she said. "But I've got you and Bridie and Petra and Luis and Madrita . . ."

"But mostly me, right?"

"You most of all." She breathed in the smell of his hair and skin, soap and almond and all that is loved.

8

In the two weeks since she'd brought Bridie home, Miranda had developed a routine. She skipped her morning shower now and clumped downstairs, set up the coffee, and woke the kids before slipping into Bridie's room to help her dress and get into the chair. Then she'd wheel Bridie into the kitchen and snug her to the table so she'd be there when Ruben and Estrella finally straggled in for breakfast. She poured coffee for Bridie, who drank it without comment. The day Bridie made a crack about the dishwater in her cup would be the day Miranda could breathe again.

Miranda had coached Ruben and Estrella to go easy on Bridie at first, told them she'd need to rest a lot and wouldn't feel like talking. When they did speak to her, her whole body strained in the effort to respond. After two weeks, it wasn't getting any easier. Estrella seemed unaffected by it, while Ruben took this new Bridie into himself like a festering thorn.

But this morning, Ruben skipped to the table and sat down, his face brighter than she'd seen it since Bridie had come home. Zeus was scheduled to arrive that night. He'd contracted an infection, and Bascomb had delayed his departure. Ruben was beside himself. Miranda tried to prepare him for the way the dog would look, but she knew his child's mind had not taken it in.

His legs swung like pendulums, and he cupped his chin in his hands.

"Aunt Bridie," he whispered. "When Zeus comes home, can we get another dog?"

Bridie didn't answer.

Miranda brought a plate of scrambled eggs to the table. Dianna Trimble had started bringing them down. It turned out that along with all Dianna's other talents, she raised laying hens, as well. Miranda set the eggs in front of Ruben. "Eat now. We'll talk about dogs later, okay?"

"But we need more dogs, Mom. Aunt Bridie can train 'em to go like Zeus."

"Zeus will need to rest awhile before he starts pulling again, Ru."

"Yeah, so we can get another dog and start training him now," Ruben said. "Aunt Bridie said you have to have a whole buncha dogs to pull the sled."

Estrella appeared at the table and slid silently into the chair next to Bridie.

"Strella wants a dog, too. We can all have one, and then we'll have a team."

"Honey, how's about you and I talk about it tonight, okay? Now's not a good time," Miranda said.

"But Aunt Bridie promised I could get a dog."

Miranda tried to catch Bridie's eye, but she wouldn't look up.

"I want one now. So Zeus will have a friend. Aunt Bridie, you promised." Ruben pulled something from his trouser pocket. "I can do the buckle already. See?" He unsnapped the Fastex buckle on the blue collar that Miranda had brought back from Alaska and left on the dresser in her room.

"Where did you get that?" Bridie said.

Ruben's face seemed to deflate.

"Dr. Bascomb gave it to me to keep for you," Miranda said. "I had it on my dresser upstairs for when Zeus got here. I meant to—"

"Give it to me," Bridie said, her hand stretched across the table.

Ruben put the collar on the table.

"The school bus will be here in a minute," Miranda said. "Everyone needs to eat now. End of conversation."

Bridie scooped the collar from the table and tucked it in her lap before she pivoted the chair and left the kitchen. Miranda stared after her until she heard the bedroom door thump shut; then she sat down next to Ruben.

He ran his sleeve across his face. "Why's she mad at me?"

"She isn't mad at you. She's mad at what happened to her and the dogs. She needs more time to get better. So we have to wait awhile on our promises, but it doesn't mean they won't come true."

He climbed off his chair and walked to the door. Miranda followed him and put his lunch bag in his hand. "It'll be all right, sweetie. Your aunt Bridie loves you as much as I do, and a kid can't be all bad who's loved that much."

"I don't like her," Ruben said.

"Please don't say that, Ru. She loves you with all her heart. I wouldn't let her be your aunt Bridie if she didn't. Just give her a little more time. Meanwhile, we'll talk about what kind of dog you want when you get home tonight, okay? We'll make a list."

He submitted to her embrace for a moment before he pulled away and walked slowly to the road. She could hear the bus grinding up the hill. She hurried back to the kitchen to give Estrella her lunch.

"Almond butter and cherry jam today," she told Estrella as she put the bag in her hand.

"He like the dog," Estrella said in English.

"Your English is very good," Miranda said, and put a hand briefly to the girl's cheek. Estrella submitted to the touch in utter stillness, but Miranda could tell it terrified her. She'd tried to initiate contact a little at a time, let the girl know she was safe in her skin, safe with Miranda. When she'd taken the girl to the clinic for the TB puncture, the nurse had tried to hold her arm and the girl struggled violently before going limp as if she had fainted.

Miranda had been relieved when the puncture did no more than redden. It was the bumps they were looking for, Beto had said. She didn't know how much of her relief was for herself or for the girl; it didn't much matter, really. The important thing was that the girl was safe.

And in the month since leaving San Francisco, Ruben had morphed into a regular little boy. She hadn't noticed before how turned in he was, and she thought Estrella was partly responsible for the change. Ruben seemed to think he'd taken Estrella under his wing, but sometimes, it seemed otherwise to Miranda. She watched Estrella walk to the side of the road where Ruben stood, and when she squatted beside him and patted his arm, he dropped his hand on her shoulder in a gesture so profoundly gentle, it made tears come to her eyes.

In high school, Catherine had been a jock, but Catherine was a physical therapist now, trained in water therapy techniques. When Miranda called her to explain the situation and asked her to work with Bridie, Catherine agreed and offered to shuttle Bridie to and from Dundee. They were supposed to start tomorrow.

For two weeks, Miranda had tiptoed through the minutes Bridie was among them. The rest of the time she stayed home but let Bridie be, thinking it was what she needed, but she had no idea how to help Bridie adjust. Miranda thought now it was because she herself had not adjusted. Bridie needed something to revolve around, a point that was fixed and stable to which she could orient. In the seconds it had taken Miranda to walk from the kitchen to Bridie's room, she imagined herself as immutable as gravity.

Miranda tapped on Bridie's door as a courtesy before she walked in, refusing to wait for the rebuff. The room smelled musty, more so than when she'd first opened the door to go over Papa's files. She kneeled on the bed and yanked the shade, let it flap up to the top unimpeded, then pushed the window up.

"Time for a bath," Miranda said. "You'll have a bath every day now. You start therapy tomorrow with Catherine. She'll pick you up at ten in the morning. The sessions last an hour, five days a week."

"This isn't going to work," Bridie said.

"You told me you'd try, and you haven't," Miranda said.

"I'm sorry I snapped at Ruben."

"Catherine says you should see a counselor, maybe get into a group session."

"So I can sit around with a bunch of cripples and whine about it? No thank you. I got enough of that going on in here." She tapped the side of her head. "It's bad enough trying to come to grips with being useless, but when I see what you meant by 'It's not what you think,' I can't believe what you've gotten yourself into. You've lost your job, which was everything you identify with, and you've gained one small child, one big one, and you're about to get a sick dog. We're all useless to you. The math's no good, Miranda. You can't do this. I'll go to Michigan."

Miranda chewed her lip, remembered what Catherine said about setting goals. "Make me a deal," Miranda said. "Just give this therapy five months, through September. After that, we'll reassess the situation. You're Ruben's godmother, Bridie. If something happens to me, you're it. And you'd better be ready."

"What are you talking about?"

"You don't need legs to love him. You just need to be there."

Bridie put her hands over her face.

Miranda leaned over her shoulder, put her arms around her. "You'll show up, Bridie. I know you will." She brushed the stubby hairs into place. "I've got to go. Petra's got something on her mind. Lunch in Dundee. I'll stop in after." Miranda held out her hand and waited for Bridie to take it, forcing her to take it, then gripped it so tightly Bridie winced a little. "Do we have a deal?"

Bridie nodded, but did not meet her eyes.

Petra plunked the cordless down on the glass-topped table and took a deep breath as she scanned the hill and valley below her. This was the kind of early summer morning she dreamed of all year, standing on the terrace in nothing more than a cotton button-down and slacks, the newspaper fluttering every so often in a wispy current of air that was so clear she could see Mount Hood and Mount Jefferson as if they were etched on glass. How odd that a mere phone call made it all look like a backdrop, a canvas that someone was about to roll up and carry away. Party's over. Move on, please.

It was the second call she'd had from the "Feering bloke," as Duncan called him. She hadn't told Duncan yet about the first one. She'd meant to that night after the tasting, but he'd been in such a snit, she thought she'd wait. And then Gagnon had almost done it in spite of her signal. He wasn't exactly the diplomat he liked to think himself to be.

This morning, Feering had asked after her health, first thing. *I could suggest a specialist in L.A.,* he'd said. She was stunned by his ability to pilfer the information. And then he'd mentioned the phenomenal figure he was prepared to offer for Ruby Throat, more than fair market value, enough to make her light-headed, enough to make her wonder what he knew that she did not. She wondered if Moore was in cahoots with the guy, since the paper had run his gossipy blip about Feering being seen speaking intimately with the new proprietor of Perry Hill at the tasting last week. Gagnon had been right to refer to Feering as a shark. Petra felt as if she were being probed, and she didn't like it, mostly because she harbored a niggling doubt that there was a chink in their armor. She had thought it was losing Carter, and possibly losing Miranda, but now Miranda was here—through no manipulation of Petra's, she was happy to say—and even so, she felt as if they were behind the eight ball.

The church bells in Dundee pealed faintly. Madrita and Luis would be there for Wednesday morning mass, which pleased her for some reason. Normally the bells pleased her, too, but today the somber notes made her shiver. *For whom the bell tolls . . .* She drained the rest of her coffee in a gulp, made a face when the grown-cold liquid hit her tongue. She was resolved to tell Duncan now. It really couldn't wait any longer.

Duncan had been in the winery since seven. She'd awakened to the screech of the big doors as he'd rolled them back. He was eager to get the new vintage lots barreled, but had to put it off for the last three days while the pressure pump was in for repairs.

Ever since Ernest died, ever since the weight on his shoulders had doubled, trouble racked him like an anxious thoroughbred. No doubt her news this morning would make him ten kinds of crazy. But since the night a few weeks ago when Gagnon had caught her out holding back on him, she resolved to take off the gloves, let him grow up. Maybe that had been the problem all along.

Duncan's assistant, Jake, and their helper, Tom, had gone to some musical event the night before. They might have dragged their young hides in by now, bleary after nights only young men could withstand. She grabbed the hamper she'd set by the door filled with a thermos of coffee and some muffins and made her way down the long steps to the winery.

Jake and Tom were late, so she braced herself for a moody reception, but Duncan smiled up at her when she found him kneeling by one of the oak barrels in the breezeway, said "Hullo, princess," like he used to do before Ernest died.

"Good morning, sunshine," she said. "Those naughty boys are dragging their feet, I take it."

"No worries," Duncan said. "They'll be along soon enough."

She set the hamper down by the office door. "I brought a basket of fortitude for in case they're surly," she said.

"Righty-o," he said, and stood to replace the bung in the barrel. "I might have a dab m'self."

She hesitated a moment before rummaging through the basket. "Muffin?" she asked. "We've got banana chocolate chip."

"Two, if you please."

She passed him a mug and two muffins on a napkin.

"I didn't know better, I'd think you had a mind to grease me."

She felt her throat constrict around the crumb of muffin she was about to swallow, but his smile was so benign, she didn't think he meant anything by it.

"You get so worked up about things lately, I try to keep the damper down. Probably the wrong approach."

"Forget it," he said. "Give us a hand, love." He gestured toward the cellar where the vats gleamed dully.

They spent a half hour straightening hoses and cleaning the pumps to prepare for draining the tanks into barrels. Jake arrived just as they finished, his face the color of glue.

"Morning, sport," Duncan said, and gave him a playful slap.

Jake peered at him in confusion, rubbed the reddening patch of skin on his face, then looked at Petra.

"Don't ask me," she said. "He's unaccountably cheerful today."

Duncan posted Jake at the pump, while he and Petra monitored the barrels in the breezeway. This was a part of the process she loved most, the smell of the wine mixing into oak, fumes rising and swirling in the breezeway mixed with the broader smells of the valley, first-cut alfalfa, grass pollen, turned earth.

"What is it?" Duncan asked.

"What?"

"That thing on your mind," he said. "Something bulging out right there." He pointed at her forehead.

"Now you're a mind reader as well as an artisan in wine," she said.

He gestured at her to plug the barrel while he moved the hose to the next. "Wine isn't the only thing Ernest taught me, eh?"

Petra ran her fingers over the warm oak staves. The hose glurked and squirmed at their feet.

"Mind that gauge," Duncan yelled at Jake, who started as if he'd been asleep on his feet. "Bloody hell, where's the other slacker? At least they could lean on each other while they're sleeping."

Petra eyed him curiously, but he didn't meet her gaze. The hose twitched again, and Duncan yelled at Jake to mind the pressure.

He leaned over the gauge, then held up bunches of fingers in a series of three.

Duncan thumped the barrel in front of him with his eyes on the pump. "Fucking wanker machine." He switched off the valve at his end of the hose, was saying something to Petra, when the pump blew. Jake shot backward more quickly than Duncan would have thought possible.

Duncan was beside him as quickly, the boy's wan hand raised like a white flag. Duncan helped him to his feet and guided him into the breezeway, where the light was better. Petra checked him over, saw no more damage than an unruly gush of adrenaline had caused.

"Go home," Duncan said to Jake. "But call that wanker, Tom, be-fore you go. Tell him to stay in bed."

Jake went to the office on unsteady legs to use the phone.

"Isn't there something else they can do?" Petra said.

"Fuck it," Duncan said. "I'll take this thing back to the shop, but I vote for a new pump. They're on sale at Drummond's in Portland."

She sighed. Another grand out the door, but relatively speaking, it was a cheap problem. "You're right," she said. "It's cheaper than medical bills."

"Hell of a lot cheaper than losing a vintage," he said.

"Besides, we can't have you missing a sale."

He laughed. She loved to rib him about his shopping phobia.

They heard Jake's old Volkswagen chatter down the gravel drive.

"So what's on your mind?" he asked.

She clenched her teeth against the pain in her hip, against her better judgment. "I'm just worried about Miranda," she said finally. "That poor dog of Bridie's is coming in tonight from Alaska, and it's going to take a lot of care. I don't know how she's going to squeeze that in along with everything else."

"Looking for Dr. Doolittle, are you?"

Petra flushed, as much from what she was asking him as from what she wasn't telling him. "I guess I am," she said. "Just until he can move around on his own. I take it he still needs a sling to get outside, and you seem to have such a way with the creatures."

"No butter necessary," he said. "I'll do it. No worries."

She put her hand on his arm. "Thank you. It'll just mean the world to me."

"I doubt that," he said. "But it's a nice go for the dog."

"I'm taking Miranda into town for lunch. I'll tell her."

"What time's the dog coming in? I might as well pick him up at the airport when I go in for the pump."

"You're a prince, Dee," she said.

He tweaked her chin between thumb and forefinger. "Better than that, I'm a pauper with a queen in my pocket."

Petra knew he would watch her go and notice the way she used the handrail to pull herself up each stair step. It wouldn't be long before she'd be telling him she'd bought a condo in Arizona. She turned when she reached the top step and noticed the thin dark line that had crested the western horizon. The barrels would need to be stowed out of the weather. But she heard the rheumy cough of a diesel engine before she'd started back down, and she saw him drive the forklift into the breezeway and scoop a barrel onto the loader. He'd be cursing the air blue for letting Jake go for the day. Between the two of them, they could have got the barrels under cover in no time.

Usually, Bridie sat out in the living room after everyone was gone. Just sat and waited until lunchtime, when she would wheel herself to the bathroom, empty her bladder, and get into bed.

After Miranda left, she rolled into the kitchen and got yogurt and bread from the fridge. She balled pieces of bread and put them in her mouth, then swilled yogurt out of the container. It wasn't exactly the diet that Miranda and Catherine had designed for her, but it would have to do. Anything would do.

She sat by the fridge for another hour. She lost track of time so easily now, it scared her. Though she had all the time in the world to think, her mind was fractious and refused to go in a straight line. She'd decided to go to Michigan because she could not bear to be part of what Miranda had gotten herself into. Miranda tried to tell her it was everything, Estrella, Ruben, Petra—couldn't Bridie see that? But all Bridie saw was fault, all hers. And as if one broken body weren't enough, now there would be two. She was so weak, she could hardly get in and out of the chair. Even if she could endure the physical effort, she didn't think her heart could encompass the raw ghost of a dog Zeus was now. Caring for him that way would require a great deal of positive energy, and she had not one watt of that. It was her fault, and he would know it.

Yet she'd promised Miranda she'd try. She wheeled to the front door and went down the access ramp Miranda had had Paul Trimble build for Bridie. The simple, hopeful gesture made her throat ache.

At the bottom of the ramp she stopped, her eyes cringing against the light. She waited until the burn in her hands subsided a little before turning the chair to follow the path around the back of the house. From there she could see the wide uphill sweep of Perry Hill, budding vines nascent in the flat afternoon light. Farther up the hill, she saw a forklift leaving the big breezeway of the winery with something stacked on the loader.

She started up the hard dirt path to the vineyard, had to set her brake at the gate in order to use both hands on the stiff latch. She didn't bother with the antiviral chlorine solution. She hadn't been anywhere else.

When she tried to get through the gate, one of the front wheels cocked around and locked up. *Cheap piece of shit.* She swore, rocked the chair as hard as she could until the wheel straightened, each motion tightening the coil of pain in her back.

She maneuvered the chair into one of the lanes between a row of vines. Long-stemmed grasses and wildflowers were cultivated in between the rows in order to entice beneficial insects and to keep the soil vigorous. She had learned that from Miranda on one of her first visits to Perry Hill—what, ten years ago? Twelve?

When she'd walked these paths before, the soil had seemed firm, but now she felt it give way under the gouging wheels. She stopped and let her arms dangle over the hard, skinny tires. With her eyes closed, her arms seemed to flop like fish, but when she looked at them, they hung abeyant, leaden and white.

A wind dervish twirled down the row behind her, pasting spikes of hair to the side of her face like pointing arrows. She tried to push farther down the lane with the wind at her back, but it passed quickly, leaving her feeling like a pylon driven into the earth.

With tremendous effort, she twisted her upper body to see how far she'd come. It couldn't have been more than thirty feet. She clamped her jaw against the heat bubbling in her eyes. A wasp crested the toe of her shoe and wobbled across the bewildering terrain of Velcro straps. With any luck, it would crawl up her pants leg and sting her dead. Instead, the wasp rose heavily into the air, then sheered off in a gust of wind.

Dark-bellied clouds swished their skirts over the Coastal Range to the west, bringing with them the smell of cut Douglas fir.

Dogs barked in the distance, probably set off by the change in barometric pressure. Zeus had been an unerring bellwether. He'd known about the storm stalking them before they'd got up out of the ravines. Pain struck her squarely in the chest, pain worse than the concrete agony of muscle and nerve. The dogs' voices rose in her head. It was her weakness they smelled, her inadequacy they announced to the roiling sky. She shivered and remembered Zeus's dripping nose drilling through the snow to her face, the smell of his blood. In dreams, Bascomb would have him put down. It was the practical thing to do.

Rising wind carried the moan from her mouth so that it seemed her shadow self cried for her, and then a different voice blended with hers, faint, calling her name. Estrella.

The girl had taken to stopping at the house when she got off the bus, before going up to Petra's. She'd appeared one afternoon, having opened the bedroom door so quietly, Bridie hadn't heard it.

"Help?" the girl said, and Bridie thought she'd needed something. She'd barely got out of Reed with her language requirement intact, and even then she'd taken French, pretty much useless in the Northwest. The girl had got behind the empty wheelchair and pushed it across the room, said, "Help?" again, and Bridie had almost cried when she realized what Estrella meant.

But the girl came every day, always with the question only now she'd ask, "Help you, Bridie?"

Bridie clamped shaking hands to the top of one wheel and forced the chair to pivot. The wind pushed at her side, her hair just long enough to needle the corner of her eye.

She wrestled the chair with soupy arms until she'd got it turned enough to move forward, but she had miscalculated the softness of the earth at the edge of the row. The chair leaned, then tipped forward as the front wheel buried itself to the shaft. She slid out, unable to hold herself back until her weight dragged it all forward, pitching her onto the ground. The chair, as if relieved, sagged onto its side, one oversize rear wheel spinning languorously in the wind.

She raised her torso onto her elbows, dirt clotted to the side of her face.

"*Estrella!*" she called, then heard her own name again, thinly, as if the girl was going away from her.

"*Estrella! I'm here.*" Her voice cracked and shrilled, and she swore at herself, dug her hands into the dirt, and tried to pull herself up against the trunk of a vine.

Then she remembered the sound that carried better than voice, could cut through wind, rage, exhaustion . . . She licked her lips and curled them inward, bracing her tongue against the back of her teeth. The sound pierced the air, sharp, insistent. Estrella stopped calling, and Bridie whistled again, calling the girl's name in between blasts.

Faintly she heard the gate slam, then saw the impossibly thin brown legs pumping toward her.

She kneeled next to Bridie. "Help you?" The wind ripped leaves from above them and blew them crosswise.

Bridie pointed her eyes at the sky, then at her legs. "No, Estrella. Bridie too *grande.*" She almost laughed at the absurdity of her speech.

"Help you," Estrella said, her face pinched, urgent.

"Luis," Bridie said. "Okay?"

Estrella started to run off, then doubled back. She shucked off her jacket and laid it over Bridie's shoulders, pointed up to the sky. "The water," she said, then took off again.

Bridie watched until Estrella rounded the end of the lane before she slumped to the ground. She lay with the side of her face in the dirt and felt the rain come smacking at her. She tried to huddle under the tiny jacket but she felt huge, bloated by dark sludge that glugged and gurgled with every movement, certain there was nothing big enough to cover the unwieldy mess she'd become.

Duncan put the forklift in the warehouse after gathering and stacking the barrels he'd carefully laid out that morning. He could have left them there until tomorrow, but wouldn't risk them getting too damp, or too dry, the staves expanding and shrinking painfully. They cost $750 a pop and could be used only for six to ten years. From the largest family-owned cooperage in the world, he ordered sixty-gallon French oak barrels, never American oak, and even the French oak must be from forests situated in poor soil so the grain of the wood would be tight, dense, slow to impart its distinct flavor to the wine. American oak had a loose grain, which was fine for cabernet or zinfandel, grapes that were already overpowering. Not for pinot. So Duncan babied the containers as scrupulously as he babied the wine.

With the barrels safely under cover, he watched from the shelter of the breezeway as the storm steamrolled into the valley. Fluke whined softly at his heels. Hazelnut branches slapped the tin-roofed shed where the mare moved restlessly about.

He couldn't help wondering why Petra hadn't told him what was on her mind. Since the night after the tasting when he'd realized she felt as if she couldn't depend on him, he'd resolved to be a partner, not a burden. He buckled down to the job, kept his fear to himself, and presented to her the countenance of confidence. Everything's apples. He sensed her relief, yet she had not been able to talk to him yet about whatever it was bothering her. He'd thought at first it was uncertainty about Miranda, but Petra had called it, all right; the girl stayed. Whether or not Petra had anything to do with the decision, he couldn't say.

He caught motion from the corner of his eye, saw the kid before she disappeared into the lower tiers of Petra's gardens, then saw her again flashing up the stone steps of the house. She came up every weekday after school, but there was something about the way she ran. . . . Duncan frowned. Probably trying to beat the storm.

He returned to the spectacle of the witches' brew in the sky. Rain began to gouge the earth like bullets. Much as he loved storms, he did not like the look of rain with that kind of force. He scanned the vineyard anxiously. It was early May, and they'd only just got over the anxiety of spring frost killing off the tender buds. This was the kind of stuff that could stymie the blossom, damage the crop.

The intercom in the breezeway gargled something he couldn't

make out. Since Petra was at lunch, it could only be Madrita. He punched the TALK button. *"Qué es esto?"*

Madrita came back at him in Spanish so rapid, he couldn't understand her.

"Qué paso?"

She blabbered at him again, but he still couldn't translate. Screw it.

"Fluke, wait," he told the dog, his hand spread wide in front of her. He grabbed his slicker from the office and took the steps to the house two at time. Madrita met him at the door, Estrella and Ruben standing behind her in the kitchen. Estrella's chest was heaving still from her run.

"Qué paso?" he asked again.

Ruben tried to squeeze past Madrita but she wedged him against the door with her hip. "That lady," Madrita said with difficulty. "Miranda's friend with no legs. She is falling and can't not go up."

"Where is she?"

"Down there." Ruben's arm thrust out from the folds of Madrita's skirt.

He looked at Madrita. "I need the girl to show me."

She went at him again in Spanish until he shook his head, looked at the girl, and asked her to show him. She ran onto the porch, wild-eyed as a colt. Duncan tried to pick her up, cover her with his slicker, but she scuttled away from him. He headed back down to the winery, motioning her to follow.

He went into the shed, plucked the bridle from the wall, and eased the mare into the corner, talking to her idly until he'd fastened the throat latch under her jaw. He looked at the saddle but decided against it. Too much time. He led the mare to the breezeway, her shod hooves pocking on the asphalt.

"I'm going to get on, then pull you up behind me," he said to Estrella in Spanish.

She nodded, her face as intent as if Duncan had told her they were going to the moon.

He almost flicked her right over, she was so light.

The mare snatched her head up, ears flat. "Easy, baby," he said. "Be serious."

Fluke stood, tail swagging expectantly back and forth. She'd probably add to the confusion. "Right there," he pointed at the ground, and she flattened to her belly, ears slicked back in reproach.

He nudged the mare into a dancy canter once they got off the pavement. They cut through the upper vineyards, slowed to negotiate the band of trees, then kicked out into the road down to Carter's house. When they got to the driveway, Estrella's hand appeared before him, pointing to the vineyard beyond the house.

He slowed the mare to a trot. When they got to the vineyard gate, Duncan yelled, *"Seguro?"*

She pointed again. He lowered the girl to the ground. *"Abre la puerta."* He couldn't remember the word for *gate*.

She struggled with the gate, the wind and rain pushing against her, then flung it back and took off. Duncan saw them now, two thin, parallel tracks in the grass, and when he coaxed the mare through the gate, he saw where they ended, the woman crumpled on her side next to the overturned chair. Acid backed up his throat at the sight of her. The mare reacted, skittered and rocked under him.

He gave the horse rein, and she spurted ahead to where Estrella crouched in the dirt beside Bridie. He yanked the mare back on her haunches and slid down all in one motion.

"You in bother?" he shouted.

She didn't answer.

Estrella crouched over Bridie's head, water sluicing from her hair, and touched Bridie lightly on the cheek with her fingertips.

He heard a sharp bark, and now here was Fluke running down on them. She stopped when she saw his eyes. He didn't have time to be angry with her now, so he gestured her to come on, and she resumed her flat-backed lope until she was among them, face poking into Estrella's, licking the rain from her downturned cheeks.

The woman's hand twined into the dog's fur.

Duncan kneeled by Bridie, his knees sinking into the soil.

"Don't let go of the dogs," she told Duncan.

"I'll have to lift you," Duncan said.

"Don't let go of the dogs," she said again.

"Estrella's got the dogs," Duncan said. "Ready?"

She pursed her lips and braced a hand against the bole of the vine in front of her.

He thought he heard her cry out, and he stopped, swaying. "You all right?"

She looked at him and nodded, her face blacked with dirt that had begun to runnel clean in the rain. He slumped her further into his arms, trying to balance the half-taut, half-limp weight of her.

The mare had moved off down the aisle, her rump to the driving rain.

"Fluke, bring it." The dog stalked the mare to the fence, where she pinned her with a wolfish stare until the mare stood still. "Bring it," he yelled again. The dog caught a dangled rein in her mouth and pulled backward until the mare came along.

"Estrella, the gate."

Once in the house, he almost dropped Bridie on the couch, swore and apologized when he saw her face bunched in pain.

"It's all right," she said, but did not unscrew her eyes. He went out to relieve Fluke of her duty and loosed the mare in Carter's barn, then went back to the vineyard for the chair and set it to rinse in the rain. He called Fluke to the porch and praised her before he went back inside.

Estrella sat next to Bridie on the couch, trying to drape a blanket over her, but it kept drooping down to her waist. Bridie's eyes were open now, her face slack.

"Chair's a right mess," he said. "Left it outside for a soak."

Her eyes were on him, flat and unseeing compared with the face he had looked into a month earlier. It unsettled him still, in spite of the difference in appearance.

The rubber boots he practically lived in suddenly felt clumsy, clammy. He looked around the living room.

"You don't have to stay," she said.

"I was thinking you'd want to spiff up a bit, dry clothes or something."

"I can do that myself," she said, holding up her arms. "I've still got these." A clump of dirt plopped from her sleeve onto the couch. She didn't notice.

He toed the frayed rug at his feet. "Well, ring the winery if you need anything."

Duncan called the dog to him as he went out, then remembered the chair. Bridie wouldn't be able to do much without that. He dispersed the thickest goo, letting the rain take care of the finer silt. It was still pounding down so hard, he didn't hear the car on the road, only noticed it when the gravel crunched alongside him in the driveway. He saw Petra's face ripple behind the wet glass.

She splashed to the porch, her jacket tented over her head. She shook herself off and waited for him to clump up the steps with the chair.

"Madrita called us at the *taquería*. Everyone okay?"

He shrugged.

"What happened?"

"She was out in the vineyard. Fell out of her chair, looks like. I didn't quiz her."

She didn't even respond to his dig, just patted his arm. "Miranda's getting Ruben. Go dry off. I'll take over until she gets here."

"It's all right," Bridie said to Petra after Duncan left. "You don't have to stay."

Petra crossed her arms. In spite of aching joints, miserable weather, the phone call that morning, she regarded the two ragged heads before her and could think only of how much they needed proper haircuts. She'd started to say it aloud, but Bridie said, "Please. We're okay." Petra heard the low desperation in her voice, like a child who's afraid its bad behavior will be reported.

"We'll get you ladies into some dry clothes at least."

She followed Estrella down the dark hall to Bridie's room, then shooed the girl off to get changed. She hadn't been in this part of the house since Miranda was a child. It was still too dark. She always worried it would give Miranda nightmares. Of course, she had enough nightmares now to make up for anything she might have missed back then.

She found a dry shirt, jeans, and underwear, didn't know if she should look for a bra or not then decided Bridie wasn't really the bra type anyway. When she got back to the living room, Estrella was there.

"Estrella, would you get me a towel, please?" The girl disappeared back down the hall.

Bridie braced herself on her arms and pressed into the back of the couch. "I can do this, Petra."

"Bridie," Petra said with a little outrush of breath. "Do you remember my husband?"

"A little," Bridie said.

"He died of cancer. Three years ago. You girls weren't around then. I took care of him for a year at home before he passed. He was humiliated every moment of it. But he never gave me any guff, never made it harder than it already was."

Bridie allowed Petra to prop her arms overhead while she peeled off the sopping shirt.

Estrella returned with two towels and held them out to Petra. *"Está perfecto, nina. Gracias,"* Petra said. She laid the towels beside Bridie and brought a bowl of warm water from the kitchen, wetted a corner of one of the towels and wiped away as much of the dirt as she could before patting her dry. She tumbled Bridie's hair with the other towel before pulling a dry shirt over her head. She was so intent on her business, she wouldn't have noticed had Estrella not tried to cage Bridie's stuttering hands between her own.

"Everything's under control. Everything's going to be okay," Petra said.

"Zeus is coming in tonight."

"I know, sweetie. But Duncan's going to take care of him for a while until he gets on his feet."

Bridie just shook her head as if she were too exhausted to argue. "I've got to lie down," Bridie said. "I think Duncan left my hell horse on the porch."

"I'll bring the chair in," Petra said. "Dry it off a little."

While Petra was on the porch, Miranda pulled in. Ruben was out of the car in a flash, running toward them.

Miranda high-stepped over the puddles and leaped onto the porch. "Is she all right?"

"Wounded pride is the worst of it," Petra said.

Miranda held the door open while Petra rolled the chair close to the couch and then helped her lift Bridie into it.

"Mom?" Ruben called from the kitchen.

Estrella watched Bridie wheel down the hall.

"The rain's let up, Estrella. Would you and Ruben go outside and play for a little while?"

The girl nodded and went to the kitchen to get Ruben. Miranda had watched the two of them outside. Estrella followed Ruben around, or squatted and waited while he brought things to her, rocks, leaves, once a tiny green snake. She seemed to have no concept of playing.

"Everything under control?" Petra asked.

Miranda nodded. When she heard Petra's car pull out, she started down the hall. Bridie would need a little rah-rah session. Miranda stopped outside Bridie's door. Her hand hovered over the knob as if it contained some repelling force. It might be worse to bother her now when she was exhausted, humiliated. Her perspective might clear after a little rest.

Miranda tiptoed back down the hall. She'd make a snack, mull some cider. But she ended up on the couch instead, listening to the sound of Ruben's gleeful shouts drifting in through the window and reminded herself to call again about Bridie's new chair. It was something tangible she could accomplish without wondering whether it was right or wrong.

That morning Miranda had promised Ruben they would talk about getting a dog. He'd been upset when he found out Zeus would stay with Duncan, so while Estrella practiced with her English tapes, Miranda settled Ruben at the kitchen table, where he crouched now, eyeing her expectantly. She picked up the pen and held it over the yellow legal pad.

"Okay," she said. "We'll make a list, just like I do when I'm buying things for the kitchen. First thing we have to think about is what kind of dogs you like."

He frowned and thought for a minute. "The kinds with fur and stuff. Like Zeus."

"What kind of personality do you like in a dog? That's very important. You know how there are some people you like and feel happy with? People react to animals that way, too. So we want to make sure we find a dog that you like and feel happy with."

He frowned again, smearing his tongue across the corner of his mouth. "I like Fluke," he said.

"Who's Fluke?" she asked.

"Duncan's dog."

"Oh," Miranda said. "I remember her. What do you like about Fluke?"

"She's nice," he said.

"Okay, so we want to be sure we find a nice dog." She wrote down *nice* at the top of the page. "What about size? Do you like big dogs? Little dogs? Skinny dogs? Fat dogs?"

Ruben giggled. "Big dogs, so I can ride 'em."

"You couldn't ride a dog. It would hurt them. What about color? Black dogs, white dogs, speckled dogs, blue dogs?"

"Ain't no blue dogs," he said.

"Aren't any blue dogs," she corrected him. "And there actually are blue dogs. Sort of."

"Ain't not," he said, blowing out his cheeks.

"Are not," she said.

"Right," he said. And now she had to laugh at how he'd caught her out.

"Seriously. What color?"

He puckered his eyes and drummed his fingers arrhythmically on the table. "Fluke's pretty."

"You like the speckles in her coat?"

"Yeah."

"Okay," she said, and wrote down *speckles* under *nice* and *big*.

They went on until she'd covered the page with words; then she wrote at the very top "Ruben's Dog," and tore it off and gave it to him.

"First a bath, then some nighty-night. You can keep this right by your bed so we won't forget what you've decided so far. Tomorrow we'll write down all the things you'll need to take care of this dog, and all the things you have to do for it."

"Let's do it now," he said.

She smiled and narrowed her eyes until he relented and plodded to the bathroom. Once she'd got him into bed, she agreed to stay with him until he fell asleep. He fingered the creased photograph of Bridie and Zeus on his night table, then slipped it under his pillow.

"Zeus is big, ain't he?"

"He's pretty big."

"How big?"

She'd only seen him lying down. "I think he's taller than my knee," she said.

He retrieved the picture and held it close to his eyes. "I like his face," Ruben said. "It's black and white."

"Yes," Miranda said. "He has a strong face. Bridie says he's very, very smart."

"I want a smart dog," Ruben said. "Can't we get a puppy from Zeus?"

"No, sweetie. Only girl dogs can have puppies. Zeus is a boy dog."

"Is Fluke a girl or a boy?"

"I think she's a girl."

"Let's get a puppy from Fluke," he said.

"I don't know if Fluke can have puppies or not," Miranda said. "Why?

Miranda tried to think of a way to explain spay and neuter, but her brain wouldn't cooperate. "Let's talk about that later," she said. "We need to be quiet so you can fall asleep."

"Strella can help me take care of my dog," Ruben said.

Miranda moved her tongue over the cracked shell of her lips. "If you don't get some rest, you'll be too tired to have a dog."

She pulled the covers up to his chest and smoothed them down on either side.

"Mom?"

"Ruben," she said, drawing it out like a warning.

He held up his hand with one finger raised.

"All right. One more thing."

"Why can't Zeus stay with us?"

"Because he's still sick from his accident, and Duncan knows how to take care of him. When he's better, he'll come live with us."

"Can I see him?"

"If Duncan says it's okay."

He was satisfied with that answer, knew as children know that he had Duncan around his finger.

Once his breathing slowed, she tiptoed into the living room, where Estrella had fallen asleep on the couch, her face pressed to the tape recorder. Miranda slipped her arms around the girl's torso and carried her to her bed. She sat sleepily on its edge while Miranda put on the girl's pajamas.

"I am pleased to meet you," Estrella said, her eyes still closed.

Miranda smiled. "Mucho gusto."

Ruben shifted onto his side and moaned but did not wake.

Miranda eased onto the bed next to Ruben, slipped the picture from under his pillow, and smoothed it across the muscle of her thigh. The familiar face smiled out at her from the picture, and next to it was Zeus's face, silhouetted perfectly against the arched drape of Bridie's arm across his shoulders. The dog's thick black tail curved neatly around his haunch, the white tip of it invisible against snow. In the background, she saw Gordon's beaming face at the edge of the crowd. She pressed a fingertip to the curve of Bridie's face, then smudged a circle around her and the dog.

With her eyes closed, she saw Bridie on the trail, the beam of her head lamp stabbing the darkness, Zeus ahead of her, a halo of lung-damp air briefly wreathing his naked face before he plunged through it, unwavering.

The steam of his breath thickens until she can discern only shapes, and then there is nothing at all but crying, and it should be the dogs, but it's a human voice she hears. She presses her hands sideways and feels cold tiles, slicked damp with steam as if she's in a bathroom. She tries to drag herself closer to the sound of thrashing water and at first it's Estrella's voice she hears—or is it Bridie?—but the sound of the dogs howling is so loud she can't be sure. Her arms will not hold against the slick tiles, and she squirms helplessly, cursing arms, legs, heart. She calls to them, their fear-whitened faces blazing close, then fading into aqueous air.

She woke with a shouted word trembling in her ear but couldn't remember what it was she'd said.

She stretched out next to Ruben, one arm draped over the rise and fall of his ribs, and tried to melt the chill in her belly.

9

Catherine Carey blotted water from the nutrition sheet on her clipboard before she continued her notes. She liked to get this part of the session out of the way while her patient warmed up in the pool.

"And today?"

There was the hesitation Catherine knew so well before Bridie said, "Toast. Two slices. Butter and jam. *Low-sugar* jam."

"Let's try again. Have you eaten *anything* today?"

Bridie finned a circle so that Catherine could not see her face. Apparently it was easier for her clients to tell the truth when they weren't looking at her.

"Coffee, but Miranda made it, so it doesn't count."

Catherine watched two geezers lolling up and down the pool in the roped-off area, marveled for the millionth time at the disparity in people's motivational capacities. In her experience, geriatrics and children tried the hardest. It was this middle-of-the-road age she had the most problems with, and athletes were the worst. She hadn't wanted to take this on, but she did it as a favor to Miranda.

They'd gone to high school together in McMinnville. Miranda had been relegated to the nerdy crowd then. Catherine was an athlete, volleyball A-team. In spite of her lack of height, she was powerful and fast. They were state champions her senior year.

But she wouldn't have made it to varsity or her degree in physical therapy had it not been for Miranda, would have failed biology, which was not good considering her career choice. Miranda had volunteered to tutor her and brought her through finals with flying colors. Of course, Catherine was getting paid for the so-called favor —Medicaid took care of that—so it wasn't as if she were sacrificing herself financially. It was her patience that was getting sucked dry. In the three weeks she'd dedicated to Bridie, she'd seen zero progress, and the thought of eking it out over two more months made her tired.

When she talked to Miranda about Bridie's sessions, she was careful to avoid letting her personal judgments slip into the exchange, though lately the temptation was harder to withstand.

Bridie had finned back around to face Catherine, who stood spread legged at the edge of the pool.

"This makes me very uncomfortable," Catherine said. "You make me treat you as if you were a child. I should be able to say, 'Bridie, this nutritional regimen will help you fight the pain and restore health to injured tissue and nerve.' And you should say, 'Okay, Catherine. Will do.' Then you should do it instead of making me stand here and lecture you as to why you're not making progress."

"I'm not making progress?"

"What do you think?"

"I'm here. I'm doing the stuff."

"You're going through the motions, *here,* anyway."

Bridie said nothing.

"Look, so you fell out of the chair. It'll happen again. Didn't you ever fall off one of those sleds? You had to in order to learn it. This is the same thing. You're just learning a new sport." Catherine sighed. "I guess Miranda's going to have to hand-feed you when she's not taking care of all her other responsibilities."

Bridie stopped finning, let the float belt suspend her in the water.

Catherine looked down at her clipboard and swore under her breath. There. She'd broken professional protocol. It wouldn't be the first time, but it would certainly be the first time she'd done it with such unprofessional intentions. It just galled her all to hell to see someone perfectly capable of making the effort, with all kinds of things to live for, but who would do nothing. She thought of children, bodies devastated by disease, trauma, in far worse condition than this hunk of a sulking human before her, yet who tried their hearts out with humor and a hopefulness that made Catherine cry.

The two geezers stood on the deck at the far end of the pool, toweling sackcloth flesh, the loosened straps of their bathing caps flapping as they worked. She sighed. She'd have to backpedal pretty quick here or today's session would be wasted.

"Look, Bridie, we've gone over this before. If you can't manage the depression, we need to get you to a counselor. The mind can be the body's worst enemy in this situation, and it looks to me as if your brain is having its way with you. For Pete's sake, you can't even bring yourself to follow a simple eating regimen."

"It's been only three weeks," Bridie said. "These things take time, don't they?"

Catherine peeked at the big clock at the far end of the pool, wondered just how long she ought to stand here and let this woman screw with both their heads. Finally, she flicked the clipboard onto a nearby bench.

"All right. Let's go through the motions. We'll start you on your back today."

Duncan took the huge syringe he'd got from the vet in Dundee and propped it in the bowl of mash he'd prepared for Zeus, who lay on the thick foam pallet Duncan had made for him, his eyes alert in a face that bristled with outgrowing fur.

When he eased himself down beside the pallet, the dog's head came up, but he would not look at the man directly. Still, he'd come a long way from when Duncan picked him up at the airport three weeks ago when he'd seen it all on the dog's face, alert intelligence in spite of pain and disorientation. He'd known instantly why Bridie had insisted on saving the dog.

Duncan stuffed the ground mess of beef, fish, and kibble into the syringe and attached the plunger. Fluke crept over on her belly and pushed her head under his arm.

"You've already eaten, Fluke. Lay by." But he let her lick the sticky mash from his fingers before he turned back to Zeus and talked to him in low, steady tones while he squeezed little gobs of food into the dog's mouth until the bowl was empty.

"Atta boy," Duncan said. "Now let's get you and your mum out for a little air." Duncan shook his head. The outings had become a daily ritual, and he had to admit, he'd got a bit accustomed to the routine.

He was lucky he had the time now. Mid-May was practically summer, and that was the only time a winemaker's job approached reasonable hours. In the vineyard, the manager and crew would train the vines by tying up shoots to the second and third trellis wires, hoe around the vines, and brush off the suckers so that the vines could concentrate on upper foliage and fruit set. The crew managed the bloom now, plucking small, white flowers from the fruiting canes so that the vines would not produce too many clusters. The fewer the clusters, the more intense the grapes. Later, they'd manage the canopy by pinching off leaves so the clusters got the best exposure to air and light. More than anything, they'd pray for the right weather at the right time.

Duncan prayed for the harvest and crush, because that was what he lived for, the endless string of sleepless weeks when the air was saturated with the smell of bruised grapes that had fallen through exhausted fingers and been crushed underfoot or tractor tire. Another, subtler odor sifted through the pomace of grape: the minted, mineral smell of Jory soil. He would supervise load after load of grapes coming in from different vineyards and different blocks. One batch into the destemmer, another straight to the crusher. He kept it all in his head, a tight folio of perfectly orchestrated music.

Summer was like a giant whirlpool. For now he spun slowly on the upper, outer rim, while each day brought him nearer to the chaotic center that was harvest, where they'd all be until the maelstrom of seasons kicked them back out to the rim.

But it was only May. Chaos was a ways off, yet. He lifted the dog to his feet, and attached the sling and harness contraption that he'd cobbled together to support the dog's chest as he walked.

Outside, the heat had concentrated itself in the truck, so he

opened the doors and let the breeze vent out the worst of it before
he gestured Fluke onto the seat and then lifted Zeus into the back
and settled him on a pile of straw and blankets. The heat would have
Luis on edge because that and the absence of rain the past weeks
could play hell with the crop.

Madrita scolded her when she went there, but Estrella liked the
smell of the winery. She liked all the smells of this new place—the
food that Miranda cooked, grape blossoms, wine, earth. She tasted
the smells in her mouth. It was like heaven for the nose. The tow-
ering fermenting tanks comforted her. When Ruben was with her,
they played on the damp concrete floor, turning the snaking web of
hoses and siphons into obstacles that had to be avoided at all costs.
Duncan never seemed to mind them playing there once he'd made
sure they knew not to touch anything.

She scampered up and down the scaffolds. Duncan didn't like that.
It was dangerous, he said, in a curious version of her language that always made her laugh to herself. She had walked the circuit of the
building on the catwalks, leaning over one tank after another to
breathe the tingling fumes into her nose, before she heard the truck
rumble into the breezeway.

She took one last breath of the wine and trotted toward the ladder, but the lights flashed on and she saw Duncan push Bridie onto
the concrete floor. Estrella crouched in the cleft between two vats
and watched as Duncan walked out, then came back with an animal she had never seen before attached to string like a puppet.
When Bridie stretched her hands toward it, Estrella remembered
seeing the dog for the first time. She had never seen a dog without
hair, and it made her feel sick and naked. The dog moved toward
Bridie with slow purpose and braced itself against her legs. Her
hands moved over and over it as if to smooth the bristle that
sprouted from its gray skin.

After a while, Bridie tried to pay attention to Duncan with her
face, but it was clear to Estrella that Bridie's mind was in the hands
that stroked and scratched the dog.

Duncan pointed at various things and talked, and Bridie nodded without interrupting the flow of her hands. Estrella heard Fluke bark outside, and Duncan stopped talking, cocked his head to one side as if Fluke had spoken to him.

"What is it?" Bridie asked.

"Fluke doesn't announce regulars." Duncan walked into the breezeway.

Bridie looked very white against the gray skin of the dog. Her hands cupped the dog's head and lifted it to see his eyes. Estrella pressed herself farther into the cleft and rearranged her hand against the tank, where it had slid in a greasy, downward streak.

She heard Duncan's voice coming near and peeked out again. She did not recognize the man who came in with him. The man's clothes were white and perfect, even his shoes. Their smooth soles tap-tapped on the cement. He must have a lot of money.

Duncan smiled with only his mouth as he introduced the man to Bridie, *Charles Feering,* and the man spoke to her as if she were deaf, tried to come near to shake her hand, but the dog raised its head and stared in such a way that caused the man to step back.

Duncan laughed, but it was a different laugh than Estrella had heard before.

"You've a spiff setup, lad. Hear you're quite the purist when it comes to your pinot. Bet you'd give a nut for a nice gravity-feed system."

"Grow good fruit, treat it right, you don't need all that crap."

"Bet you wouldn't turn it down if it bit you in the arse."

Duncan did not respond.

"For the price I've offered, you could have it all. I'd want to keep you on, of course."

"I'm sorry?" Duncan said.

"I should think three weeks is enough time to consider. I just wanted to see if you and the mistress had come to any agreement."

Duncan's face was red. Bridie had stopped stroking the dog. Her eyes followed Duncan like arrows. The man continued as if he did not notice the way their faces had changed.

"The deal I put together's sweet as they come. But I'm sure she discussed that with you."

"She doesn't fancy your plonk any more than I do."

"She seemed of another mind when we spoke."

Duncan shook his head; not even the bottom of his face smiled anymore. "We're all 'of a mind' here."

"Good working relationships are few. Cherish that, lad."

The man looked around at the vats once more. "How's about a little something to slake a man's thirst? I wouldn't mind sampling the new Perry Hill."

"Private tastings are by appointment only," Duncan said. "Check with my assistant in the office."

The man shoved his hands in his pockets and turned down the corners of his mouth. "Out on my bum like an old swaggie, eh, lad? No need for that. It's just business."

"I couldn't agree more," Duncan said.

"Well, tell the mistress I dropped by. She has my number."

After the man left, Duncan stalked the vats one by one. Fluke stayed at his heel, her face turned up to him. When he finally came to a stop, Fluke circled around to face him. Duncan leaned to her and rubbed the sides of her face.

"What is it?" Bridie asked.

"Bloody ocker swaggers in here in his cricket whites like his pockets aren't daggy as mine. What the bloody hell's his game?"

"Maybe he's just trying to drive a wedge," Bridie said.

"Beg pardon?"

"Psych you out. Generate bad blood. Between you and Petra."

"Maybe," Duncan said. "She's been a bit off lately. Worried. Never seen her worried like this."

"Why?"

Duncan looked away.

Bridie persisted. "You're her partner. You must have some idea."

"She keeps telling me there's no problem. The business is fine. Sales are good. I know she's been worried about Perry Hill."

"You mean Miranda," Bridie said.

"She's got a tough go of it."

"What with all her obligations."

"That's not it," Duncan said.

"Of course it is," Bridie said. "But you've all pitched in at the gold donor level. I know Miranda appreciates it."

"That's not . . ."

Bridie turned her chair toward the breezeway and called the dog's name in a low voice.

"I'll have to get a ride back. Sorry." She wheeled herself into the breezeway.

Duncan put the sling on the dog and helped him across the concrete before he flicked off the lights at the door.

Estrella shivered in the pungent darkness until the sound of the truck faded.

Now she heard Madrita's voice, thin and shrill in the distance. She scrambled down the ladder and ran up the steps to the house, careful to circle around to the kitchen entrance so that Madrita would not know she had been in the winery.

She stood in the doorway as Estrella skidded to a halt. Madrita stooped to her and caught the child's chin in her strong hand. "Are you hungry, starveling? There are *arepas*. There is fresh bread, also."

She could not nod with her chin trapped in Madrita's hand, so she smiled and inhaled the spices on Madrita's fingers.

"Ah," Madrita said. "I thought so. Come inside. Feed the belly."

As she ate, Estrella thought of Bridie's face. When Bridie came, there had been a nothingness to her that Estrella understood. But it was different now. The air around Bridie had thickened; shadows shifted across a face that had been still and white. Estrella did not understand this Bridie, or the anxiety that vibrated her spine like a tuning fork.

Blossoms floated Perry Hill on a cloud of umber light. As a child, Miranda had thought it the most beautiful sight on earth. Now she scanned the canes, trying to decide which blooms to flick off and which to keep, to decide how much each vine should bear in order not to overcrop. Normally the pruning took care of that, but this year Luis felt the blossom was too strong, and so they cut back again. It had to happen quickly since the fruit set roughly two weeks after bloom, so they'd hired some extra crew. And she knew, too, that from bloom time, it was 110 days to harvest. Petra used to call Ernest her 110-day husband because it was the only time she could count on seeing him with any regularity.

They still had not found a manager, so she was compelled to pitch in. Luis now thought Hector might be able to fit the bill after all. *With you here, he does not have so much pressure while he learns the thing. You will make the decisions, but he will tell you how. You work together, see? Like with Carter. Like with me and Ernest.*

A mid-June heat wave concentrated the air around her as she crept along, trying to remember what Luis had taught her. Just when she'd learned enough to really do something in one field, she'd had to start at the bottom again. She missed the adrenaline, the heat of the line, plating 150 meals at perfect temperature, all flawless in appearance.

She intended to interview at restaurants in Portland this week. After talking with Petra and doing a quick perusal of the establishments, she'd winnowed it down to the three places she thought were closest to her sensibilities and high-end enough to make it worth her while. She'd thought of applying at Niko's in McMinnville, but his was a family-run business, and he did not have enough house space to accommodate a full-time chef. There were plenty of restaurants in Seattle that would fit the bill, but that was too far away.

Once you're in the current, Petra said, *we'll start looking for investors so you can do your own place.* She knew Petra was trying to give her heart, but all Miranda saw was a long climb up rope that made her hands bleed. She flicked the blossoms to earth and moved to the next vine. As soon as bloom was over, there would be no use for her. Under Hector's careful direction, the regular crew could handle the work.

One of the men called her from a few rows over, and she squatted down to see him since she was unable to see over the high trellised vines. He squatted also, calling to her through the shaggy trunks. The girl, Estrella, was whistling from the house, he said. Bridie had taught the girl that. Miranda felt a pall settle in her head, something that had become too familiar in the past weeks when dealing with Bridie even for moments. It was like throwing herself open-armed at a thicket of cactus. It required a force of will she thought existed only in biblical tales. And while their contact was more and more brief, the resulting enervation dragged on for hours.

Miranda thought she would resent the attention Bridie allowed from Estrella and Duncan, but what she felt instead was relief, and even that was tainted with the realization that she had come to dread the company of a soul who was once her greatest solace.

When Estrella whistled again, she shucked off her gloves, threw them at the base of the vine she'd been working so she'd know where she left off, and hiked down the aisle.

Miranda stared out at the widening valley as she walked and imagined what it looked like to the French Canadian trappers who were the first whites to settle the area. What had they made of the summer heat when they were so used to cold and snow and the necessity of furs? Surely they hightailed it up to the Cascades in the summer to escape.

Miranda tried to remember what year it was that Papa's grandfather first brought the family from Wisconsin to these hills, which were settled even then, and how the vista would have looked to them, exhausted after months of privation on the Oregon Trail. Papa used to tell her stories.

But right now she had on her mind a glass of cold water, and when she flung open the kitchen door, she headed straight for the faucet without noticing Estrella, who stood with her back pressed to the wall and didn't see her until she'd swallowed two glasses down, her eyes aching from the cold. What did they call that sensation? Ice-cream headache?

Estrella said her name softly.

"Yes, sweetie?"

And before she had a chance to kneel to her, she heard a crash from the back of the house.

Estrella's eyes darted sideways before returning to Miranda. "She fall," Estrella said. "She is very angry."

"It's okay. I'll go talk to her."

Estrella nodded. Miranda touched the girl's cheek. "She's not angry at you. You know that, don't you?"

Estrella said nothing. Miranda's heart twisted at the thought of how the emotions of others leached into children even when the emotions had nothing to do with them.

"Hey," Miranda said. "I made something special for dessert tonight. Would you like an ice-cream sandwich?"

Estrella's eyebrows twitched together. "Sandwich?" she said.

"Yes, but with ice cream. I made them this morning. Chocolate. They're sweet."

Miranda unwrapped one of the thick rounds she took from the freezer and put it on a small plate that she set on the table. "Try it, and tell me what you think."

Estrella sat in front of the plate and looked at Miranda.

"With your hands," Miranda said, miming in the air. "Eat it like a sandwich."

Estrella put her nose to the dark cookie top and inhaled, then picked up the sandwich in her hand and scraped her teeth gently across the edge.

"Me gusta mucho," Estrella said, and smiled for the first time since Miranda saw her in the *taquería.*

"Estupendo," Miranda said. There was another crash from the back of the house, and Estrella put the sandwich down. "No," Miranda said. "Please eat. I'll go talk to Bridie now."

"She is in the toilet," Estrella said.

"Do you mean *on* the toilet?" Miranda asked.

"No. Baño. Cuarto de baño."

"Bathroom," Miranda said. "Your English is getting so much better."

She brushed her hand over the girl's lengthening hair and walked down the hall.

The bathroom door was closed, so she tapped on it, could almost feel the cactus spines on her knuckles. "Bridie? I'm coming in," Miranda said.

"Don't," Bridie said.

"Are you hurt?"

Bridie's laugh sounded like a bitter bark. "Depends on what you mean by hurt."

Miranda's stomach churned. She was hungry, and the cold water had done nothing to mitigate that. "Do you need help?"

"No."

"What's all the banging about?"

"Nothing. I'll get out of here eventually."

"All right. I'll just get some lunch, then."

"Lucky you," Bridie said, and the tone of her voice made Miranda's skin prickle.

She turned the doorknob in spite of everything in her that wanted to leave it be, that wanted to go to the kitchen and slice up a pear, sprinkle it with a little vinaigrette and roll it up in one of Madrita's flour tortillas with slices of the pork tenderloin left over from last night's supper, then sit down next to Estrella while she ate, ask her about school, and say something that would bring back that tiny little smile she'd seen as the girl tasted the ice cream sandwich.

But she opened the bathroom door instead and found Bridie, blood trickling from a nick at her temple, her body jackknifed into the corner between the toilet and the wall, trapped there by the wheelchair, which was tipped and wedged between the toilet and the bathtub.

Bridie took one look at Miranda's face and made that bitter sound again. "I told you not to come in."

"What happened?"

"Blowout," Bridie said. "I had the handles off so I could slide over, and the tire went flat."

"What happened to your head?"

"Guess I hit something on the way down."

She had removed one of the leg rests from the chair and was trying to bash the chair free, but she was cramped so tightly in the corner she couldn't get enough of a swing going.

Miranda wet a washcloth to clean the blood from Bridie's face, but Bridie blocked her reach with the leg rest. Miranda stood back.

"What's the problem?" Miranda asked, and tried to keep her voice cool against the heat she felt in her hands.

"We're all a problem, aren't we?" Bridie said. "Me. Ruben. Petra. Estrella?"

Miranda closed the door so Estrella wouldn't hear them. "Estrella *thinks* she's the problem. I'm losing my mind because I think *I'm* the problem, and Ruben's heart is breaking for the same reason. But it's not them, Bridie. It's not me."

"I told you not to do this," Bridie said. "I didn't want this. But here you are playing lifeguard because you think you have to make up for your mother."

"What are you talking about?"

"For Christ's sake, that's why you took on Estrella, isn't it? And me? To make sure nobody gets left out as you were?"

"I wasn't left out. That has nothing to do with what's happening here."

"Smell the coffee," Bridie said.

"You're wrong," Miranda said. "It's not true."

"You didn't come to my rescue with maternal feelings and a child's remembered heartache? You didn't scrape Estrella out of that barn because of some awful fear ringing in your head?"

"I know what I see, which is that you're not trying."

"You've got something to try with. You have options. You can work. You can love and be loved. I'm trapped."

Miranda grabbed the edge of the chair and pulled it free, then put her arms around Bridie and hauled her onto the john.

"Wasn't that easy?" Bridie said. "Well it's easy for *you,* but you had to come all the way down from the vineyard to do this easy thing, so the level of difficulty mounts. It's not easy to ask you to do it, so the level of difficulty mounts again."

"And it keeps mounting when you make it hard to help you."

"Helping me makes *you* feel better."

Miranda said nothing.

"It's not your responsibility to make up for the bad behavior of others, not your mother's, not Estrella's father's, not mine."

Miranda blinked as if she'd been slapped. She looked at the damp washcloth she still held in her hand. The emptiness made her stomach feel swollen. She put her hand on her belly and turned to the door.

Bridie swore softly behind her, *"Goddamnit,"* but Miranda continued into the hall and closed the door behind her, kept walking to the kitchen, where Estrella sat in front of the empty plate, a few smears of melted chocolate darkening the edges of her lips. Miranda smiled at her and used the washcloth to wipe the corners of Estrella's mouth and it was only then she realized that tears had trickled down the girl's face to mix the chocolate into paste.

"What is it, sweetie? What's the matter?" And no sooner asked the question than knew the answer.

She leaned closer to the girl. *"Ay, niña,* this is not your trouble. Bridie's not herself, but she will get better. All you need to do is eat and get strong, okay?"

Estrella ducked her chin and nodded.

"Mira," Miranda said. "I'm hungry."

She put a small pot of water on the stove to boil and covered that with a plate, then put one of Madrita's tortillas on the plate to warm to room temperature. She never put food in microwaves; they made it tough and rubbery, especially bread. She rubbed her fingertips together for the soft, dusty feel of the flour left there from handling the tortilla. She sliced the pork tenderloin thinly, peeled and sliced a pear, and layered the fruit and meat on the tortilla before she sprinkled on the vinaigrette. Once she'd rolled it up, she sliced it in half and put one half on Estrella's plate.

Miranda sat beside the girl. "Eat with me," she said. "Tell me if you like it."

But her attention was on Bridie still. Miranda heard her drag herself to her room, where she kept the tire pump, then drag herself back to repair the flat.

An absence of feeling gave her a sense of suspension, weightlessness. Miranda had never questioned her life. She'd been happy growing up in circumstances that seemed normal to her; but she also knew the mind was capable of hiding things from itself. If what Bridie said was true, it meant everything she'd done had been dictated not by free will and a sense of what was right and wrong, but by some hidden agenda, instead. Miranda brushed some crumbs from her lap and told herself it was just Bridie striking out, taking liberties with the one person who would allow it.

Her face softened into a smile at the sight of Estrella chewing slowly, eyes closed, and Miranda felt her belly conflate around the food that had settled into it along with love and despair.

Bridie had grown used to noise in the house, but tonight she was glad Miranda had taken the kids to a movie. Silence was the perfect hell. The pain had pooled in her legs now, something new, and the pulse of it would not let her sleep—that and the remembered feel of Zeus's stubbled skin under her hands that morning in the winery, the bristle-brush feel of him prickling her palms. And then the humiliation. She had actually begun to anticipate Duncan's visits. She found herself listening to his long explanations, taking them in, questioning things as if it might interest her. But of course, it was a fantasy. Of course, everything was being done for Miranda's sake.

Bridie took a double dose of the pain medicine Miranda doled out to her. No tears now, no choice but to lie under a blanket of agony so heavy it drilled her to the bed, helpless against the memory of that afternoon. She had watched herself slash at the one person who anchored her to earth, wanted to obliterate the thing she had become, but could not flail free of the rage that battered Miranda until Bridie had looked into her eyes and seen nothing, not even herself. When Miranda left and closed the door, Bridie'd gone so cold her teeth rattled.

She felt herself melting, melding into the air around her. The drugs were good for that. It didn't matter if she were mush anymore. She ceased trying to restructure herself. Now she was muscle and sinew bound to bone and brain in perfect working order, and she ran with the dogs through forest, over tundra and ice, the shrinking bite of cold in her mouth.

She had settled in to take her eight-hour layover at the Cripple checkpoint according to plan, but then she'd got the news from one

of the volunteers: the second-place racer was only two hours behind her. She'd thought at the time, it was impossible—she'd had an
eight-hour lead at the previous checkpoint—but between the alarm
bells and exhaustion, she knew only that she'd have to revise the
plan. Gordon would be pissed, but she had taken the most important things into consideration, the dogs. They had rested and eaten
well, and the vet who'd gone over them said he'd never seen a team
in such good shape. They wanted to go. If she got the jump on this
stretch of trail, some of the worst in the race, and made it to Niko-
lai, her lead would be assured. She and the team would lope into
Nome alone. She was sure she had enough daylight to get her
through the worst of the icy ravines and switchbacks before coming out onto the Burn. And if the storm came on up there, she
knew the team was used to wind and snow in their faces. This was
the time to take advantage of where they were from. It was a risk,
yes, but as long as she felt she wasn't compromising the dogs, it was
a risk worth taking.

She harnessed the team and bootied every paw, her hands so hot
she'd had to take off her gloves, though at 10 P.M. it was already well
below zero. The forecast called for a hell of a blow, but she thought
she could make it to the Burn before the worst of it hit. The dogs
were restless, snappy, mirroring her attitude. She stepped away from
the sled a moment and tried to empty her heart of everything but the
trail and the team before yanking the snowhook and calling on the
dogs to run.

The trail was worse than she remembered it. Getting to the river
bottom was a hell of switchbacks, glare ice, and miserable, killing
work. It had been the worst few hours of her racing career, the first
time she'd ever truly feared for herself as well as the dogs. She'd
stopped the team once they were up on the Burn, because she
wanted to give each dog a snack break and a good going over before they continued. The darkness of the Farewell Burn was eerie
with no stars to reflect from the snow, and she'd gotten goose
bumps. It looked like the edge of nothing.

She pulled the team off the trail and walked up the line, stopping
to rub and encourage each dog while she doled out fish-and-lard

Popsicles. They were in good shape except for the pulse of heat and the suggestion of swelling she felt in one of Zeus's forelegs. She went over it again and again in case the cold had caused her hands to lose their sensitivity, but it was unmistakable. She unclipped him from the gang line and walked him out along the trail. He didn't favor it, but the heat was there, and that meant an injury had occurred or was imminent. She stood in the gathering dome of blackness and lost no time in making the decision. The storm would come on any time now. She could feel it in the dead still of the air.

Sorry, buddy. You're going to have to sit out this dance.

She walked him back to the sled and rummaged through her medical kit for the liniment she prepared specially for the dogs and rubbed it into Zeus's leg before hefting him into the sled bag. He watched her as if she were a traitor of the cruelest sort while she moved Zorba and Stella into tandem lead. They would need each other's fortitude when the storm hit. The crystallized ice in the river bottom had shredded their booties, so she changed them all and snacked the dogs again before asking them to run.

Though she can hardly see now for the dense curtain of snow driving directly into her face, she knows the motion so well, it's as if she can see forever. In the light of her headlamp, she catches glimpses of Stella and Zorba in the blur of white air, heads low, tails straight, working the trail. And then in a quick lull of wind, she hears them keening and feels the sled jump forward. She knows what that means; it's happened before. She tries to whoa the dogs, screaming against the wind, and jams the foot brake down to slow them, but knowing soon enough that it won't make a difference. There's nothing much to do but point the wobbling light ahead until she sees it in the trail, coming up fast.

The moose starts to move off the trail and into the brush, and the dogs veer off after it. The sled continues straight at that speed, and she grips the handlebar hard with one hand and squats as much as she can while holding on to Zeus with the other, but the sled whips to the side so hard, it flips and sends her flying into the brush.

She scrambles through the deep snow in search of the sled, willing her lungs to reinflate so she can breathe. She can hear the dogs in brief interludes and can tell by their voices that the moose has turned and they are on it. She finds the sled just off the trail, dumped against a wind-gnarled stump. Zeus is crouched by the sled, looking as stunned as she. She checks him quickly for injuries and finds nothing. She tells him to stay while she tears into the sled bag and finds the smooth wood right where she's lashed it for safe-keeping. She yanks the ax free and starts toward the sound of the dogs until she realizes Zeus is following her. She walks him back to the sled and tells him to stay. He's the only one of the team she's trained to more commands than stop and go, left and right, so he crouches there as she's asked while she staggers away again. At least he'll be safe.

What she finds in the cone of her headlamp just about stops her heart. The more aggressive dogs had gone in on the moose, dragging the less willing ones in the harness. Two of them are already slack in the tangle. Their lifeless bodies snap and twitch like puppets in response to the frantic struggles of the other dogs. They are tangled in a giant snapping ball amongst the moose's legs, and it's kicking and stomping to save its life. She doesn't halt her forward motion. With ax upraised, she focuses her cone of light on the moose's long bearded neck. She knows her only chance is the jugular. She crouches low, trying to avoid the swoop of its giant head as she sidearms the ax inward and feels it bite into flesh only momentarily before she is in the air, then down in the snow, where sounds becomes muted and murky, even the sound of her own scream when the weight drives into her spine, drilling her pelvis deeper into the snow.

Dogs. She hears them screaming, their voices part anger, part fear. She summons her voice, deep from the belly—*Here! Hike up now!*—tries to give them something to focus on other than their anger, but her mouth is full of snow. She tries to turn her head, clear her mouth, but there is no place to move where there is not snow. When she tries to move, a burning brand sears her back.

There are the dogs again, screaming, their voices fully agonal. But there is one voice above the others that pricks her. She tries to call his name, but she can't breathe, can't move, and now it's her own fear she hears, puling damply into the snow. Then a sharp scratch across her cheek and hot steamy air and she spits out the snow so she can breathe, an effort that causes her to cry out. She smells him, feels his breath on her face, and smells something else, too. Something thickly sweet that she cannot name.

Hold on. Don't let go. She grabs hold of his damp fur and does not let go.

Bridie woke sitting up, her eyes wide open to the glare of morning sun through the screen. She covered her eyes against the pain of pupils asked to dilate too quickly, of memory returned in a tidal wave.

10

Miranda hadn't noticed it before, how the Toyota stank like moldy vinyl in the heat. She wasn't sure if vinyl could molder, but on the hour drive back from Portland with the windows down, the pulpy smell assaulted her along with the insidious odor of baking asphalt and car exhaust until she'd got back into the hills. There the stench was mitigated by blasts of sun-drenched earth. It was the Fourth of July, and there had been no substantial rainfall for five weeks.

She wished she hadn't wasted the time driving in for the interview that morning. It was nothing but what she'd come to expect over the past two weeks. There was nothing open at her level. *You're overqualified for a sous chef.* The chef she'd interviewed with today, a woman, told Miranda she'd come into town underqualified, spent ten years getting overqualified, then couldn't find a job upward. She didn't want to move to Seattle so ended up making her own niche, and a nice one it was, a small, Panhellenic-based restaurant with a bit of daring but emphasis on the basics. It had taken her five years to get the backing for the place. *Industry's still pretty conservative here, but you probably already know that,* she'd said.

Miranda hadn't anticipated just how conservative it was. Nor had she anticipated how fast she would blow through her savings. She upgraded Hector's salary to a starting manager's position. He had a family to feed, just as she did. There were swimming lessons for

Ruben, Estrella's language classes, and though Catherine had tried to refuse it, Miranda had insisted on supplementing the Medicaid payments for Bridie's therapy. There was still a cushion from the sale of last year's crop, but she needed to maintain it as just that. Income from the fall crop was still three months off, late October, and she couldn't bring herself to take Petra up on a fifty percent advance, even if it was the usual contract with other growers. Papa hadn't done it that way, and neither would Miranda.

As Miranda wound up the hill to Perry Hill, she saw a scrim of dust hanging over the vineyard, thickened to a point she couldn't see. She thought at first it was the Bordeaux mixture Luis sometimes sprayed in the vineyard, a sulfur dust he used to keep down the powdery mildew that raged through vineyards in the damp climate. But it was anything but damp now, and she couldn't imagine him spraying if it wasn't absolutely necessary. She was so focused on the dust, she almost slid out of the ess curve just before the house and ended up braking to a stop just shy of the ditch. No wonder the teenagers and hot rodders lost so much rubber on this curve. Her hands slithered down the steering wheel as if they'd been greased. She wiped them dry on her pants, a habit she'd picked up from so many years in the kitchen, before she pulled back onto the road and drove the remaining fifty feet to the driveway in low gear.

She had groceries to unload before she headed to the vineyard. The Trimbles were coming for dinner that night, so she'd shopped in Portland. Fresh king salmon which she'd bourbon baste, spinach and red pepper timbales, baby red potatoes steamed and tossed with a little parsley and anchovy butter . . . She'd made a mouth-cleansing lime mousse that morning, and she thought of how the pale, celery-colored cream lay on her tongue like cool, smooth flannel. Her fingertips tingled pleasantly in anticipation of the smells, the feel of the food in her hands, the looks on the faces of her guests and the assortment of fireworks Paul Trimble promised to bring. Ruben had never had much in the way of holiday excitement; she was always too busy at the restaurant. But ultimately Miranda hoped the gathering would spark something in Bridie, who had changed in the two weeks since she'd fallen from her chair in the bathroom. Before that, the sullen smolder had been difficult to live with, but at least it had substance. Now there was a nervous cordiality that made Miranda queasy. She was neither engaged nor distant, just an automation of Bridie.

After stowing the food, she hiked up to the vineyard, looking for the genesis of the dust cloud. She could hear the tractor as she went, though she still could not see it through the haze, which she knew now was not spray because there was none of the metallic smell of sulfur in the air.

When she finally found the tractor, there was a man driving it whom she did not recognize. She introduced herself and asked where Hector was. The man, Ignacio, said Hector was with Luis in the northwest block at Ruby Throat. Ignacio had been hired yesterday to fill out the skeleton crew so they could get the aisles clean-cultivated only to prepare for watering. She remembered Papa clean-cultivating only once in the years she grew up there. It was a low-water summer, and they'd tilled the aisles clean of the beneficial plant material they normally grew, which also competed for water when it was scarce. Ignacio said they were bringing in the water trucks the next day. The fruit was beginning to set now, and it was a critical time for the vines.

Ignacio kept talking faster and faster, looking very uncomfortable, until Miranda realized that her face had creased in a frown as he talked. She relaxed her forehead and smiled. *"Esta bien,"* she said. She'd talk to Hector later. Luis, too. He'd taken on training Hector, even though he'd said he had no time. Obviously she was not so necessary to the operation as Luis had insisted she would be. It made her peevish to think she'd been manipulated as if she were twelve.

And then the frown returned as she thought of how much money the extra crew would cost. If Luis feared for the crop enough to clean-cultivate, her worries were justified. They had managed the bloom in anticipation of too many berries. What remained had to be saved at all costs. It was one of many risks associated with undercropping.

She saw the pint-size school bus creeping up the road to Perry

Hill, and she headed back to the house. She liked to be home when Estrella returned from her language classes so she could talk to her and make her a snack before they went to Petra's to pick up Ruben. She liked to watch the girl's face when she ate, see the way she held the food in her hands and licked her lips with her eyes closed. It reminded Miranda of when Madrita had fed her after school when she was a child, and she meant to make those kinds of memories for Estrella.

Since the day Feering interrupted them in the winery two weeks earlier, Bridie treated Duncan with bland indifference when he brought Zeus down to see her. She'd say she was too tired, and would he mind just leaving the dog for a while? Zeus could walk now without the aid of the sling. Physically, he was recovering like a champ, and that was the only thing Duncan was supposed to care about, wasn't it? Still, he lay at night with Fluke breathing lightly against him and found himself figuring out some way to force Bridie to come out, and when he found himself succeeding in his imagination, he was annoyed by the flush of heat in his skin and the way his heart tocked a touch too quickly. And then he reminded himself that it was only a natural desire to help that had spilled over onto her. Nothing more.

He sat on the mare and stared down at the white clapboard house. He knew she'd returned from her physical therapy. She was always back by ten-fifteen. This was probably the most ridiculous thing he'd ever done in his life, but he'd committed himself to it, so he touched up the mare with his legs and let her amble through the vineyard on a loose rein until he got closer before he squeezed her into a canter, just enough so she'd be blowing a little when he pulled her up outside the kitchen. He called Bridie's name through the open screen door as he slid from the saddle, putting enough urgency in his voice to flush her out. He saw the vague outline of her wheeling from the living room into the kitchen, and then she was at the door.

"Sorry to bother," he said. "The dog had a night last night. He's a bit down. I didn't want to risk moving him. Maybe you should have a look."

Bridie looked at the horse and then craned her neck sideways, searching for the truck.

"Truck's at the winery. I'll lead you on the horse," Duncan said, and saw how quickly her face scanned from concern to resignation.

"Porch'd make a nice mounting block," Duncan said. "Wouldn't take much to slide you on from there."

"She's a little feisty for me, don't you think?"

"She does fine with Ruben," Duncan said.

Her cheekbones sharpened in the shadow, and then she swung the door out and rolled onto the porch.

"How much—?" He gestured at her hips.

"I have feeling from the tops of my legs up."

"Then you can balance. That's most of it." He was surprised by how easy it was to get her in the saddle. "Just let your legs hang," he said.

"Not a problem," she said. "That's all they do."

He started off slowly, the reins wound tightly around his hands, and kept his eyes ahead while he chattered. "He's made good progress. I had him walking without the sling, but he's backsliding, seems to me. Like his mind isn't coming along with his body. Like he's got no will."

"He needs something to do," Bridie said. "It's always been the way with him."

"Your uncanny eye for dogs."

Bridie said nothing, and Duncan didn't risk pushing it, just continued on with his hand cinched tightly under the mare's chin. He wanted to make sure he was close enough to grab something in case the mare spooked and Bridie started to slide.

It struck her as soon as he led the horse through the gate. The view. She could see again as she used to see, looking ahead and out instead of always at somebody's crotch or up at something she couldn't possibly reach from the chair. There was air up here, and she sucked in the heat of it, felt hot gusts moving against her face. When she looked at Duncan, she saw the neat flex of his shoulder outstretched to the mare's bridle and the way his hair thinned slightly on top of his head. This was how she'd lived her life, watching things move before her because she was moving also.

Her hips cramped slightly, and she realized she'd been willing her legs to tighten themselves against the mare, though the mare had not responded—which meant that the tightening in her thighs had not translated from command central to the platoon. It was phrasing Catherine liked to employ, and it sometimes caused the beginnings of laughter to convulse in Bridie's throat.

The constant ache in her spine began to ratchet up a few notches in spite of the mare's easy gait. Bridie clenched her jaw against it. On the vines, grapes the size of small peas had formed randomly along their stems, and she knew from past visits that they would close ranks as they grew into the classic cluster most people recognized. Their tiny green surfaces looked hard and perfect, and she wanted to touch them, but that would have required interrupting the horse's movement, so she let them go by, using only her eyes to caress them.

When they arrived at the cottage, the dismay she had grown so accustomed to rushed back when she looked at the three small steps leading up to the door. She didn't even have her chair to get into. What was she supposed to do, slither inside?

"Can you bring him out?" she asked.

"Not necessary," Duncan said. "Just push yourself sideways, and then push backwards. I'll take it from there."

She looked at his arms held up to her like thick, brown scoops and remembered her father teaching her to swim at the local pool. *Just jump, girl. I won't let you go under. Promise.*

And now she was a little girl again in a woman's body that wouldn't be so easy to catch. She looked away from the sad slant of Duncan's eyes.

She felt pressure on her leg, and when she turned back, his hand was there.

"Hiked you a better distance than this. Remember?"

She nodded.

"Come on, then. Sideways first."

She slid backward as slowly as she could, lest her weight fall on him at once. He scooped her close to his chest, his hand around her rib cage palpable and hot, the one around her outside thigh evident only as pressure. He said nothing as he thumped up the steps and hooked the screen door open with a boot.

"Let's see how the old boy's doing," he said, and eased her into a tattered old recliner. The smell of earth and woodsmoke and dog rose around her, making her feel oddly calm.

Zeus had risen from his flat-out position on the pallet to a half-sit, his ears perked as much as they ever did.

She stretched out her hands. "Zee," she purred, "how's my buddy?"

The dog used his front end to heave up the rear and ambled toward her.

"I'll be shikkered," Duncan said. "He wouldn't get up for me this morning."

Zeus leaned against her legs and let his head hang when she moved her hands over him. She felt his face, probed inside his ears and ran her fingers around the inside of his mouth. The dog sighed when she finished her examination, and he looked up at her before dipping his snout under her hand and asking for more.

"Everything feels right," she said. "There's no bunching at the suture sites, no excessive buildup of scar tissue . . ." Zeus smiled at her. "You old hound," she said. His tail whooshed back and forth, looking like a bottle brush with its thin spike of new-grown fur.

The fingers of her free hand trailed the pronounced ridge of the dog's spine.

"You've worked miracles with him," Bridie said.

"My uncle's ranch, any animal hurt as badly as that would have been shot where it lay. Never had the stomach for it, but it wasn't my place to say so. Dad always made that clear."

Bridie rubbed Zeus's head. "When I was a vet tech in Alaska, I had to assist with the . . . terminations. I'd bring them into the room, one by one. I always thought they knew. I'm *sure* they knew. Some of them fought it; some of them seemed to apologize. They watched you with this face that said you're God, I'm in your hands.

"I didn't want to be God. I told Bascomb I couldn't do it anymore. I thought she was going to fire me, but she didn't. Then I got into the racing thing and quit anyway. But I never forgot their eyes. When Zeus . . . after the accident . . . I saw his eyes, and I said death would have to take him, not me, but I had to give him every chance to beat the odds."

"That's it, then," Duncan said. "He doesn't need me anymore."

"What do you mean?"

"It's you what's got him in bother. He needs to be with you. He can walk on his own now. You've got the spiffy ramp, so he won't have to negotiate steps."

Bridie hesitated.

"Right. I'll bring him down later with the food and whatnot."

She could not look at him. There was the matter of thanks for all that he'd done, and she did not know how to say it without sounding fatuous or girlish—or worse, not grateful enough.

"Duncan," she started off.

"Not necessary," he said. "Just promise I'm not out on my arse like an old swaggie now that I'm no use."

"Swaggie?"

"A bum."

"Then bums are sometimes great hearts."

Red seeped into the smooth brown of his face, and she thought she saw in his smile something she hadn't hoped to see again.

Miranda set up dinner on the patio. It was always Papa's favorite place to be on summer nights. She had learned to cook passably well by junior high school, and often Luis and Madrita bore the trials of her progress. She remembered the night Luis had taken his first mouthful of a nut-crusted halibut that she'd worried over all afternoon. He exchanged a nodding glance with Madrita that told her more than anything he could have said aloud.

Tonight she was as apprehensive as she'd been fifteen years ago, and she fussed over the table as if an award committee were on its way to her restaurant. It was Dianna she meant to please, and with the woman's sense of ingredients and texture, she wanted perfection. She'd kept the menu simple, each element boasting its own bright, clean flavor, but all meant to concert in a powerful finish.

Estrella hovered at the edge of the patio in the shiny purple warm-up jacket she'd found at Goodwill last week. She rarely took it off now, even in the heat of the day. Ruben trotted onto the patio in his underwear, his hair still dripping wet from the bath.

"Oh, sweetie, the Trimbles will be here any minute. Why aren't you dressed?"

"Whaddya want me to wear?" he said.

"You're supposed to pick it out yourself, remember?" She'd been trying to give him more rein in that department.

"I help him," Estrella said.

"Great. That would be nice."

Estrella led him back through the living room, her purple coat fading into the gloom.

Miranda lit torches at the corners of the patio, though it was hardly sunset. Still, she didn't want to bother with them later, when she was ready to serve.

After dinner, Sonny and Ruben scurried into the yard to play. Estrella stood at the base of the hickory tree and watched them. Miranda wiped the last of Dianna's lingonberry buckle from her plate with the tip of her finger. It was a perfect complement to the lime mousse, and she had been impressed by the simple elegance of it. The biscuit had been mounded on intermittently, allowing the juice to bubble through and pool darkly in between the islands of dough, but the biscuit itself was worth eating on its own. Dianna had mixed it with hazelnuts she'd toasted in butter and sea salt, and they contrasted brilliantly with the airy cinnamon-sweet of the dough.

Miranda complimented Dianna again on the confection.

"Have you ever thought of doing this for a living?" Miranda asked.

"Yeah, but I'm a happy grunt. I don't have the patience for up-front work. What I fantasize about is getting hooked up with a good restaurant that I can supply and have some say in, but only from behind the curtain. I sell to some of the upscale restaurants and delis in Portland now, but it's not consistent. None of the chefs around here have made a full commitment to good, seasonal ingredients."

"I've interviewed with most of them lately," Miranda said. "They're afraid of the market. I'm interviewing in a couple of days at the French place on Salmon Street. They just lost their chef."

"Bon Vivant?" Dianna said. "God, it's eighties traditional. Heavy, saucy, and unrecognizable as food."

"I know," Miranda said. "A stain on France's otherwise impeccable taste in everything."

Paul covered his face with his hands. "Jesus, I should have known better than to let you two loose on this subject."

Bridie tapped the table with her hand. "No, let them go on. They're obviously having a good time. They should start their own restaurant, call it Great Minds Think Alike."

Paul leaned back in his chair. "Perfect," he said. "Consign them to their own perfect hell."

Bridie had sat through the meal in silence and even smiled in response to Dianna's stories about her job as a mail carrier. That afternoon she had broken from her usual routine of staying locked in her room, intending to help Miranda prep for the dinner, and while Miranda would have welcomed it before, she hadn't known what to say to the dusty cloud of a person sitting not five feet away from her. Once, Miranda was certain she would recognize Bridie anywhere, in any situation, but the outline of her friend had begun to soften and blur, and Miranda could no longer draw her in her mind.

So Miranda couldn't tell what startled her more, the fact that Bridie had spoken more than seven consecutive words in the space of seconds or that she had actually reacted to something.

Dianna was still ranting about Bon Vivant. "You'll be wasted there," she said.

"A single mother of one without a job does not go over well with the state when it comes to adoption."

"Estrella?" Dianna said. "But can't that wait until you've found something more in line with your credentials? Working at that place will break your heart."

"Every minute I wait is a minute we risk losing her to Immigration. They don't call it *de-Portland* for nothing."

Dianna chucked Estrella under the chin. "You're some lucky kid." Dianna rose and began to clear the plates, which she piled in the crook of her arm as she went. Miranda stood up to help her but Paul waved her down.

"She who cooks does not clean. That's the rule in our house."

"And a fine rule it is," Dianna said. She set the stacked dishes in Bridie's lap. Bridie stared at the dishes amassing there and said nothing until Dianna tapped her on the shoulder in passing and said, "We'll have these done in a jiff," and sailed off toward the kitchen.

Estrella drifted into the range of soft light and said, "Help you, Bridie?"

Bridie shook her head. "No, Estrella. Bridie's okay."

She flipped the brakes away from her wheels and negotiated the chair smoothly into the living room after Dianna. Miranda hadn't noticed how adept she'd become at maneuvering the thing.

Estrella sat with Miranda and Paul in the soft light of the torches and put her chin on crossed hands.

"What's wrong, sweetie? Where are the boys?"

"They are play," Estrella said.

"Do you want me to talk to them?"

Estrella shook her head.

"You could see if Bridie and Dianna need any help. I think there's a little of that dessert left they might need somebody to eat."

"Yes, please. No. I mean thank you." She unzipped her purple coat and headed into the house.

"So, how's that going?" Paul said.

"I think she's doing great, don't you?"

"Absolutely, but I meant the dog racer."

"I don't know, Paul. I used to think she'd come back."

"Not without precedent," he said, "but probably the wrong thing to expect. I expected the same Dianna after her accident, but that's not what I got."

"Accident?"

"She hasn't told you about that?"

"No."

"Twelve years ago, she had just started carrying mail for the P.O. Bad winter up in Washington. We had snow a few times that year. Crappy road conditions out where she drove. She just doesn't have a way with ice. I always teased her about that. Kid came out from behind a parked vehicle, and she went over an embankment to avoid hitting him.

"The car acted like it was going to bend in half, but it bent only far enough for the steering wheel to cut into her pelvis. Just crushed it. Long and short of it is they said she'd probably never walk again or if she did, it would be poorly. She was in a body cast for a long time. Hell, I don't even remember how long. Then we found out about this surgeon, and the surgeries began. Fourteen altogether. They grafted and spliced and pinned and built, and five years later, she was on the pins again. Seven years later we had Sonny. C-section, of course. Docs wouldn't let her deliver. But we sure as hell never thought that could happen. Thing is, though, the thing I'm getting at is that I thought when she got over the pain and the initial awfulness, she would be the woman I knew again. And she still is in some essential way. But she changed. She used to seem, well, big, as in presence. When Dianna walked into a room, she filled every crack, and when she left the room, the cracks were still full. After the accident, it's like she shrank, or got sharper, maybe *focus* is the word I'm looking for. Like when you try to find the way with a piece of wood and then you find out what it wants to be, and it takes a very specific shape. Maybe Bridie's just taking shape, Miranda. All's you have to do is get used to it." He paused. "Uh, I think somebody's here."

Miranda hadn't even heard the gravel crunching in the driveway.

She stood up to leave, then turned back to Paul and gave him a quick squeeze before continuing.

By the time she got to the kitchen, Duncan was already sidling through the door with his arms full of dog food, flanked by Ruben and Sonny, who were carrying bowls. Bridie held the door until all were inside, then eased it shut and wheeled into the living room. Miranda heard the front door open and then the sound of the chair whizzing down the ramp.

Duncan tapped Dianna on the shoulder as she continued to wash dashes. "Lo, neighbor."

"Nice to see you, winemaker. It's been a while."

"Yes, indeed. We'll have to remedy that." He turned to Miranda. "Sorry to bother. I just came to bring Zeus home. We thought he was ready."

"We?"

"Bridie and I talked about it this morning. I think he needs to be with his mum. And the nippers will cheer him up."

His eyes flickered over her shoulder to the living room, and she saw his face meld into a boyishness she hadn't seen there before.

"Mom, look at Zeus," Ruben said.

And when she turned, Bridie was there with the dog beside her. With his fur half-grown out, he looked like an old hairbrush, but definitely better. The dog let his hind end down with a groan. Ruben and Sonny crouched beside Zeus and ran their hands over his head as if they were afraid he would break.

Duncan hunkered down in front of Bridie and recounted the feeding procedure and the schedule the dog had been on. She watched him intently, nodding at each ended sentence. The cool pale of her skin seemed sharper against the outline of dark red hair, but then Miranda realized it wasn't that so much as the light in her face that made it seem so. Dianna mumbled something behind her, and when she turned, Dianna was leaning against the sink, watching them.

She winked at Miranda. "Are great minds thinking alike right now?"

And Miranda said, "Yes. Yes, they are."

11

"Call me crazy," Catherine had said that morning, "but I'd swear you've been practicing."

Bridie had to turn her back so Catherine wouldn't see her face and the slow smile that spread there.

Back at the house, Bridie insisted Miranda leave Ruben and Estrella with her when Petra called her up for a meeting. In the weeks since her recall had returned, Bridie had wanted to tell Miranda what happened, tell her that the dam of memory had broken into air and she saw it all now, how misinformation had caused her to make the decisions she had, not bad judgment. The knowledge pumped her body full, and she relished it after months of limp desuetude. But every time she started to tell it, she saw Miranda's face, dense and rigid as a solid door, so Bridie left off. The door was her fault, and it would take some time to open it. Bridie had time.

After Miranda left, Bridie gathered Ruben and Estrella and Zeus and wheeled outside. She had begun to do laps around the yard with Zeus, but since the kids were with her, she decided to go into the vineyard, make it a little more interesting for them.

Ruben skittered along out front, ducking in and out of the vines while Estrella pretended to hunt for him. Bridie wished she could see above the tops of the vines and found herself scanning the slopes. Duncan would be out there now with Luis as he had been the past few days, checking clusters. She wished she were on the horse now. Every time she rode again, she felt the elation of sight and motion, and she couldn't tell which she looked forward to more, the vista or the time when Duncan put her on and off the horse.

By the time they got back to the house, Bridie's clothes were wet through with sweat. She settled Ruben and Estrella in their room with the Legos and went to the bathroom to wipe herself clean with a damp cloth. Two baths in one day were too much to ask. She had just about gotten herself dressed again when she heard Zeus growl, a noise she hadn't heard in many months. Unlike most dogs who barked at any provocation, he'd always had the knack of discernment and had never bothered himself with threats that weren't real.

She finished buttoning her shirt quickly and wheeled into the hall, looking both ways. She could hear the clack of Legos from one direction and nothing from the other. She went to the kids' room and put her finger to her lips before she pulled the door closed; then she wheeled into the kitchen.

A man stood behind the screen door, head swiveling this way and that. Zeus's eyes followed the man's movements like a metronome.

"Can I help you?" Bridie asked.

The man snapped his attention inward. "Oh," he said, "you startled me."

"Ditto," she said.

"Well, apologies all around. I'm Mark Blend," he said, and rummaged in his jacket pocket. "INS." He flipped out the badge he'd been looking for and pressed it to the screen.

Bridie rolled closer to the screen and peered at it, then at the man's face. "Okay, so what?"

"We're just doing a regular survey of area businesses. Checking papers and whatnot. Do you have any crew?"

"I'm not the mistress of the house," Bridie said. "I'm just staying here."

His eyes scanned her legs. "Mind if I look around?"

"It's not for me to say," Bridie said. "You could come back some other time when the owner's here."

"When would that be?"

"She doesn't discuss her schedule with me. If you have business, you could make an appointment like everybody else."

"Everybody else?"

Bridie hesitated before she realized he was used to flustering people, flushing them out, and it made her angry. Zeus growled softly behind her.

She turned her chair away from the man. "Excuse me a minute while I put the dog away," she said, and rolled to the back of the house, calling Zeus after her.

She wheeled into the kids' room, bringing Zeus in with her, and closed the door. "I'm leaving Zeus here with you."

"What's wrong, Aunt Bridie?"

"Everything's okay, honey. This man's just looking for some-body we don't want him to find. He might get the wrong idea if he sees you guys, so don't come out until I tell you, and don't make a sound, okay?" She looked at Estrella. "Estrella?" The girl nodded.

Bridie wheeled back to the kitchen, where the man had let him-self in and stood just inside the door.

He'd removed his jacket, which lay draped over one arm. "I asked myself in," he said. "The heat and all."

"Like I said, I can't help you. Call later if you want, but you'll have to go now. I'm really not comfortable with you in here. Your behavior is very unprofessional." She looked at herself and back at him. "Know what I mean?"

He flapped his hands in the air and backpedaled through the door. "Sure," he said. "Sorry for the intrusion." Bridie enjoyed re-turning the fluster.

"What's your name?" he asked.

"What does it matter?" Bridie said.

"I just thought . . ."

"Not a good idea," Bridie said. "So long."

She watched as he walked back to the car, which he'd parked by the road, flipping on his jacket as he went, and she waited until the sound of the engine had faded completely before she went back down the hall and tapped on the door. It cracked open enough for one liquid eye to peer through; then the door swung open all the way.

"He's gone," she said to Estrella. Bridie pressed the girl's thin shoulders between her hands. "Are you okay?"

Estrella nodded.

"Where's Ruben?"

"Tiene mucho temor," she said.

"Where is he?" Bridie asked again.

Estrella opened the closet and crouched, peered into the darkness, then back at Bridie. *"Está aqui."*

Bridie could see the outline of him balled up in the corner. "It's okay, Ru. You can come out now."

He didn't move.

Estrella put her hand on Ruben's arm and said something to him in Spanish that Bridie didn't understand. He relaxed and raised his head. She hadn't even realized he'd been learning the language.

"Ready?" she asked.

He nodded and held out his hand to Estrella, who took it and walked him slowly down the hall.

Duncan and Luis drove to Petra's. They'd been out since six, checking clusters, hands running gently over the berries as they watched for signs of drop. But the grapes had held firmly to their stems, which meant they had got enough water at the right time. The prospect of harvest was good.

Petra sat by the window, a thermos of coffee at arm's length, a tray full of fruit, cheese, and Madrita's dark bread beside it. Luis removed his boots on the porch, apparently not in the mood to vex his wife that day, and he sat now to tear off hunks of bread, which he layered with cheese and slices of fruit.

They revised tonnage predictions and forecast harvest dates while Petra made note of everything in the logbook. The news was good, better than good, but Petra had not raised her eyes since the meeting began, and Duncan couldn't shake the feeling that he was in the dark with no sense of horizon.

Luis leaned back in his chair and sighed. The tray was empty now.

Petra capped her pen and slid the logbook onto the table, beside a pile of papers.

Duncan squirmed in his chair. "Anything else?"

"Pierce's disease," Petra said. "It's been reported in the Umpqua Valley. We won't be affected this year, but by next year, who knows."

Luis sat up in his chair. "I have been reading on this," he said. "It is a very interesting problem." Luis started talking about disease vectors and something else Duncan didn't understand.

"There is no cure, Luis," Petra said. "The guys at UC Davis have been on it for years."

"There is something," Luis said. "There is always something."

She shook her head, thrummed her fingers once on the table. "I don't know but that we should reconsider Feering's offer," she said, and in the aftermath of her speaking, the air seemed to repeat her words in a hollow rhythm.

"Some of us don't know the specifics," Duncan said, "so we can't exactly *re*consider anything."

Petra took in the sarcasm without a twitch. "The deal is sweet," she said. "Both of you would retain your roles here as well as the money that your shareholdings reflect. I'd be out of the loop, of course, which is just as well." She shook her head. "These corporations can't stand to let anybody else have a piece of pie. Stick their dirty fingers in everything."

Duncan squeezed a hunk of bread in his fist. *It's all there in black-and-white,* he remembered his dad saying. And Duncan couldn't help thinking there was something. He was certain there had been something, but it kept hiding in the furls of cloth around his mother's body. In frustration, he'd flung his tea at the window, watched as the glass spidered around the impact. There was nothing he could do. He was eighteen, and he'd worked his balls off since he couldn't remember when, and now there was nothing to show for it but the daggy mess in his pockets.

Fuck it, Dad, he'd said. *Let it go, then.*

Duncan had not noticed it before, his father's face, crumpled, weary. *The money's good enough,* his dad said. *I'll take your mother into Melbourne. Wouldn't mind a break m'self. A fellow gets tired, duking it out all the days. Maybe we'll stay at that fancy hotel awhile. She always wanted to go there.*

"Don't look so glum, Dee," Petra was saying. "I'm only fifty percent of the vote. Nothing happens without everybody's say-so."

"Why are we having this discussion?" Duncan asked.

Petra shifted in her chair and could not keep the grimace of pain from her face. "I'm trying to look ahead," she said. "And I don't see anything pretty. Pierce's kills like lightning. Are we prepared to take an extended hit?"

"I don't think it's Pierce's that's got you rattled," Duncan said.

Petra fingered a paper from the tabletop, one of the industry newsletters, and looked at it.

"Have a look at this," she said, and shoved it across the table.

Duncan scanned the article quickly and then popped off his chair like a jack-in-the-box.

"What the bloody—?"

Petra shook her head. "I have no idea. No one's talked to me."

Duncan heard the kitchen door open and close behind him.

"Miranda, thank you for coming up," Petra said.

"What's going on?"

"We're taking a beating's what it looks like," Duncan said. "This raggedy-rag says our whole line's in question, we're in trouble financially and so don't have the wherewithal to install irrigation, and it's going to cause a setback in the crop."

"But that's not true," Miranda said.

"It doesn't matter what's true," Petra said. "Perception is everything. I've had calls from three distributors already this morning."

"Call the newsletter. Make them retract," Miranda said.

"More important, where are they getting this information," Petra said.

Duncan looked at Miranda. "Has anybody spoken to you?"

"Lots of people talk to me."

"You've been interviewing in Portland at these restaurants," Petra said gently. "Have they asked any questions about the winery? Perry Hill?"

"No. They mention it. They're complimentary. But they haven't asked me anything specific."

"Is there any conversation you can think of that might have given somebody cause to make these speculations?"

Miranda shook her head.

"She like the old man," Luis said. "She don't give nothing away."

Duncan sailed the newsletter across the table. "The little wankers," he said.

"What?"

"My trusty assistants, Jake and Tom. Shickered in some club, blabbing like kids. I bet that's what this is about."

"Talk to them," Petra said, but he was already on his way out the door.

Miranda rose as if to leave, but Petra touched her arm. "Stay awhile, would you? Have lunch with me?"

"If you're cooking, I'll be happy to stay," Miranda said.

"I was hoping you'd do the honors," Petra said.

"I thought so," Miranda said.

Miranda headed into the kitchen.

Petra called out from the living room. "Light on the salt, please."

"I remember," she said, and turned her attention to the smell and feel of the food, the life in her hands.

Jake and Tom had whined like puppies when Duncan found them in the office. *No way, Duncan. No freaking way. We know better than that.* They were lousy liars when they lied, but their earnestness was not faked. Duncan believed them. He tried to resist the scour of worry in his mouth by sampling some of the better batches and making meticulous notes, but his palate was off, and he wasn't sure what he was tasting. He stabled the mare and put Fluke in the truck before he drove down to the house.

He found them in the yard under the hickory tree, Bridie in her chair pitching a plastic softball to Ruben. Duncan called to Zeus, and the dog actually trotted across the yard and gave him a quick nosing before he moved to Fluke, who stood with her ears half-perked, her tail high and waving. Ruben clutched Duncan's knees with entreaties for a ride, but Bridie caught up with him and insisted on lunch first.

"It's too hot," Ruben said.

"We'll eat something cold," Bridie said.

"Aw, *man,*" Ruben said.

"Maybe Duncan will eat with us," she said, and arched her eyebrows at him over Ruben's head, and he'd nodded. It was too bloody hot to do anything else.

Duncan positioned himself behind the chair, but she wheeled off before he got his hands on the grip, calling the dogs along with her. He watched Zeus's ears, alert and happy.

She sliced cucumber and spread cream cheese on bread before piling the thin green wedges on top.

"Something my mother used to make when Dad was laid off at the plant," Bridie said. "Cucumbers were cheap. She used to make soup with them, too."

Duncan grimaced.

Bridie sent Ruben and Estrella off to the living room with their sandwiches, so they could watch a video.

"He's doing well," Duncan said, nodding at the dog.

Ruben came into the kitchen, put the plates on the counter, and started out the kitchen door.

"Ruben?" Bridie said.

"Goin' outside."

"Absolutely not," she said.

"But it's okay now. You said."

Estrella hovered between the living room and kitchen.

"I know I said, honey, but we should still be careful."

"Strella can come," Ruben said.

"It's too hot to play outside. Let's wait awhile."

"Aw, shit," he said, peering out the door.

"Better not say that when your mom's around."

"I know," he said.

"Better to not say it all."

He crossed his arms and peered out the door.

"Why don't you play Legos for a while. Then we'll go out again."

He scuffed back to the living room.

Estrella hovered still.

"You okay?" Bridie asked the girl.

"I go," she said.

"No outside without a grown-up, okay?"

Estrella looked at her a minute longer, then turned away.

"You're a strict one," Duncan said. "I wouldn't have thought it."

"Some INS guy was poking around earlier. I don't want them outside, in case he's lurking around with binoculars or something."

"When was this?"

"A couple of hours ago."

"What'd he say?"

"It was a 'routine survey,' something like that."

"They don't poke around unless they've got reason to. Did he say anything else?"

"Just asked if he could see the crew, so I figured he wanted to check their papers."

"And?"

"And I blew him off. Told him I didn't have the authority to say anything but to check with the owner. I was more worried about Estrella than about the crew."

"Right," Duncan said. He didn't know what the situation was with the kid and didn't think it was his business to pry, unless of course it meant that INS would start bothering them.

Bridie frowned and pushed the heels of her hands into her thighs.

"What's that?" Duncan said.

"Just some new and interesting pain. It comes and goes."

Miranda's car pulled into the driveway, and Duncan stood up. "I'll be going then," he said. "You going to tell her about this morning?"

"Yes."

"Very good."

Bridie pointed at the couch, and Miranda sat, obedient as a dog, while Bridie told her what had happened.

But for the purple rime under her eyes, Miranda's face was streaked and ashy, like those first months after Dario's death. It was as if the two of them hadn't existed between then and now, as if Bridie had just appeared.

Miranda's fingers trembled when she smoothed her hair. "They'll take her away, put her in some godawful foster care, make her a ward of the state if she's lucky. Or else send her straight back." Her eyes lit on Bridie's for a second, then fluttered away. Bridie remembered the tic well, remembered what it meant.

"Look, what I said in the bathroom that day about your intentions, your mother? I was wrong."

"It's going to take a lot of money," Miranda said, as if she hadn't heard Bridie.

"We'll work it out," Bridie said.

"With what?"

"We'll work it out," Bridie said again. "And the money, too."

"I can't let her go," Miranda said.

"We won't."

Bridie wanted to yell, as if volume alone would make the difference. But learning to navigate in the emotional world was going to take as much work as getting around in the physical one. It was slow and steady, either way, so she choked down the volume and said instead, "I'll help you in any way I can."

"Help you, Miranda?" Estrella had crept silently into the living room.

Miranda held out her hand. "It's okay, Estrella. Everything's fine."

"I will go," Estrella said.

"It's all right. We're finished talking now. I was going to make you a snack. Would you like that?"

Estrella nodded and headed back to the kitchen.

But Miranda sat still on the couch, her eyes on the tips of her shoes.

"Ran, it's going to be okay. We'll work this out."

Miranda's eyes augured into Bridie's as if to anchor themselves to something, so Bridie held on, and didn't look away.

12

The next day Miranda took Ruben to his swimming lesson and dropped Estrella off for her last day of language class. Miranda was going to pick her up instead of letting her ride the bus home, but Estrella had pleaded softly. She liked to ride the bus like the other kids, she said. Bridie thought they should stay home, but Miranda said that no, she wanted them to feel like everything was normal. When Catherine came to pick up Bridie, Miranda waved to her out the kitchen door. Everything normal. Everything fine.

But she couldn't shake the queasy feeling that had crept over her when Bridie had tried to apologize. Miranda thought she'd put away the slap of Bridie's rage. That Miranda now doubted her every move, every thought, was not Bridie's fault. Bridie was just the medium. But Miranda hadn't separated the message from its bearer after all.

So she'd moved through the past weeks, acting on convictions that felt as weak as rotten mortar—everything normal, everything fine—because there was no other way to act. There was no alternative.

She had to interview that morning with Bon Vivant, so she made arrangements with the school to have the bus drop Estrella at Petra's. Madrita said that Petra was out and agreed to pick up Ruben at the pool.

During the interview, Miranda scanned the menu with dismay as the owners spoke to her. She sampled their signature dishes prepared by the sous chef. Coquilles St. Jacques and beef Wellington. The foie gras stuffing was distinctive, and the puff pastry had been prepared perfectly, she had to admit, but it all sat in her belly, twisted and immutable, through the rest of the interview. *What happened to your chef?* she'd asked before she left. Heart attack, they'd said. And she'd thought, *No damned wonder.*

She'd tried to think of Madrita's spiced rice as she drove home, the way each flavor announced itself on the tongue with a polite bow, or the fresh nut-and-sour feel of Dianna's goat cheese in the pockets of her mouth, the smell of lavender and mint and basil in her garden. She'd managed to hold on all the way home, negotiating traffic as if she were in driver's ed.

But when she pulled into the driveway and turned off the ignition, the reflux was unstoppable, and she had to fling open the door so she wouldn't vomit in the car. She wiped her mouth on the back of her hand and dried her cheeks with a sleeve before she went inside.

The midday heat seemed to cancel all sound. Not even the house itself spoke in its usual snaps and groans. The silence mesmerized her, her mind quite empty now. When the noise of the phone thundered in her ear, she felt electrocuted. It continued to ring as if it could see her there and would not stop shouting until she answered it.

"Come up to the house," Petra said when she finally held the receiver close to her ear.

And she'd just said okay, replaced the receiver gently in its cradle lest it shout at her again. She got back in her car, careful to kick gravel over the puddle of creamy bile she'd left there earlier.

She came in through the kitchen door after leaving her shoes on the porch. She filled a glass from the tap and let the cool liquid seep down her throat, slowly at first, and then sucked it down in greedy gulps.

When she turned from the sink, Madrita was there, hands on hips in that way Miranda knew from childhood. The hair on her arms stood away from cooling skin.

"*Qué pasó?*" Miranda said.

"She did not come from school," Madrita said.

Petra came down the hall from the bedroom wing. "I just got Ruben down for a nap."

"I'll call the school," Miranda said.

"They said she left before the bus. That she was meeting you to go to the doctor."

"Why would she say that?"

Madrita rolled her eyes at Petra. "All that work for nothing," she said. "We raised an idiot."

Petra squeezed Madrita's arm, said to Miranda, "Can you think of any reason why she wouldn't come home?"

Miranda brushed her hand across her face as if at a pestering fly and remembered the previous day, Estrella saying, *Help you, Miranda? I will go.*

"Somebody from INS came by the house yesterday. Bridie hid the kids and told him to beat it. We didn't tell Estrella anything, but she must have put it together."

"What's INS doing here?" Petra said. "We've never had any trouble from them."

The sound in Miranda's ears turned to buzz. It couldn't be Beto. He'd treated Estrella. He knew what she was up against. He worked in a free clinic. She was certain he wouldn't have called Immigration. But how could she be certain about somebody she barely knew when she wasn't even certain of herself?

Madrita's voice cut through the buzz. "She is afraid. She will hide."

"But she's safe with me—she knows that."

"Not if the boogeyman comes in the door. I am calling Luis," Madrita said. "He will know what to do."

Petra led Miranda into the living room.

"Tired?" Petra asked.

"And then some," Miranda said.

"I feel like I'm looking at myself twenty years ago, only I didn't have so many . . . encumbrances."

"They're not encumbrances."

"Of course not."

"Was I unhappy as a child?"

Petra grinned. "Only when you couldn't get your seat at the Problem-Solving Place."

"You know what I mean."

"No, sweetie. You were fine. How could you not be with so many parents looking over you. Are you thinking of your mother?"

"No. Yes. I mean I never thought of her. It didn't seem to matter. I thought I was happy."

"What makes you think you weren't?"

"All this. Dario, Estrella, Bridie. Am I trying to make up for something I didn't think I had?"

"I think you try to perpetuate what you had."

"Perpetuate?"

"Everyone took you in. Your world was one of total acceptance. Luis, Madrita, me, Ernest. No doors were closed on you, so you think that's how the world should be for everyone."

A plume of dust rising over the gravel road announced Luis's arrival. He came in through the kitchen with his boots on, Madrita following in his shadow like a wrathful magpie.

He looked from Petra to Miranda, not bothering to ask why he was called away from his work.

"Have you seen Estrella?" Petra asked.

He shook his head and sat down.

"It seems that she left the school, but never came home. I hoped she might be with you."

He placed his dusty cap on the table in front of him, his hair matted damply to his skull. Madrita snatched it up and took it to the kitchen.

"Maybe she's with Duncan," Petra said. "Madrita says she likes to play in the winery."

"I see him earlier with Bridie on the horse," Luis said. "The child is not with them."

Miranda gawked at Luis. "Bridie? On the horse?"

And then she heard a familiar voice in the kitchen, and tires bumping across the tiles, until Bridie's face erupted from the gloom with Duncan behind her.

"Estrella didn't come home from school," Miranda said.

Luis kept his eyes on the vineyards, his jaws shifting back and forth, before he looked at Duncan. "We will check the winery first."

Duncan drifted out of the room.

"What if she's not there?" Miranda asked.

"You've got some decisions to make," Petra said.

"Like what?"

"You can let it go."

"Like everybody else in her life?"

"Or you can try to find her."

"Oh, I'm going to find her," Miranda said.

"She will hide," Luis said. "But she will hide where she knows."

"She knows *here*," Miranda said.

"Someplace where it is not danger for you or Ruben."

Had everybody seen it but her? Miranda blinked and looked away; she could not fathom such selflessness in a child. Duncan returned.

"The cellar workers checked the winery, top to bottom. She's not there."

"She will go where she knows," Luis said again.

"The camps," Miranda said.

"Yes."

"Ruben'll be up soon," Petra said. "We've all got a lot of work to do."

Luis gave Petra a look over Miranda's head, and Petra nodded at him. He crooked a finger at Duncan, but waited until he'd left the room before he patted Miranda on the shoulder and left.

"It's possible Estrella wasn't happy here," Petra said. "Have you considered that?"

"She was scared at first, but I think she was getting used to us."

"I think Luis is right," Bridie said. "She left because she thought she was getting us into trouble."

"I can't let her go," Miranda said. "I just can't."

"Even though it may be the best course?" Petra said.

"You didn't leave Miranda alone," Bridie said to Petra.

"This is different," Petra said. "I didn't have all the responsibility. And Miranda had her father, *three* fathers, really."

"Well, Estrella will have three mothers," Miranda said.

Madrita carried in a tray of fresh tortillas and corn salad. "She will have four mothers," she said, and set the tray on the table.

"Don't encourage this, Madrita," Petra said.

"Why not? You didn't listen to me when Miranda comes. Why does she listen to you?"

Petra put her hands in the air. "Okay. You all go ahead and do what you want. You will anyway." She got up and went to her room.

"Don't mind her." Madrita waved her hand. "She is sticky after meetings this morning."

"What meetings?" Bridie asked.

"Who knows. They are always these meetings. She is tired." Madrita reached across the table and grasped Miranda's hand. "You find Estrella. But you will not go by yourself."

"No," Miranda said. "I won't."

"Maybe not such an idiot after all," Madrita said, and mounded corn salad onto a tortilla before folding it into a tidy pocket and pushing it into Miranda's outstretched hands.

Miranda tried to read Ruben to sleep, but he ended up crying himself senseless. He wanted her to read *Goodnight, Moon,* and she hadn't thought of the implications until he asked to say good night to Estrella.

"Estrella's away for the night, honey," she explained to him again.

"Call her."

"There's no phone where she is right now."

"Everybody has phones."

"Seems like it, doesn't it?"

"I'll go see her and say good night."

"How?"

"With the car," he said. And she was so touched by his certainty, her eyes started to water.

"What's wrong, Mom?"

"Nothing, sweetheart. We'll have to wait a little while to see Estrella. You can say good night later."

And that's when he'd started, must have heard the fear in her voice. She scooched up next to him and pulled him onto her lap, wrapped him to her chest and let her upper body drift back and forth.

"Is she mad at me?" he chittered between sobs.

"No, honey. She just thought there was something she had to do. But we'll find her. Remember Mommy told you she'd find her?"

"Can't we go now?"

"Not in the dark, Ru. It'd be too hard in the dark."

"What if she's scared?" Ruben said, and then cried so hard, he could no longer speak. She kept drifting back and forth, tears collecting at the point of her chin where it rested on his head. When he finally fell asleep, she moved him onto the bed next to her and pulled a sheet over his legs.

She turned off the bedside light and shuffled to the hall, almost stumbling over Bridie, who'd been parked there.

Bridie reached out and steadied her, then wheeled to the living room. Miranda followed.

"Everything set for tomorrow?" Bridie asked.

"Beto will meet me here, and we'll go to some camps. He knows people there. It might make it easier." And easier to see whose lips were loose, Miranda thought. His dismay on the phone sounded genuine, but she wanted to see it in his face. Faces didn't lie.

"It's good you're going with him," Bridie said.

"There's nothing to worry about," Miranda said. "I could go on my own."

"But I'm glad you're not."

"I want you to call Duncan tomorrow, have him stay with you while I'm gone."

Bridie laughed. "It's not necessary."

Miranda turned on her. "I'm serious, Bridie. No screwing around."

"I know you're too stressed to notice, but I'm not screwing around." Bridie wheeled closer. "Everything you were trying to make happen for me did happen. Okay? You did the right thing in spite of my worst efforts."

Miranda felt like she was hearing Bridie through a thick pane of glass. Unbidden, her hand searched the air between them.

She heard a car approaching, and when the driver accelerated into the curve, the engine hammered so hard, it made the windows rattle.

Bridie patted her arm. "I'm going to make some coffee. You want?"

"You're not supposed to have caffeine."

"The way you make coffee, I haven't. But let me worry about my regimen. Right now I feel like something deep, dark, and hairy."

When Bridie turned the chair toward the kitchen, Miranda thought she had never seen her so clearly. "Bridie?"

Bridie pivoted the chair neatly back toward Miranda and wheeled close enough to touch her arm. "That's right. I fired that bitch who was standing in for me. I'm here now. That's what it's about. That's all it's ever about."

13

Miranda rocketed from sleep with adrenaline stinging through her. It took her a minute to realize where she was. She heard birds at first, then the sound of voices, a child's and a woman's. It was the smell of coffee that brought her fully awake.

She stumbled down the steep farmhouse stairs to find Bridie in her wheelchair pushed against a cupboard while Ruben used her lap as a stepladder to reach the cereal.

"I can see I'm not needed," Miranda said.

"The more swollen faces, the better," Bridie said, steadying a wheel with one hand and Ruben with the other.

"Can I get that for you?" Miranda said.

Ruben snagged the bag of Miranda's homemade granola with both hands and waved it triumphantly in the air, the contents fanning across the kitchen with each swipe.

"Looks like we've got it," Bridie said.

Ruben's face started to crumple. Miranda took the bag and held it up. "Plenty left for breakfast, Ru. Don't worry."

She sat him at the table with a bowl while Bridie got the milk.

"Coffee's ready if you are," Bridie said.

"I'm ready, all right." Miranda poured them both a cup and sat next to Ruben, frowned and swallowed hard when she sipped the coffee.

Bridie laughed. "First decent cup of brew you've had in ages. Admit it."

"I'll admit I need milk, nothing more."

"What time do you leave?" Bridie asked.

Miranda yawned and looked at the clock. "An hour."

"Catherine'll be here in an hour."

"I asked Petra to keep Ruben today. It's okay."

Bridie put the milk back in the fridge. "Why don't I keep him? He can come to the pool with me."

"Yeah," Ruben said. "I wanna go."

"Honey, Bridie has to work in the pool."

"It'll be all right," Bridie said. "If you don't trust me, you'd at least trust Catherine."

"I didn't mean it like that," Miranda said.

"I know," Bridie said. "So let up. We'll take good care of him."

The coffee stung her lip where she chewed it. "What about when you get back from swimming?"

"What about it?"

"I'd feel better if you'd ask Duncan to come down."

"The man can't spend his life baby-sitting me."

"What are you talking about?" Miranda said.

"Look, I'm out of the black hole up here"—Bridie pointed at her head—"but the world is not going to be a wonderful place for me. There's a lot to get used to. I'll do my best, I promised you that. I promise myself that. I'll get what I can of what's left, but I don't make the mistake of thinking it's going to be normal and that's going to include . . . Let's just say romance isn't going to be part of our conversational fun like it used to be, okay?"

Miranda held up her hands. "Okay. But you started it."

"Didn't hear a word I said."

"Yes, I did. I'm sorry."

"That's better," Bridie said.

Zeus moved closer to Bridie's chair.

Miranda looked at the dog. "I wouldn't have thought it was possible from what I saw at Bascomb's."

Bridie bent her face to his, brushed her cheek against the top of his head.

Miranda showered and dressed, careful to wear her work clothes. She didn't want to stick out in the camps. She scribbled Beto's cell phone number on a piece of paper and gave it to Bridie.

"Do not be afraid to use that," Miranda said. "No matter how stupid it may seem."

"I won't, Mother dear. And if it'll make you feel better, we'll go see Duncan for a while."

"Just tell me what I want to hear," Miranda said. "Every mother's dream. We'll be back by supper."

"I'll try to get something ready. You may remember I'm not much of a cook even under ideal circumstances."

"I'll pick up something on the way home."

"Bring Estrella," Bridie said. "That'd be the best thing."

Miranda thought of the picture Ruben had drawn of them all and cursed herself for neglecting to take pictures of the kids. It would be easier if she'd had something to show, the girl's slim face in the palm of her hand.

When Petra got back from the bank in Portland, she parked the car and walked into the vineyard without bothering even to change her shoes. After a while, she'd taken the shoes off and left them somewhere, she couldn't remember. She was in the south block now. She hadn't walked this much in ages, but she'd kept going in spite of what felt like screws tightening in her hips and knees. She stopped every now and then to run her hands over the fully shaped clusters, which had come into color now, morphed from green to purple. The French called the process *veraison,* "true color." She ran her thumb over one of the small orbs, wiping away the cloudy film on its skin. She rubbed her fingertips together and fancied she could feel the wild yeasts.

She was on one of the steeper slopes now and stopped again. She passed a hand over her mouth, letting a fingertip rest lightly over the gap between her two front teeth. This was where she'd rolled the tractor all those years ago when she and Ernest first started working the land to accommodate the plants. She didn't know anything about pitch and grade then. She had no idea the tractor could roll sideways as well as forward. She'd had to hike a while before she found Ernest, and by then her shirtfront was soaked with blood.

She remembered the look on his face when he'd turned and seen her coming, how he'd thrown down his shovel and come at her, running. Despite her fear of the pain and the blood, that look had calmed her, told her she was valued, loved, necessary. Rather than leave her and go for the truck, he had carried her the three quarters of a mile to the rough road they'd hacked up the hillside, and she was no small package, not even then. She could smell him now, the sumptuous must of his sweat as it soaked through her shirt while he carried her.

She stopped at the end of the aisle, swaying uncertainly, and grabbed the cable stay of the end post. She held on to the cool, twisted steel and lay her cheek against it, the smell of him still in her head, not as he was dying but like that day on the slope so long ago. *We've made something here, haven't we? It's for you. Don't let go.* And she hadn't, not for his sake, or even for hers, but for the meaning of what they'd done together, the part of it that would go on. But all of that was in jeopardy now.

She pressed her cheek to the wire and cried like a teenager, frustrated at the way life shifted so insensibly. She cried until the sound of the air horn finally cut into her thoughts, two blasts intermittently, which meant she was needed up at the house. She wiped her face with the edges of her hands and tried to smooth her hair as she moved slowly up the end lane. It wouldn't do for a farmer to be seen thus, puffy eyed as if she'd sat through a silly romance movie.

Gagnon paced the hearth. Spit gathered in the corners of his mouth. "And I'm telling you, this is not nothing," he said. "He came to my winery today. Asked for a personal tour. Yes, the things he asked could be anyone, but they were not. First he makes an offer on Ruby Throat—now he come for me." Gagnon shook his head.

"We are not so far from garagiste, you know. We are barely market-size business these days and have little legs to stand on. We think we are independent because we are small, that we are strong because we are independent. But this not all the ways true."

"Feering's got you right addled," Duncan said. "Nothing more entertaining than a hot Frenchman unless it's a shickered swaggie trying to walk uphill."

"Has he made you an offer?" Petra asked.

"No, but he will. I feel it in his eyes."

"Do you want to sell?"

"I am plain as your nose," Gagnon said.

"Then refuse the offer. That's what we did," Petra said.

"This man does not make hay for an answer."

Luis laughed. "Even my English better than his."

"You make amuse, Luis, but look at article in newsletter. Just silly newsletter, not even *New York Times,* and suddenly you are in shit. We are all supposed to be knowing something, and it continues to be that we know nothing. When the sharks circle, it is better if we are together."

"We *are* together," Petra said.

"But as business, we are not. We are weak," Gagnon said.

Petra stood up. "If there's a point, get to it."

"There is strength in group," Gagnon said.

"Here it is," Duncan said.

"What?" Petra said.

"He's about to suggest we make our own little merger."

"It is smart business," Gagnon said. "We are same philosophy. It is no-header. We are strong if we are big. Problems are smaller; profits are bigger."

Petra turned to the window. Now would be the time, of course, to tell them. The segue was near perfect, but much as she loved Gagnon, he was not quite family. She didn't think Duncan and Luis would take it well.

When she turned her attention back to the living room, they were all staring at her as if a question had been tossed her way and she'd neglected to catch it.

"You've said your piece, Jean-Paul," Petra said. "Nothing's going to come of this now. Let's see how things settle."

Gagnon snorted in exasperation and hung his head. "My God, cowboys, every one of them."

Luis and Duncan started to file out after Gagnon until Petra touched Luis lightly on the shoulder. "Stay a minute, Luis, would you?"

Luis looked up at the slice of sky he could see through the door and then turned back to the living room. Petra smiled in spite of her gloom. Luis never wore a watch, and he always knew what time it was by the light.

She called Duncan back before he got out of earshot and sat by Luis, trying to compose what she had to tell them in the most efficient terms possible.

Duncan sank to his haunches in the dim recesses of the winery and pressed the heels of his hands into his forehead. He could see the tips of Fluke's white paws in front of him as she stood guard. He remembered the day he'd got her, how those paws had come up on him as he sat behind his uncle's house, where he'd gone to say good-bye to the family there.

His mum and dad had long moved to Melbourne, and he'd been three years working as an assistant at Henning's winery, three years making mediocre plonk to saturate a mediocre market. But even in that, he'd known he had a knack. Now he was off to France to do it right. Still, he was a little unsure of himself. He had waited out back for his uncle and cousins to come in after his aunt had radioed them that Duncan was there. Though he could see dust rising in the middle distance, it would be a half hour yet before they hit the gate. Distance was deceptive in the outback. His years in the Barossa had not shrunken his perception.

He'd put his head down and nodded off, but the pup had wakened him when his uncle arrived. It was her white paws he'd seen first through the splayed fingers of his hands. She couldn't have been ten weeks. When his uncle and the boys had tumbled onto the back porch, the pup ran, and he'd known the story before they shouted and took off after it.

The bitch had been destroyed for some reason, and the pups had been systematically destroyed, as well, all but the one who'd got away. Duncan had risen from his chair, slightly stunned with sleep yet, but in the instant he saw the pup's gray speckled rump pumping across the yard, the boys after it, he'd decided that this one would make it.

He'd whistled after his cousins, *Leave it be.* And his uncle just shook his head. Soft, just like he'd always said.

But Duncan didn't have to care about that anymore. He was going away.

Well, well, his uncle said when Duncan scooped up the dog, *you win by a fluke.* When Duncan had left the station, Fluke was on the seat next to him, and she'd been there ever since.

He wished just now that she could speak. With all her doggie smarts, she would surely know what to do. He reached out a hand without looking up and stroked the fur under her chin.

When Petra said the bank had been sold and was restructuring, he'd just blinked dumbly at her. *What's that got to do with the price of tea in New South Wales?* But when she'd said they had called in the loan on Ruby Throat, he'd almost fallen off his chair. He was so caught up in his cellar and barrels and bottles, he hadn't even remembered the loan.

It's my fault, Petra said. *I couldn't let him die in the hospital alone. Even if I'd known then it would come to this, I still couldn't.*

We all agreed, Luis said, and kept patting her knee. *That is not for blame.*

I would give anything to make this go away, Petra said. *But all I have is this. It's all we have.*

Christ, there's a million banks, Duncan said. *We'll just go somewhere else.*

It's not that easy, Dee. I've been to four already. We had a sweet deal with the bank in Dundee because they were small. We've been with them since we came here. Big banks are corporate. Everything's paint by numbers. Our numbers don't fit into their formula.

What the Christ, we run a steady business. What's not to fit about that?

We're not growing, Petra said. *They want to see a sound business plan that ensures growth of assets.*

Our assets are growing, he said, flinging his hand at the vines. *Right bloody there.*

Luis had looked at him almost sadly and said, *This is not what they mean, Duncan.* He'd felt like a stupid kid.

His head was a mess of alarms that refused to be sequenced. When he thought he'd isolated one thing to chew on, something else would pop up. He remembered just now talking to his dad last year. They'd got onto the subject of the old place and comparing it with the way Ruby Throat was so carefully tended. *Not like that bloke took over our vineyard,* his dad said. *Bled the bloody hell out of it. Now it's nothing but bungalows with a lime tree and barbie in every backyard.* The new owners worked the land to the bone, then sold it to developers, but what did that have to do with anything?

Fluke rose, her nails scritching on the cement, and butted her head against his shoulder. Her tail plumed slowly back and forth.

"Right," Duncan said. He retrieved his clipboard from the floor where he'd laid it and continued down the row of barrels.

Bridie was exhausted when Catherine dropped them off after therapy, but Ruben was hypercharged after swimming. Bridie managed to coax a little lunch into him.

Grilled cheese and tomato soup? he'd asked.

No, sweetie. It's a little hot for that. So they'd settled on a couple of bowls of cereal.

Then he'd wanted to find Duncan, and it had taken all her persuasive powers to get him off the subject. She needed a nap, she'd told him. It was very tiring to do all that she had to do without using her legs. She got him to lie down in his room while she stretched out on Estrella's bed. Zeus commandeered the rug between them, and she told Ruben about her first Iditarod when Zeus had brought them home in third place.

"It was like we were blessed," she told him.

"What's that?"

"It feels like God is right there with you no matter how stupid you are."

"What happened?"

"It was toward the end of the race. There's a part where you have to go out on the ocean for a while."

"Can't do that," Ruben said.

"In the winter you can. It's so cold there, even the ocean freezes. To keep from having to take the long way around over land, you can cut across this big bay on the frozen ice. But before we left land, I knew there was a storm coming."

"How?"

"Because we were in a little village, and they had radios and stuff to let the racers know what's going on when they come through on the trail."

"Why'd you go out in the storm?"

"I took a chance," she said. "If I made it across the bay, even in the storm, I'd be way ahead of the other racers. And I had Zeus. He gave me confidence."

Ruben rolled onto his side and stared at the dog where he lay flat on his side, snoring.

"When we took off, it was beautiful—dark and cold. I could see every star except the part of the sky where the storm was coming from. In that direction, it looked like the end of the world. It takes about four hours to cross that ice if all goes well. It's pretty bumpy in spots, but you can do it. But the storm hit about three hours into the crossing, and it was so bad, I finally had to stop the team. I turned the sled on its side to help break the wind, and I gathered the dogs around me to wait it out. I had to put on my survival suit and zip myself into the sled bag. I couldn't fit the dogs in there with me, but they were huddled up right outside.

"I tried to sleep, but when the wind blows that hard, it's hard to really fall asleep. I felt something pushing at the bag, so I unzipped it a little. It was Zeus, poking and pawing at me. I thought he wanted to get in the bag with me, so I tried to pull him in, but he kept pulling the other direction. I told him to lie down and stop bothering me. Every time I unzipped that bag, I lost a lot of body warmth. But he wouldn't stop bugging me. I don't know if I did it because I was mad or because I knew in my heart that something was wrong, but I got out and set up the sled again, got the dogs all spread out in their harness, and told Zeus to do the best he could. We were going for almost an hour when I felt something funny under the runners. When I pushed against the ice with my boots, they sank in."

"Why?"

"Because the storm had come from over land. The wind blew so hard, it had started to blow the frozen ice away from the shore, and the ice was breaking up into pieces so that water could seep onto it. Zeus must have known it somehow. If he hadn't made us leave when we did, we would have floated out to sea, if we were lucky, or fallen through a crack in the ice. But we got off it just in time. He saved our lives."

Ruben climbed off his bed and sat next to Zeus, ran his hand over the stiff fur of the dog's back, then curled up to him on the rug and closed his eyes. If she could have, Bridie would have done the same.

Instead, she slept with her face turned to the boy and the dog as if she could encompass them that way.

When Duncan finally emerged from the winery, late afternoon sun had buttered the hillside. He shaded his eyes, found them roving automatically to the old farmhouse below. He clucked at himself. *Go on, you old peeper.*

He hupped Fluke into the truck and drove to the cottage, where he saddled and bridled the mare. He left her out front with Fluke on the watch while he went inside and came out with a bottle of Burgundy. It was a nice pretext. Perfectly natural. He crunched his teeth back and forth a few times. Fuck it.

He moved the mare off, Fluke leading the way through the Perry Hill vines to the gate behind the house. He pulled the mare up and sat a minute with the bottle balanced carefully on the saddle in front of him. The wine would start to sulk in this heat if he didn't get a move on.

When he pulled up abreast of the kitchen door, he could see them inside. He extended one arm, the bottle dangling between the fingers of one hand. "Hello in the house."

Bridie's face came closer to the screen, the boy's appearing next to it, flanked by Zeus.

"Did we miss a birthday?" she said.

"Made it through another hot day," he said. "Reason enough for celebration."

He leaned from the saddle and set the bottle on the porch. "We could chill that a bit while I give the lad a ride."

Ruben shot out the door, which cracked shut behind him like a rifle shot. The mare crowhopped stiffly to the side, leaving Duncan with only a leg over the saddle. He slid the rest of the way down, but she continued to crab sideways so hard he dropped the reins.

"Fluke, bring it," Duncan said.

Fluke came around and locked eyes with the mare until she came up against the fence, nostrils flared and glowing like coals. Duncan walked up on her slowly, talking low nonsense until he had her reins.

"Lay by, Fluke," Duncan said, and the dog backed off before sinking to her belly.

He led the horse back to the porch.

Ruben stood with his back pressed to the clapboards.

"Tell him, Ru," Bridie said.

"I'm sorry," he said.

"Not a drama, lad. Just remember about that door in future, eh."

"Yes, sir."

"Ready?"

Ruben turned to Bridie. "It's okay, if you want," she said.

Ruben stared at the horse, then at Duncan. "Maybe she doesn't want to ride now."

"Just had a little fright," Duncan said. "She's all right now."

Ruben hesitated.

"We'll just stay inside the fence. I'll lead you," Duncan said.

"Okay," Ruben said. "Aunt Bridie, you wanna watch?"

"Yeah, buddy. I'll meet you out back."

Duncan shunted the boy into the saddle and started off in a circle around the house. Fluke followed in her usual position. They passed Bridie and Zeus at the base of the ramp.

"Lookin' good, little man," Bridie said, and pushed her thumbs up.

Bridie followed at a safe distance so as not to spook the mare, until she parked under the hickory tree out back. When they came around again, Duncan stopped a few feet away.

"We'll rest her a bit, eh?" Duncan said to Ruben.

"But she ain't tired."

"I am," Duncan said.

"Aw, *man*."

"Patience, lad. We'll go again in a bit."

Duncan clamped Ruben's rib cage in his hands and whisked the boy down.

Fluke poked her snout into Zeus's ear, then reared with her paws in Bridie's lap.

"Fluke," Duncan said. "Manners." She slicked back her ears and reversed her course.

"It's a dog-friendly zone."

"Okay," he said to the dog, and she went back to Bridie's lap for a scratch. "I'll put the mare in the shed and get that wine," Duncan said.

Ruben went with him.

He returned alone with the wine and two tumblers. "Kid's watching a video," he said, and handed her a tumbler.

"You'd think there'd be a wineglass in the house," Bridie said.

"No matter," Duncan said. "I've got a balls-to-the-wall Rhône red, a '98 Perrin Beaucastel that would taste good drunk from a stone."

"Nice description."

"Gen-Xers would rate this a Three Dude beverage. Or perhaps you'd prefer the sort who compares wine to movie stars, which would make this a Sylvester Stallone meets Gary Cooper kinda thing." He stepped over Zeus, who lay at Bridie's feet, and swirled the blood-thick wine into her glass. "It's young yet. In a coupla years, the Gary Cooper will balance out the Rambo."

"Why do wines get better with age?" Bridie asked.

"Not all wines age well. Big reds, Châteauneuf-du-Pape, Bordeaux, Burgundy, Shiraz . . . most Rhône-style wines do well with a bit of dust on them."

"But what happens to the wine itself that makes it better?"

He tried to explain the chemical histograms of wine, how certain properties derived from a grape's skin and juice and pulp—sugar, acid, pigments, and flavoids—were volatile in young wine and danced separately until they ceased to conflict and bound together in chains of polymers that lengthened and strengthened over time.

But that was only the tangible explanation, the boring one, so he told her the story that passed around the houses of Burgundy, of the negociant who came into the business thinking recipe was everything, that all you needed were the best equipment and the right ingredients. One of these negociants had done everything "according to Hoyle," and still, the small farmer down the road with only a few barrels and a musty cellar made consistently better wine. One day the negociant couldn't stand it anymore and went to see the old man to find out what was his secret.

When confronted, the old man asked simply, "Do you love your wines?"

The negociant shook his head. "I don't understand."

"Do you love your wines?" the farmer asked again. Finally, the negociant returned to his gleaming, state-of-the-art winery, convinced that the old man had no secret—he was just lucky.

"That's the intangible binding property of a great wine," Duncan said. "The one you don't usually talk about lest you be thought daft by your colleagues. But all the great winemakers have that secret. You can taste it in their wine.

"Swirl the glass a bit, so," Duncan directed. "Now stick your nose in it; breathe in with your mouth a little open."

She followed his direction. "Smells great," she said. "But I don't know why."

"Doesn't matter," he said, "long as it tastes as good as it smells."

The smooth frontage of her throat bunched as she swallowed.

"What am I tasting right here?" She stuck out her tongue and pointed to the base of it.

He waved his hands in an arc. "Everything around you," he said. "*Terroir* is what the French call it. Air, water, other plant growth, soil."

"You-are-what-you-eat for plants?" she said.

"Yes."

She sipped again, eyes closed. "There's something kind of spicy and clean."

"Pepper," he said.

She looked at him askance.

"That's what they call it."

"There's something else," she said.

"Leather," he said.

"There's something else," she said. "A kind of all-over thing."

"The creator loved his art," Duncan said. "I'd be happy to put my name on this bottle."

"You do well for Ruby Throat."

"I just make the wine. That's all I'm good at. Petra and Luis, they do the rest."

"You talk as if you're not important to what happens here."

"You can always find another winemaker," he said. "Not a drama."

"Everyone's replaceable," Bridie said. "The thing is to make sure nobody else gets lucky." Bridie put down her glass. "But you're not here to give a wine lesson."

Duncan grinned. "You're not thinking I came here to liquor you up, are you?"

"No, I'm thinking Miranda asked you to come."

"She didn't," he said.

"Petra, then."

"If you'd prefer to be alone . . . ," Duncan said.

"It's not that," Bridie said.

"You're on the mercy thing again, then."

"No. But there's something more on your mind than a glass of vino with a crippled chick of a summer's evening."

"Know anything about loans?" he asked.

"Only that I'll never qualify in hell to get one. You've got to have something to give them in return. Collateral, right?"

"Right," he said.

"One of my race sponsors was a bank president. He used to lecture me about saving and starting a business of my own one day. He'd say, 'The business plan is the thing, Bridie. Just come up with something that looks like growing gold, and the bank's in your pocket.'"

"Well, that's very helpful information," he said.

"Best I can do without a script. Do you need a loan?"

Duncan scanned the slopes above them. "Sort of," he said.

Ruben's face appeared at the window screen. "Can we go again?"

Duncan looked at Bridie, head cocked.

She sighed. "If you're up for it."

"Yeah, buddy," Duncan said. "We'll go again."

"Can I go by myself this time?"

"I'll just go along beside you, but you can hold the reins." Duncan fetched the mare from the shed and swung Ruben into the saddle.

"Watch, Aunt Bridie."

"I've got to go in for a sec," she said. "I'll be right back." But Ruben was already swaying in the saddle, deaf to anything but the blood thrumming in his ears.

They'd already gone a couple of circuits by the time she wheeled out again, Zeus at her side. She waved at them, but Ruben would not take his hands off the reins to wave back.

When she got to the bottom of the ramp, she tried to turn off, but the front wheels cocked around and pitched her to the ground. Duncan yelled at Fluke to hold the mare. The dog lay down facing the horse, held the mare's eyes with a wolf's stare. Duncan ran to where Bridie had already struggled to a sitting position.

Duncan righted the chair, but when he tried to lift her into it, she waved him away.

"I've got to get used to doing this by myself," she said. "There isn't always someone around to pick you up."

He squatted in front of her.

"You don't have to sit right there," she said.

He stood up and moved the chair closer to her. "Don't do that," she said.

"Kinda hard to just stand around," he said.

"I know, but somebody's got to do it."

Fluke barked a short yip behind him, but he kept his eyes on Bridie.

"Duncan," Ruben called.

"Hang on a minute, Ruben."

Fluke barked again. "Fluke, lay by," he said sharply, and tried to inch the chair closer to Bridie with the toe of his boot without her seeing. She had herself halfway to the seat when she slipped back, clipping her hip on one of the footrests. She swore an impressive blue streak.

"Nice language proficiency," Duncan said.

"More where that came from if you're interested," she said.

The truck was almost abreast of the yard by the time they noticed it, carburetors opened wide as the driver wound it out in low gear. When gears shifted, the engine sputtered in coarse, staccato bursts. Duncan swung in time to see the mare gather herself on her haunches. He started toward her, thinking he could grab the reins in time, but she shot from her crouch and headed for the fence in a blind panic before he'd gone two steps. He yelled at Ruben to hang on, thought the horse would stop at the barrier, but she'd hurled herself across it, not quite clearing the top rail, which splintered to either side of her gathered body.

"Fluke! Bring it!"

The dog's gray-speckled body coursed like a bullet over the grass. The mare's legs splayed wildly on the asphalt as she tried to keep her footing to leap the roadside ditch. Ruben was still upright, though canted at a forty-five-degree angle, and Duncan knew he'd go off when the mare took the ditch. His eyes rose to follow the trajectory of the dog's blurred body over the fence, caught the movement in the corner of his eye too late, but shouted anyway, *"Fluke, wait!"* and was already running to the fence when the second vehicle came out of the curve and started to swing sideways from the pressure of locked brakes. He reached the fence when the blur of gray disappeared under the front of the car and then tumbled out behind it like a tattered doll. Still the sound of tires screeching did not cease as the car straightened and accelerated up the road.

He vaulted the fence, calling Ruben's name, and when he saw the boy sit up in the ditch, he veered away toward the motionless bundle in the road.

The tire had tracked across her midsection, leaving her sunken between hip and shoulder, her body squeezed like a tube of toothpaste that had been opened at both ends. Fecal matter slicked the silver feather of tail; blood already darkened the white fur of her chin. She lay with her head stretched in the direction she'd been asked to go, legs curved as if to follow his order still. He bent his body over her, hemmed her in the wide arc of his arms. When he gathered her to him and stood, her head flopped over his shoulder like that of a sleeping infant.

He carried her to the porch and laid her down as gently as he could, unkinked the ear that had turned inside out, and stroked the fur smooth before he stripped off his shirt and covered her body. When he went back for Ruben, he found Bridie already wheeling back across the road, the boy sobbing in her lap. He vaulted the fence again, lifted the boy from her lap and carried him to the house, but took him in the kitchen door so that he would not see the dog or how Zeus had planted himself beside her like a sentinel.

Duncan went back for Bridie and found her uselessly shoving the chair against the lip of the ramp like a windup toy that was running out of juice, the features of her face sharpened by anger and slicked wet with tears. Wordlessly he tipped the chair back until its front wheels cleared the lip, then pushed her up the ramp and into the house, where Ruben sat sniffling on the couch.

"I have to go." He gestured across the road where the mare had disappeared. "Wait here."

She heard him in the kitchen, rifling the refrigerator, and then the screen door slammed. She caught sight of him through the front windows, the carrots in his back pockets outlined against the bare brown of his back.

Ruben started to cry again. Bridie wheeled to the couch and held out her arms to him. "Where's Fluke?" The words stuttered out as he climbed into her lap.

"She's on the porch, sweetie. Zeus is watching over her."

"I wanna see Fluke."

"Maybe not such a good idea right now, Ru. She's awfully hurt."

"I wanna see Fluke." His voice pitched high, and he started to wail.

"Okay, sweetie. But let's get a blanket for her. Will you get me a blanket?"

He nodded and slid from her lap. A thin rope of snot stretched between her shirt and his mouth before it broke and clung to her.

She sighed when she saw the blanket he'd brought. "Oh, sweetie, maybe you should get something else. That's your baby blanket."

"It's for Fluke," he whispered, and tears began leaking again down his face.

"That's very nice of you. But I want you to stay here while I put the blanket on her. Then you can come out, and we'll say a prayer for her, okay?"

Zeus rose when Bridie wheeled onto the porch, but he kept his head low to Fluke's body. Bridie leaned down to remove the shirt, her teeth clenched at the pain. She let her fingertips glide over the silk of Fluke's haunch before she covered her with Ruben's blanket.

She looked across the field in the direction Duncan had gone. She could not get his face, drained white, impassive, out of her mind. She knew well the coil of agony in his belly. She put out her hand to Zeus, who pushed his dry nose against it, then called Ruben.

He inched up behind her, his hand hot and clammy on her shoulder. "Is she there?"

"Yes, honey. Would you like to say something to her before she goes to . . ." She'd almost said *Heaven,* but stopped herself. She didn't even know if he knew what that was. "Let's tell her we love her so her spirit can be free."

His hand tightened on her shoulder.

"Want me to go first?" she asked.

"Yeah."

But when she opened her mouth to speak, her throat turned gummy and tight. It could have been Zorba, Boone, Stella, or Spy under the blanket. It could have been Zeus. She reached for Ruben's hand and pulled him into her lap, pressing his face to her so that he would not see the ghosts in her eyes.

14

The way Beto drove the back country roads, the battered green Suburban felt about as stable as a water balloon balanced on a marble. Miranda clutched the edges of her seat, not quite trusting the frayed web of the seat belt.

He looked at her briefly and smiled. "You get used to it after a while. Put a lot of miles on this baby out here."

"I can tell."

Men worked through oceans of seed grass, some with canisters attached to their backs.

"What are they doing?"

"Roguing. They'll flame or spot-spray patches of weed before they spread."

She tried to nod, but her head was already bobbing constantly, like one of those dogs in the back windows of cars with their necks set on springs.

They were headed for Hillsboro where the strawberry harvest was in full swing. The processor there preferred hand-harvested berries for shipping to the European market and hired picking crews brought in daily by contractors. Visiting workers in the field was the best way, Beto said. *Contractors don't like it, but they're not around during the day.*

They'd already canvased two nurseries, Miranda feeling each time as if she'd spy Estrella's small frame around the next corner. But so far, they had not even come up with a lead.

Beto parked the van on the road. "Better to just slip in without going through official channels." He took his cell phone out of his pocket and locked it in the glove compartment.

"I thought the whole point of having one of those was so you could be contacted all the time."

He grinned at her. "You'd think. But in this case, I find that it distracts people in a bad way. Makes them think I'm getting a call from the INS or something. Besides, I've got voice mail."

She followed him down the row, the dense tang of crushed berries rising around them. Beto stopped short, and she almost ran into him. He gestured at a crew of pickers in a block a hundred yards distant.

"Try not to talk this time, eh?"

She nodded. She'd been a little overzealous on previous visits, questioning anyone she could get close to. Beto suggested it might be better to chat them up a little and talk about the medical problems they'd supposedly come for. *It wouldn't hurt to play nurse for a while.*

They started off again, his big medical bag slung over his shoulder and banging his hip as he walked. Miranda's head began to feel like a baked ham, and she cursed herself for the hundredth time that day for forgetting her hat. She couldn't imagine being out in the blaze all day with a bare head. Most of the crew had wide-brimmed hats, or else covered their heads with wet kercheifs.

Beto set down the bag at the edge of the block, where work was in progress, and she waited beside it, squatting in the dust. She watched him move through the rows, jumping back and forth until he'd spoken with each person, his smile so bright, she could count his teeth from where she waited. He returned to her finally and squatted, waiting to see if anyone would take a chance and come over.

An older man and woman left their boxes in the row and made their way slowly toward them. The woman wore a brightly patterned apron over her pants and shirt; the man had cinched his oversize polyester trousers around his waist with a rope. His arms and neck were burnt to chocolate. When they drew closer, the trenched skin of his face accordioned around a broad smile.

The woman stood to one side while the man talked to Beto. The woman was his wife, he said. She'd been having some problems with her legs and feet, swelling, pain. The man laughed, said it was just because of the work, but the way he escorted her closer, with his hand on her elbow, made Miranda's heart ache.

Beto took her vitals, checked the glands around her throat and in her mouth, as solicitous with the woman as her husband had been.

He looked up at the husband. "I will need to check her glands here"—he clamped a hand to his armpit—"and then check her legs and feet. My nurse will help us."

The man nodded and looked out at the fields.

Miranda and Beto helped the woman sit down; then Beto stepped away, his back to them, while Miranda tried to explain what he was doing. The woman seemed surprised when Miranda spoke to her in Spanish.

When Beto was finished, Miranda asked the woman when was the last time she ate.

"This morning," the woman said. "Some berries. A little bread."

"I think you have a problem with your blood that we can fix," Beto said. "It is called diabetes. It is a common thing among workers. We could take a little blood to do a test that would tell us for sure. Then I will bring you medicine for the problem."

The woman shook her head, smiling.

"The medicine is free," Beto said. "The government pays for it."

The woman got her husband's attention, and he squatted beside them. Beto explained to him what he'd told the wife.

He looked at Miranda, who nodded. *"Es cierto,"* she said. "There is no cost. Nobody will know of this. There is no paper."

The man rubbed the stubble of his chin, patted his wife on the arm. She smiled at Miranda. "Yes, okay," she said.

Beto opened the bag and rummaged through it until he found a stick kit, took a small drop from a prick in the woman's finger. Her calluses were so thick, she did not even flinch.

Five other workers had drifted close to them.

Miranda helped the woman rise and brushed the dirt from her apron. "We will bring the medicine next week," Miranda said.

The woman took her hand and squeezed it. *"Gracias, doctora."*

"De nada," Miranda said, then put her hand on the woman's arm as she turned to go. *"Abuelita.* I am looking for someone. A little girl of about twelve. I brought her to live with me and my son because she had no family. Her father died." Miranda tried to put into her voice everything she imagined had happened to Estrella so that the woman would know. "Immigration came to my house asking questions. Now she has run away. She is afraid."

The woman's face went blank.

"If they find her . . . I am afraid. She is only a child."

The woman's eyes pooled within raisined folds of skin. "I will ask my husband," she said.

Miranda waited while the woman lumbered away and then returned with her husband. "Where we live, there are many of us. Fifty, sixty. Same contractor for everybody. He does not allow children, but he does not really know. My husband says there is a little girl in one of the barracks, maybe twelve, thin, short hair."

Miranda put her hand to her throat. "Where are the barracks for this crew?"

The husband explained the directions to her, and she thanked them both, promised again to bring the medicine next week.

They finished seeing all the workers who had come to them, then walked back across the hot fields to the van.

"I didn't get any leads," Beto said as he settled himself behind the wheel.

"I did," Miranda said. "The old woman and her husband. They said there's a little girl who fits Estrella's description in their camp. The contractor doesn't allow children supposedly, but they're there."

"Where is it?"

"Cornelius."

Beto looked at his watch. "Do you need to go home?"

She eyed the glove compartment where he'd locked the cell phone.

"Oh, yeah," he said, and retrieved the phone. He peered at the LED display, then pushed a few buttons and listened.

Finally, he pocketed the phone and started the truck.

"Just stuff for me. It can wait." He rocked the truck off the shoulder and onto the road, Miranda swaying hard in her seat.

"You handled that well," Beto said. "I'd go so far as to say you have a knack. Maybe you should go into nursing, forget about this restaurant stuff."

"But I have a knack for that, too."

"Guess I wouldn't know about that. Haven't had a chance to sample the fare."

His eyes strafed her briefly before he turned his attention back to the road. She nodded and tried to concentrate on staying upright in her seat.

"What will happen to that woman?" she asked.

"If there was a clinic in this area, she wouldn't be so far gone. Her organs are already affected. Medicine won't buy her much time now."

It was one of the older camps with buildings erected in barracks style. Each building housed twenty-five workers. The grass around them had been worn away, leaving packed dirt that was dry and cracked. The metal siding had probably been white at one time, but it was hard to tell now. Cars and trucks were parked helter-skelter around the buildings. There were three trees amongst the buildings. Most of the workers were gathered in the shade of the trees, eating from paper plates.

Beto tried to pass himself and Miranda off as distant relatives looking for a family member, so as not to arouse suspicion. They had canvased two groups so far, but nobody offered any information. They stood now near the group under the third tree.

Miranda noticed the old woman and her husband from earlier that day, met their glances but did not greet them. She smiled and squatted by a group of men.

"My husband and I are looking for our niece. She came here with my husband's brother and we'd like to say hello, see if they need anything. The child is twelve years old. She wears a light-weight purple jacket."

"What is her name?" asked a younger man.

"Estrella. She is maybe this tall now." Miranda held up her hand to show the girl's height.

The man wiped hamburger grease from his chin and kept chewing. "Don't know the name," he said. "But there's a skinny kid running around last couple of days. Maybe they just arrived."

"Yes," Miranda said. "They've only just come here. It would have been two or three days ago."

The younger man consulted with a couple of his buddies, then said, "Don't know which house she's in. Sorry."

"Mind if we have a look? We'd hate to come all this way and miss them."

The man shrugged, looked at his buddies, who shook their heads.

"Gracias," she said, and threaded through the crowd to where Beto stood talking to an older man.

She waited until he finished his conversation, a bland, subservient smile on her face, then hooked her arm through his as they moved away from the crowd. "Guys over there say there's a kid who looks like Estrella," she said.

"Yeah, this fellow says the same thing," Beto said.

"I asked the guy if we could look around. They didn't seem to mind. I'll check this building," she said, pointing at the structure nearest them.

"It would look better if we went together, no?"

She squeezed his arm and smiled. "Of course, *querida.*"

He laughed. "This is the easiest relationship I've ever been in. *Poof.* You're married. Just like TV."

"Savor it," she said. "Those marriages last only thirty minutes."

He pressed her arm to his side. "Gee, honey, don't break my heart just yet. I could get used to this."

They sauntered to the door of the nearest building and walked up the rickety box steps.

It was a good fifteen degrees hotter inside, though all the windows were open. Old metal army cots lined the walls as if it were a boot camp. Clothes were scattered everywhere, hanging on strung wire. There was an efficiency kitchen across the rear of the barrack.

Several women prepared food and replenished the containers that covered a picnic table. They darted quick looks at Miranda and Beto, but did not acknowledge them further until they were confronted directly.

Beto went through the spiel while Miranda kept the wifely smile plastered on her face. The women looked at each other and consulted. Maybe there was a girl—they couldn't be sure. Didn't know whom she was with, but surely it was temporary; there weren't supposed to be any children in this camp.

Miranda fingered one of the tortillas from a plate and smelled it. "Homemade, no?" she asked.

One of the women blushed and smiled. Yes, she said. She had made them that afternoon.

"I can always tell," Miranda said. "The texture, the smell . . . May I try one?"

The woman nodded. Miranda folded it in a neat square, dipped a corner into a bowl of mole sauce. She chewed a minute, closed her eyes.

"Perfecta," she said. She dipped another corner and offered it to Beto. He took the offering and practically mooed in ecstasy.

"We have not eaten all day," Miranda said. Sweat trickled between her breasts and ran down her belly.

"Please sit down," the woman said. "We have little to spare, but there is enough."

"Just a bite," she said. "We should be getting on."

The women asked questions about their relatives, and Beto offered up most of the answers. Miranda had to admit he was remarkably quick on his feet when it came to making up stories.

Finally, he rose, rubbing his belly, and thanked them for the food as he pulled Miranda's elbow. She looked up at him and gestured at his pocket. "Should we leave the number for in case somebody sees them?"

"Oh, right," he said, and fumbled for a pen in his shirt pocket.

She took one of the paper napkins and thrust it at him before he'd got one of his cards out. "Write it here," she said, and he scribbled the cell phone number on a napkin.

"She has a purple jacket, with gold trim like this," Miranda said, tracing a line on her chest. "We sent it to her last Christmas. She might have brought it with her." She handed the napkin to the woman who made the tortillas, who folded it carefully before she tucked it in the pocket of her apron.

Outside, the sun had just begun to rest on the back of the Coastal Range. Miranda looked at her watch.

"We'll check the other buildings. Then we'd better go."

The second building was pretty much empty of people. Most everyone had gathered under the trees by then. They walked through as quickly as possible, saw no one.

They perused the final barrack, said hello to the two women left cleaning in the kitchen, paraded their story, which had become more detailed each time. The women said they had not seen any children. They looked tired, worn out, and Miranda didn't have the heart to pump them, so they turned and headed for the door. She might have missed it had one of the women not said something and caused her to turn back. It was on the floor by the cot nearest the door, pushed into the corner by a battered suitcase. She froze at the sight of it, squeezed Beto's arm so hard, he swore under his breath.

"Ah," he said softly when he followed her gaze, and repinned her arm so that he could steer her outside.

"What are you doing?" she said. "The jacket's there."

"I know. Just keep moving to the van."

When they got in, he started the engine, turned the fan and the AC on HIGH.

"*Hijo de puto,*" he said, peeling the shirt away from his chest.

"What are we doing?" she asked.

"We're playing it cool," he said. "No pun intended. We should leave. Come back tomorrow. If we make a ruckus now, it won't go well."

"But she's here. We know she's here."

"Exactly," he said.

She stared through the dusty windshield. "What if she takes off again?"

"I'm betting she won't."

"Stiff gamble when a kid's life is at stake."

"Does this look like a den of iniquity to you?"

"No."

"She'll be fine. They'll take care of her. Let's not blow it now."

Miranda scanned the area, hoping Estrella would magically appear so Miranda could at least see her.

"Okay," she said finally. "Tomorrow?"

"Much as I look forward to another episode with my TV wife, I can't come with you tomorrow. I've got a full day at the clinic. But you'll be fine. You should bring Ruben."

"Ruben?"

"You said they were close, no? There's nothing like a carrot to lure a rabbit."

They drove out of the camp slowly so as not to raise too much dust. Once Beto accelerated on the hardtop, Miranda rolled down her window and let her head rest against the doorframe.

"You know, TV husband, I don't even know where you come from, how you grew up."

"Pretty old story," he said. "Immigrated with my family when I was six. Made a few false starts. We ended up in Idaho and got field-work weeding onions, shucking corn. You know the routine. We were able to go to school, though. I went to college, Boise State. That's when I woke up to what was happening. I guess I had a little help from my uncle. He's in California, went through the grape boycott. Chavez was his hero."

"But not yours?"

"One of my sisters died from an infection when she was ten. Could have been avoided with a simple course of antibiotics, but my parents were afraid to take her to a doctor. My father had hypertension and died of a heart attack at forty. What the hell did we know? So when I woke up, our health was the problem I attacked."

"How did you end up here?"

"Went to PA school in Seattle. Started working clinics in Washington. Then found a good job in Portland."

"Good thing," she said.

"Why's that?"

"Good thing for us, I mean. For everybody. Estrella."

He shot her a look, then turned his eyes back to the road. "Glad you approve. But what about you, TV wife? What should I know about you?"

Miranda watched the land roll away through her window. She'd always thought of herself as uncomplicated, focused. Her life should be easy to explain, but when asked to cache it into a paragraph, she didn't know where to start. Half of what she would have said four months ago no longer seemed true. *I'm a chef, a good mother, good friend, good daughter* . . .

Beto must have taken her silence as a blowoff, and he fished his cell phone from the glove compartment to check his messages. He listened intently for a few minutes.

"Your friend called," he said. "Ruben fell off a horse."

"When?"

"Hour and a half ago. She said he was fine, just misses his mom."

She leaned forward against her seat belt as if to get out of the car, then sat back.

"We'll be there in half an hour."

"Can we go any faster?"

"Not in this bucket."

She unclipped her belt and was out of the car before the brakes stopped grinding. She ran into the kitchen and saw the front door wide open. Zeus was on the porch, lying next to Ruben's old blanket as if he'd been left to guard the bloody mess. She lurched backward against the wall and slid down when her legs melted from under her.

Beto squatted beside her and fingered the blanket. "*Ay, querida,* relax. It was a dog that was hurt. See the fur here?"

But Miranda looked away. Beto laid the blanket aside before hooking her under the arms and hauling her up.

"Let's get you some water before you pass out on me."

She found them both asleep in Ruben's room, Bridie sitting in her chair next to Ruben's bed. She touched Bridie awake and signaled her into the hall, where Bridie explained what had happened.

"Is Duncan okay?" Miranda asked.

Bridie shook her head. "I haven't seen him since he took off after the horse. Is Fluke—?"

"She's gone," Miranda said. "I saw the blanket and almost passed out."

"Sorry," Bridie said. "Ruben insisted on giving her that. Duncan must have come for her while we were asleep."

"Beto's here," Miranda said. "I'll fix us something to eat. Hungry?"

Bridie shook her head. "I think I'll just lie down, okay?"

Bridie lay on the bed and fingered the broken webbing of Zeus's racing collar. Her left leg was on fire, so she guessed she should be grateful the right one only throbbed. When she'd seen the doc about it at Catherine's insistence, he'd said it was a normal reaction, whatever the hell that meant. *But if I feel pain, doesn't that mean—?* In some cases, it meant that the nerves were repairing themselves. If that was happening to Bridie, it wouldn't happen all at once. The process would be incremental. Inscrutably incremental.

She lay on the bed fully dressed and waited until she heard Beto's car pull away, waited longer until Miranda had cleaned the kitchen and gone upstairs. And waited longer still to be sure Miranda was asleep before she dragged herself into the wheelchair and let herself and Zeus out the front door and down the ramp.

It was not so far if she'd gone straight up the hill. She'd been doing distances like that for a month now. But she had to zigzag back and forth so that the slope wasn't so daunting, and this doubled the distance. She stopped every now and then to stretch her arms and bring her heart rate in line. Zeus nosed her, and she stroked his head, then felt her jacket pocket and was reassured by the bulge there.

She thought of how she'd lain in the hospital and rehab for weeks on end and battered herself into even worse shape over what had happened to the dogs. No one had asked her about it. No one had understood the assault of guilt over the deaths of her team. A moose could have appeared anywhere on the trail, regardless of the weather, regardless of whether she had stuck to her plan. It happened all the time. She didn't know if having the gun with her would have helped. The time it had taken her to get to the sled for the ax was the same time it would have taken her to get the gun. And then what? What if she'd missed, or made a poor shot and enraged the animal further? The questions orbited her head like hamsters on an exercise wheel. They were unanswerable, which left her with nothing but the facts to bear. Shoulder the knowledge and go on, or not.

She continued her zigzag course through the vineyard. There was no light on at the cottage to guide her, but she knew the way. She had traveled it enough as she sat in her chair at the window. As she rounded a trellis post, she felt the chair tip slightly. She shoved harder at the wheels to keep herself from sinking in the soft dirt, but the chair began to tip anyway. She shifted her weight to the right to keep it from going over and tried to pivot on the right wheel until the left one came back to solid ground but succeeded only in digging in the right tire, as well.

She slumped forward. She could slither to the ground and crawl, dragging the chair to solid ground, but her arms were so tired now, she didn't think she could haul herself back into the chair. Zeus sat in front of her and batted her leg with a paw, keening softly. She saw the gray brush of tail swing tightly back and forth.

She raised her hand to his face. "You think so, hound?"

He whined again.

"It's worth a try."

Bridie removed her jacket and looped the sleeves between the dog's front legs and back up his chest before tying them across his shoulders. It wasn't much of a harness, but it would have to do. She bunched the rest of the jacket in her hand and looped her free arm under an armrest.

"Well, hound, if you're willing. *Hike.* Let's go home."

Zeus bounced against the pull of her as if testing the weight, bounced again, and she was about to whoa him back, thinking it hurt him, but he threw himself against the harness a third time and did not let up. She felt the familiar surge and hung on, her back screaming at the strain. He'd pulled her twenty feet before she was able to whoa him. He turned to her, his tongue flopping from the side of his mouth as if to say he was just getting started.

Her hands shook so hard, she could hardly untie the jacket. She scratched the dog's chest. "Save it, buddy," she said softly. "We'll do this again."

15

Duncan dug the grave plenty deep and square enough so that Fluke would not be cramped. He brought her stiffening body from the back of the truck and laid her carefully in the red dirt, tried to uncurl her legs a little. He removed her collar and flung it away, then smoothed her neck ruff. It took a little spit to straighten the cowlick at the top of her withers as he'd done when she was a pup.

He retrieved some things from the cottage—knuckle bone, blanket, pallet, bowl, a handful of kibble—and laid them alongside her, the food at muzzle's tip, then sat at the edge of her grave, his legs hanging inside it. He sat so long, his sweat-drenched clothes dried on his body, but his face would not follow suit.

She was all he had taken with him from Australia. She was all he'd cared to bring. Every strange place he'd come to since then had been easily demystified by the things he did for her on arrival. Find the best vet, proper food, a place to live that allowed for dogs' lives as well as humans'. She needed plenty of exercise, so he always knew the land well.

He clutched the loose red soil in his hands and pressed it to his face, the dirt turning to lachrymose mud under his palms.

He gathered himself on his knees and began to fill the hole by hand, arranging each fistful before pushing in another, patting the dirt around and over her as if sculpting a figure of great delicacy.

Dark had gathered around him before he was finished. His stomach felt shrunken and dry. He should get up, he thought. Put on a shirt, make something to eat, but Fluke always ate with him at night. Instead, he fetched a bottle from his stash in the root cellar, a Burgundy. The '85 Chambolle-Musigny was one of a case that he had managed to get for a relative song, which still required a huge outlay. It is an investment, was what he thought at the time. Tonight such forward-looking moves were not on his radar.

He went back to the freshly tamped mound of dirt and sat down. He pulled the cork and drank directly from the bottle. Very improper procedure, but he hardly gave a toss. This was how wine was meant to be drunk anyway. After water, it was the original beverage of life and had been consumed in this way for thousands of years by humans who were tired, happy, sad, sick, celebratory.

He automatically cataloged what his palate told him about the liquid in his mouth—earth, a touch of pepper, a slow caress of violet—but what mattered to him at the moment was the warmth of it in his throat, the slight cessation of clenched muscle in his belly.

What had chilled him most about Petra's news that morning was not the news itself but the delivery, the resignation and release in her voice. It was as if some evil scientist behind a curtain had suspended the properties of gravity, freeing all the elements of the universe to collide at will in a chaos he had not felt since he was eighteen. He had not intended to feel that helplessness again. Yet here he was, stupid as the day he was born.

The only way out of the mess he'd been able to think of was an impossibility. Ernest and Carter had seen to that. There were codicils to the land titles of both Ruby Throat and Perry Hill that specified the land could not be broken up. It was a stipulation Ernest and Petra had agreed to when they bought the land from Carter. Duncan had suggested that morning that these things could be got around legally, but only, Petra pointed out, with time and money. The bank had given them thirty days, and the upcoming harvest required a tremendous cash outlay for extra crew and for the crop from their ancillary growers.

When he felt the dog's cool nose against his arm, he thought he was hallucinating and tightened his grip on the bottleneck as if the feel of the smooth glass in his fist could retrieve reality. But then he heard the tread of the rubber tires crossing the packed dirt of his driveway, and while he was certain that was real, it was not possible. He closed his eyes and put his hand to the side and felt the stiff brush of fur on warm skin and pulled the dog to him.

"Zee," he said, softly. "There's a dog."

He felt the heat of her hand on his bare shoulder. He closed his eyes again, this time against the rush of water accumulating there at the thought of what it must have taken for her to get there. He wanted to say something but was afraid of the squeak his voice had surely become, so he covered her hand instead with his and waited for control to return.

She slipped something into his lap. "It's for Fluke," she said. "From Zeus."

His hand recognized the stiff webbing of a dog's collar. He leaned forward and smoothed it across the turned earth before him. He felt the warm cup of her hand smoothing his hair, crown to nape, crown to nape.

"Must be a sight, me out here tipping the bottle like an old swaggie."

"Bum, right?" she said.

He nodded under her hand, which had gone still now, but was still there. He passed her the bottle. He heard her swallow, first quickly, then slowly.

She smacked her lips. "There's that dirt," she said. "And something like flowers."

"Violets," he said. "The hallmark of truly great Burgundy."

She passed the bottle back to him. "Ruby Throat's in trouble, isn't it," she said.

"Yes," he said.

And in spite of Petra's admonishment to silence, he could not stop himself from telling her everything: the newsletter bashing, Gagnon's rage, the bank loan.

"When bad things piled up like this, the natives in the village used to say the evil spirits were hungry, and they would offer them something. It had to be something choice, something you really didn't want to part with, like your last hunk of meat."

"S'pose I could bash the rest of this case of Musigny over my head or something," Duncan said.

"That's not necessary," Bridie said. "Because sometimes the spirits take things from you anyway, before you get a chance to decide. And when that happens, you get to rewrite the myth. When that happens, you get to take something back."

Duncan said nothing.

"I was thinking about what you told me today. Not the story about the lucky guy, but the scientific stuff. There's more story in that than I realized."

"How's that."

"You said the elements in young wine fight with each other until they join together in chains that lengthen and strengthen over time."

"Binding properties," he said.

"Yes."

"Mergers?"

"Exactly."

"But Gagnon doesn't know about the loan being called in. He'd never go for it."

"Everybody knows everything around here, and you can bet your ass he knows about the loan."

Duncan's stomach grumbled. "You hungry?" he asked.

"It's like Miranda always says. Food belongs with wine."

"Come again?" he said.

"You know, food and wine belong together."

Duncan stood up so quickly, Zeus rose and growled, thinking something was wrong. "The business plan," he said.

"What?"

"Your banker friend said you needed a good business plan." Duncan moved behind the chair and started pushing her toward the steps. "We'll eat," he said, "drink a bit, and I'll tell you a story."

"I should be getting back," she said. "I'm pretty tired."

"You're here," he said, and crouched in front of her. "You should stay."

"I guess I can manage a meal," she said.

"I mean after." He curled his hand around the back of her calf. "Will you stay after?"

"You realize I can't even feel your hand," she said.

"But you know it's there."

"You could do better for yourself," she said.

"You said bums sometimes have great hearts," he said. "Mine does its best. Will you stay?"

Still she hesitated. "I can't even walk in your door."

He lifted her from the chair. "Not a drama."

Miranda leaned across the car and unbuckled Ruben's seat belt.

"Where is she, Mom?" he asked.

"We have to find her, sweetie. That's why we're here."

"Is she mad at me?"

"No, Ru. She likes you very much."

"Is she mad at you?"

"I don't think so."

"Then why'd she run away?"

"Because she's afraid. Because there are a lot of people in this world who think Estrella shouldn't be here."

"Like that man?"

"Yes. That's why we have to find her first and make sure that man knows she can be here."

"He's the boogeyman, ain't he," Ruben said. "That's what Luis said."

"Well, he's right. Sort of."

Ruben put on the cap that Petra had bought for him, another "just like Papa" item, while Miranda tied one of his sneakers that had come undone.

"We'll go slowly and quietly, okay, Ru? We don't want to scare her."

She took his hand, and they moved toward the closest barrack, the one where she had seen Estrella's jacket. Miranda's mouth was dry as the day she'd interviewed for Eric six years ago.

When she tried the barrack door, it was locked. She doubted anyone was inside, since the windows were also closed, but she knocked anyway. She tried to peer in the windows, but the buildings were set off the ground on blocks, making the windows too high to see into. The buildings were skirted round with tattered roofing paper. She got down on her knees and pulled one of the flaps aside to see into the crawl space. Shafts of light shot across the dirt from various cracks and flaps, but it was dark enough so that she could not see the whole space.

She sighed and looked at Ruben. "Let's go get the flashlight out of the car."

When they returned, she stationed Ruben at one of the flaps and squirmed under the building. The beam of the flashlight wandered over the space with the movement of her hand, making her feel like she was in some crazy disco.

"*Mom!*" Ruben stage-whispered.

"What?"

"Didja find her?"

"No, honey. Not yet."

She could see a part of the structure at the back end of the building that came all the way to the ground. She instructed Ruben to walk to that end and pull one of the flaps aside so he could see her. As she crawled toward the structure, she could see that the bottom two feet of it was not actually wood but another skirt of tar paper. As she got closer, the stench was obvious. Contractors were supposed to supply a battery of portable toilets for the workers. This one had tacked an outhouse to the building, meant to make do for twenty-five people.

As she crawled closer, the odor was so intense, she had to hold her breath, stopping every few feet to breathe into her sleeve. She wanted more than anything to back out of there and get into the sun, but if she didn't look everywhere, she'd never be sure. Just a few more feet, and then she'd peel back the flap and hope she didn't faint before she fanned the light across the space.

Now she was there, and the fetid smell was so strong, her eyes watered. They probably threw some kind of chemical in the hole to mitigate the stench, but it only added to hellish atmosphere. She took another deep breath from her sleeve before she pulled the tar paper aside and heard an unmistakable wail. Ruben.

Miranda rolled to the side and dragged herself into the light. Her eyes convulsed shut so tightly, she couldn't see, and she walked straight into the side of the building.

"Ruben!"

She heard his voice, farther away now, calling Estrella's name, and turned in the direction of the sound. She covered her eyes with her hands and peeked through the crack between two fingers just in time to see Ruben disappear around the corner of the farthest barrack.

She ran toward the sound of his voice.

When she rounded the corner, a man was on his knees in the dirt, peering through the tar paper skirt just as she had done minutes before. He must have laid his suit jacket on the ground beside him, because Ruben had picked it up and was flailing him with it, yelling words that were indistinguishable from one another.

She grabbed the jacket and threw it from her before snatching Ruben up in her arms.

"It's him, Mom!" Ruben said. "It's the boogeyman."

The man stood up and thanked her for rescuing his jacket.

"Who are you?" she asked.

He dusted off his jacket and produced a badge from one of the pockets. In the photo on his INS ID he looked grim, older. But in broad daylight, he looked like a big farm boy who'd been paraded out in his best Sunday suit. His hands were callused in all the right places. His hair was light brown and thin at the crown where he'd already started doing the comb-over.

She squinted into the young old face. "You're the one who came to my house and terrified my friend and my son."

"And the illegal," he said, hooking a thumb behind him. "Don't forget her."

"She won't be illegal for long," Miranda said. "I've seen an attorney. He's ready to start the paperwork. Trouble is, we can't start adoption proceedings without someone to adopt. I've been looking for her ever since you scared her away."

"I know," he said. "I've been following you."

"And I don't know why. Our vineyards have always been oper-ated aboveboard. But I'm sure you know that."

"Yes. But how do I know you're not bullshitting me about the adoption thing?" He blushed and excused himself.

"Do you have a cell phone?" she asked.

"Yeah."

"I have the attorney's card in my purse. You can call him right now. He'll fax the startup documents to your office."

"I believe you," he said. "But I'll take the number down anyway. Check it back at the office if I have to."

"If you believe me, then why are you hounding us?"

"We got a call on the tip line that you were harboring. We have to respond."

"Who?"

"It's a tip line, ma'am. Anonymous. We couldn't tell you even if we knew."

"What's this *we* business? I see only you and me and this boy. Who called?"

He stared at the dusty toes of his shoes and said, "Look, I didn't even hear the recording. We just get the report on our desks. For-eign gentleman called in at such-and-so o'clock on such-and-so day to report that such and so—that would be you—was harboring an illegal."

"How do you know the caller was foreign?"

"Accent on the recording, I guess."

"Everybody's got an accent around here. That doesn't mean they're foreign."

"Not Spanish," he said. "English. And you didn't hear that from me."

Miranda set Ruben down. "If I get you that number now, will you leave so I can find this child? I don't know how long it's been since she's eaten."

"Yeah, sure. I'm kinda hungry myself."

After he'd copied down the number and peeled off in his department-issue Olds, Ruben said, "If he was the boogeyman, why did he leave?"

"I guess he wasn't in the mood for boogeyness today. I guess we just got lucky."

She retrieved the flashlight where she'd dropped it under the building, then went back to the place where she'd found Ruben swacking the agent with his jacket.

"Are you sure you saw her go under here, Ru?"

He nodded.

"You're going to be my carrot, okay?"

"I don't wanna be a carrot."

"We're going to pretend that Estrella is a rabbit, and you know what rabbits like to eat, right?"

"But I don't look like a carrot."

"You will to her, sweetie."

Duncan stepped into the steamy interior and took a deep breath of brine and beer. John didn't work this late at night. There was another guy shucking oysters behind the big counter whose name he could never remember. He waved at Duncan and pointed toward the back, but Duncan shook his head.

"Waiting for someone," he said.

The guy grinned. " 'Bout time, buddy. Thought you'd never spark up."

Duncan grinned. "Business, not pleasure."

"Too bad. You know what they say about oysters."

"Saving up for later," Duncan said. And he would have brought Bridie tonight, but he was afraid it would queer the deal. There would be another time. He was certain he had that luxury.

"The usual?" the guy asked.

"Yeah, but double up. My associate might be a bit peckish."

" 'My associate,' " the guy said. "What a kicker."

Duncan went to the back bar and ordered a bottle of sauv blanc, but they were out, so he ended up ordering a bottle of his own pinot gris. The bartender was new and didn't recognize him, or Duncan would never have done it. Just didn't think it looked right to be out and about ordering your own wine.

Duncan was into his second glass by the time Ken Moore came in, looking as if he'd slept in his clothes for three days. Duncan poured him a glass of the gris, and the man kinked his eyebrows together.

"They were out of the sauv blanc," Duncan said. "This is the only other thing I trust in here. Let's get a table. Took the liberty of ordering you a dozen Yaqs. Didn't think you'd whinge about it."

"Whinge?"

"Whine with a *g*."

Duncan signaled the guy behind the oyster bar, who nodded and whistled up a waitress, one of the younger girls. Thank God Betty didn't work nights.

"Thanks for coming," Duncan said. "It'll be a good harvest this year. Best ever."

"You didn't drag my ass over here to talk about harvest."

"That I didn't."

"Editor said you wouldn't take no," Ken Moore said. "Better be good."

"It's better than good," Duncan said. "Might just cork you into the big leagues."

"And what's in it for you?" Moore said.

"Cynical bastard," Duncan said. "And not without justification. But I'm not the only one interested in exposing Feering. Besides, you'll be a regular fucking hero, Moore. Here's the deal."

Duncan explained his suspicions, giving as much detail as he had to give.

Afterward, Moore sighed and blew his nose in his napkin. "I do *news,* Duncan, not op-ed. What you're talking about is pure opinion. You got no facts."

"I thought news required a little digging, time to time," Duncan said.

Moore rolled his eyes and slurped down a few more oysters.

Duncan pushed harder. "I guarantee that nose of yours will lead you from the bank sellout to BevCorp and Feering. And I bet you've got a contact at INS who can rustle up a recording of that rat-line call-in where you'll hear Feering's voice."

"I wouldn't know Feering's voice from yours," Moore said.

"I do," Duncan said.

"What about the libelous articles in the industry rags?" Moore said.

"Bloody hell," Duncan said. "You a reporter or not?"

Moore shoved the empty shells around on his plate. "And we're talking about a case of the '85 Chambolle-Musigny for my troubles."

"Almost a case," Duncan said.

"Right. And how do I know these precious bottles exist?"

"They're about three blocks from here, ready to go home with you."

"I don't suppose you'd throw in a vertically arranged case of Perry Hill?"

"Have to see Petra on that. I'd say, however, if it puts Feering closer to cliff's edge, she'd be right inclined."

Moore nodded agreeably. "I can't guarantee this'll go to print."

"I know it will, Moore," Duncan said, and went in for the final stroke. "You've got the golden nose."

16

Between the truckloads of grapes and cement equipment rumbling up the road, Petra felt as if the house were permanently shaking. She looked up from her paperwork, her eyes scanning the vineyard in a long-practiced sweep, which took in the umber-leaved vines of early October, the beginning of harvest.

She'd have to go down any time now for the dedication. They were pouring cement for the second level of the gravity-feed winery today. The original plan had been to put the facility on Gagnon's property, but his land was configured such that the only possible location ran into zoning no-no's with his neighbors. And hadn't he grumbled. *You get the winery* and *the restaurant* and *the tasting room. It is not fair.* He'd sounded like a little boy, but oh, how it made her laugh. She hadn't laughed like that in months.

She would have laughed at his bookwork skills now had she not been about to go crazy over the mounds of files before her. Merging their history was proving to be a hell of a lot more difficult than merging their wineries. All the latter had required was a lot of fine print and a few signatures. Even getting the new loan had seemed like a walk in the park in comparison. The business plan Duncan came up with made that certain.

She watched the crew moving through the vineyard, their hands flashing in and out of the vines as they cut clusters and placed them into plastic tubs. Because of the drought, the yield was lower than even their usual undercropping allowed, but Duncan and Luis had assured her that the grapes were more intense than ever. This vintage would be a banner year, one that collectors screamed, and paid, for. Once they got the new irrigation system on-line, lack of rainfall would go to the bottom of the long, long list of worries that would always plague growers.

She heard the airhorn—two short blasts—and pushed herself up from the table. While she slipped into her rubber boots, she imagined the house for the millionth time as it would be soon, full of tables and comfortable chairs and people enjoying food and wine together as if they were at home. She could have sworn Ernest had designed it for this eventual purpose, always the seer.

Everyone was there by the time she arrived. Miranda sat cross-legged by Bridie's chair, laughing at something Bridie had whispered to her. Since Bridie and Duncan had—well, she didn't know what to call it . . . "hooked up" is what youngsters called it these days—the place had seemed about to burst.

She tapped Duncan on the shoulder. "Where are the babies?"

He jogged off to the winery and returned a few minutes later with Estrella on his shoulders while Ruben and Sonny tore around like dervishes.

The masons had smoothed the cement to perfection. She called out for everyone to line up at the edge of the pad. Maybe they thought it was corny, pressing their hands one by one into the smooth glurk, but she didn't care.

She'd done it thirty years ago when they poured the pad for the old winery, but there had been so few hands then. Now there were many.